The Stand-In

my life as an understudy

ALSO BY ELIZABETH STEVENS

The Stand-In

my life as an understudy

Elizabeth Stevens

SLEEPING DRAGON BOOKS
ADELAIDE

Sleeping Dragon Books

The Stand-In
by Elizabeth Stevens

Print ISBN: 978-1925928198
Digital ISBN: 978-1925928181

Cover art by: Izzie Duffield

For my sister,
You can't have my chocolate, but you can have my kidney.
P A K I D G E!

Contents

Stand-In, Stage Left

"Ella!" a voice called, the tightly denim-wrapped body it belonged to hurrying towards me. Lindy's face fell as she got closer and saw me around the giant canvas in my arms. "Oh, it's you…"

And that was how most of the world greeted me. Full of disappointment as though they'd been expecting Narnia and only found the back of an old cupboard full of musty coats. I couldn't blame them, personally. I'd been looking for Narnia all my life, too.

"I'm looking for Ella."

That was another thing people often said to me, in much the same manner as they were affronted I even existed. But I was used to it. That was my life and, when it came to people like Lindy, I didn't much care how little they thought of me, both in what they thought about me and the amount of time they actually spent remembering I existed.

"I don't know where she is," I answered, rearranging the canvas so I didn't drop it. Damn thing was big and awkward if not particularly heavy. "I thought you had last lesson with her?"

Lindy flicked her plait over her shoulder as though she were heavily flirting with someone. I did a quick scan of the hallways, but it could have been any of the guys pushing through the throng of students. Certainly none of them seemed to be flirting back and I hid a smirk.

"Well we need to get to the committee meeting, or all her plans with be for nothing," Lindy sighed, like it must have been my fault for locking my fair princess of a sister up in the tower. I had no idea what said plans were and I was happy to keep it that way. "We're going to be late!" Lindy stamped her foot.

I nodded, not really sure what Lindy expected me to do about it. Ella ran on Ella time and not even an adoring crowd waiting on her was going to make her run to anyone else's schedule. "Okay. Sure. Well you two have fun with that."

I made to move past her as I hefted the canvas, but Lindy stepped in front of me with a bored expression. "Can't you, like, call her or something?"

I mentally rolled my eyes and managed not to drop the canvas on her head. "You'll have better luck getting through to her, I'm sure."

Lindy looked around like she was about to do something really dirty – like, you know, talk to me some more – and I huffed, deciding to save her the bother.

"I'm sure you're fast approaching your quota for being seen with a nobody for the day, so why don't you run along and I'll see if I can find Ella?" I asked, making myself sound chipper and helpful like the good secretary I was.

Lindy gave me a grimace I expected was supposed to pass for a smile on that face and flounced away, her skirt bobbing dangerously close to flashing her arse. I hurriedly looked away before it became a train wreck I wouldn't be *able* to look away from.

I hoisted the canvas back up and pulled my phone out of my pocket with my other hand, hoping I could keep hold of everything. Just as I was sure I had a handle on everything, my bag slid off my shoulder and almost took my phone with it.

"There you are!" someone else called and I looked over, feeling rather frazzled. But the paint-splattered face that matched that familiar voice made me smile. And this time when they got closer, they didn't pout like I'd ruined Christmas. "I've been looking everywhere for you. I told you I'd help with that!" Rica chastised.

She shook her head at me with an exasperated sigh and grabbed the other end of the canvas before I dropped it as well. I gave my best friend a thankful smile and reached down for my bag. As I hoisted it on my shoulder, I hit Ella's number.

"What's up?" Rica asked, already amused by my predicament.

"The harpy is required by her minion, I just have to–"

"Where are you?" my older sister snapped. No 'hello' or 'how are you, fair sister', just outrage I hadn't followed whatever order I was supposed to have read in her mind.

"Ella, hey!" I laughed awkwardly into the phone.

"Thank God. I've been trying to get hold of you all day," she scoffed. I pulled the phone away from my ear; no missed calls or texts…

"How? Telepathy?" I mumbled, shaking my head at Rica's questioning look.

By the time I put the phone back, Ella was ranting. "…busy, so you need to go in my place."

"Sorry. What?" I asked.

She grunted in annoyance. "I am busy," she enunciated loudly and slowly, like I was a foreign exchange student. "You have to go to the Formal Committee meeting for me."

"Uh, can I ask why?"

Rica made more questioning gestures at me and I shrugged.

Ella grunted again. "Elijah Sweet is taking me to the formal and I need someone to make sure Milly stays away from him."

"Does…Elijah Sweet know this…?" I asked slowly as though talking to a very large idiot. In fairness, I was.

"Oh my God! Can't you just do this *one* thing for me?" she cried. "It's in the Willis Theatre, okay?"

I rolled my eyes at Rica. "Sure. Keep Milly away from him. Although if he's already taking you, what does it matter?"

"He hasn't asked yet, duh. So talk me up and make sure he does."

Uh, no thank you!

But, no wasn't an option here…

"Uh, great–"

I pulled the phone away and looked at it. In true Ella form, she'd hung up on me without even waiting for me to answer because she just expected I'd do what I was told. Again in fairness, I was going to.

"What did she want now?" Rica asked as I took hold of the other side of the canvas and we frog-marched to the art rooms.

"Apparently I'm required at the Formal Committee meeting to make sure Milly keeps away from Elijah Sweet."

"Why?"

"Because he's asking Ella to the formal, don't you know?" I asked her like it was obvious, duh.

Rica snorted. "And *does* Elijah Sweet know this?" she asked, wanting to know as badly as I did.

I shrugged. "I would expect not."

"And you're on guard detail?"

"Wooing detail. He is apparently yet to ask."

Rica looked at me knowingly and I could see her fighting a smile. "Because that's going to go well for you."

I gave her my most withering glare. "Thank you. I'm aware."

"Well, good luck with that."

"Oh, shut up."

"Girl, I love you. But talking to boys is not your strong suit…"

I huffed a piece of hair out of my eyes. "Just in case I hadn't noticed…"

"How are you feeling?" She barely contained her snort.

I hardened my glare at her and wished some people didn't know me so well. "Fine right now. Thanks so much for your concern."

A smile tugged at her lips, but she kept the laughter at bay at least. "What time's the meeting?"

I shrugged again as we wrestled into the art room. "Don't know. Now I assume. Lindy was panicking about being late."

"Sure the ho wasn't talking about her period?"

I sniggered. "Uh, I don't even want to begin to contemplate that, so…hopefully not."

Rica took the canvas from me and set it up on her easel. "Thanks for getting this for me. You should have waited though."

"Eh, I wasn't doing anything." I looked at my phone for the time. "I'd best get to this meeting then. I'll see you Monday."

She shook her head, but smiled fondly. "Why do you always do what people say?"

"Says the girl who now has her new canvas." I waved my hands at it like the girl who gets the letters on 'Wheel of Fortune'.

Rica tried to frown, but failed. "I'm serious, Gin."

I nodded, my gaze roving across the classroom at the various pieces of art; sculptures, paintings, pottery, all sorts of things I didn't even know the names for. "You know why."

"Because life goes quicker that way," she intoned in what was supposed to be a mockery of me.

"It does," I laughed at her half-arsed attempt at an insult. "I'm just waiting for those neon lights, Rica. Eighteen. Freedom. No more understudy. I can live my own life."

"Yeah, except you won't know how after spending eighteen years being a carbon copy of her majesty." Rica meant well, but the conversation was always the same.

"I've got my list. I've got my plan. Less than twelve months and I'll be the star of my own life."

Rica hugged me. "Well, I already think you're a star."

I snorted. "Sure. The star of the understudy programme."

Rica shook her head with a laugh and pushed me towards the door. "Go, be the stand-in, and woo that handsome prince for the petty princess."

"I think you mean pretty princess."

Rica scoffed. "I think you know I don't."

I grinned and hurried out, jogging through the emptying hallways until I got to the theatre. I pushed my way in and saw there were a whole bunch of kids already milling around and there were chairs on the stage. I jogged up the centre aisle, watching Milly as she was sorting something on a table to the side and talking animatedly with Brenda.

I dropped my bag at the base of the stage and went to pull myself up. But a hand popped over the edge and I found a guy with a green splash at the front of his almost black hair grinning down at me. His smile lit up his nut brown

8

eyes and I told myself that, yes he might have been quite cute, but it was still possible to not make a fool of myself.

"Need a hand?" he asked and I was fairly sure I recognised him, but my brain seemed to not know where from for a moment.

"Uh, thanks…" I smiled, pleased I managed two words without word vomit.

He grabbed my hand and helped haul me up.

"You know, they have these nifty things called stairs. They make scaling great heights much easier," he said in wonder once I had both feet on the floor again and had managed not to fall over.

I nodded, looking down so he wouldn't see me blushing. "Oh, hey. I've heard of those. But me and new-fangled technology just don't get on."

He snickered. "I'm Govi."

I blinked as I looked up at him, then realised why I recognised him. *This may have been a fortuitous meeting after all.* "Chloe."

He scrubbed his hand along his chin. "What're you in Winters for, Clo?" he asked, looking me up and down. "I don't reckon we have any classes together."

"No, that'd be because she's not supposed to be here," Lindy said, stalking over and glaring at me.

I gave her a sour smile. "Ella sent me on *the mission*." I tapped the side of my nose as though that would make any sense to Lindy. Amazingly, it seemed to.

Lindy went from being scary bitch monster to acting like my best friend faster than I assume a Mustang goes from zero to one hundred. "Oh, of course. I forgot," she tittered, grabbing hold of my arm and grinning maniacally at Govi.

I looked down at my arm as though I'd suddenly lost feeling in it or it no longer belonged to me. I sort of wished either of those situations was true… "Uh, yeah. Good…"

"So you know each other?" Lindy asked, still staring right at Govi.

"Sure. This is Chloe. We go way back," Govi answered, giving me a smile.

I smirked, but looked down to hide it.

"Can we sit down and get on with it please?" Milly called, exasperated.

I yanked my arm out of Lindy's grasp – it took a while, she had a grip like a limpet – and headed for a random seat. Lindy dropped into the one next to me, crossing her legs and sticking out her meagre chest like all the boys must be watching.

"Right. Thanks for coming…" Milly paused, "everyone who actually turned up. I know it's…" She petered off and

I looked up to find her staring at me. "You're not Ella." She was caught in some unholy mix of surprised and put-out.

I nodded and swallowed. "No. Uh, she sent me to stand-in because she couldn't make it…" I replied, looking firmly at Milly and no one else.

Milly looked at me with interest, like I was a jar of Ella's secrets and Milly was going to find them out one by one and use it to crush her. Did it make me a terrible sister to say I was okay with that?

"Okay…?" She waited for my name.

"Chloe," Govi offered.

Milly's gaze flickered between me and Govi. "Chloe Cowan?" she asked and I nodded. "How unfortunate." Then I was dismissed as she looked down at her clipboard. "Okay. So, like I was saying–" She paused again. "Eli, nice of you to *finally* join us," Milly drawled, clearly trying to impress him with how unimpressed she was with him.

My heart felt like it stopped in my chest and I looked up sharply as Elijah Sweet walked out of the wings, grinning like he knew he'd just wet every pair of pants in the room.

"Sorry, Mil. I got here soon as I could," he replied, suave as always.

I was in the same room as Elijah Sweet and I had no idea what to do. Lindy elbowing me wasn't helping either.

Like, *yes, Lindy. Thank you. I have eyes!*

11

And those eyes were not about to miss Elijah Sweet. I didn't imagine there were many eyes that missed Elijah Sweet.

Elijah was the hottest guy in school, hands down. He had dark blond hair cut so it fell endearingly into his eyes, which were this amazing contrast of a light honey colour and framed by dark lashes. He had a face so beautiful it would make the Madonna weep, and the voice of a damned angel. And no, that's not just hyperbole; the guy sung like a Greek god and was as sinful as they came. He was born to be a rockstar and well on his way to becoming one on the world stage with his band Quicksilver.

I was embarrassed to say that I – like, most likely, the whole school – had a huge crush on him. It was a good thing I'd never had a chance to speak to him because every time I saw him smile, my brain melted into this little giggly puddle that was useless for anything. It was disgusting really, but I had no control over it. I knew he was the worst sort of guy – arrogant, conceited, smarmy, arrogant, a player, shallow, did I mention arrogant? – but my eyes refused to believe that a guy with that much gorgeous smoulder could be such a twat.

You see now why my wooing him for Ella was going to go so terribly well and why I wouldn't have been surprised had Rica laughed in my face.

Well, I suppose she had in the end...

I snuck a look at Elijah as he dropped into the chair next to Govi, giving the Quicksilver drummer a fist-bump and a smile. At least I might have an in with Govi; I seemed to be able to put two words together in front of him.

I felt Lindy nudge me and I blinked. She was waving a stack of papers at me in exasperation as her eyes darted furiously between Elijah and me. I nodded, took the stack of papers, took the bundle on the top that was paper clipped together, and passed them on.

"Okay. So, your schedules," Milly was saying. "We're going to be meeting every Monday, Wednesday and Friday for the next four weeks, then every afternoon in Week Ten. We have decorations to sort, posters to make, tickets to sell, final donation drives, it's all go from now people. I need one hundred per cent commitment—"

"In which case, I vote Eli out now," Govi chuckled, throwing his hand straight up in the air, and Elijah smirked.

Milly glared at them, only just managing to act like she didn't care one whit that they were semi-rock royalty. "He can't be out. You're playing and he agreed as front man to be your spokesperson. *You*, on the other hand, Gabriel, can leave anytime you wish."

I had the distinct impression Milly would prefer that option even as I had the distinct impression she wasn't

13

letting Elijah out of any commitment that put them in the same room if his life depended on it.

"I'd be happy to stand-in for him," Govi replied, throwing me a wink like stand-ins were suddenly a thing and possibly cool.

I jumped in my seat as Lindy nudged me again and I glared at her while Milly and Govi kept up what I'm sure was witty banter.

"Are you quite right?" I hissed, knowing full well the answer was no but not quite having the heart to tell her; unlike my sister, I did try not to be a bitch.

"Gabriel Costa is the drummer for Quicksilver!" Lindy whispered, far too up close and personal.

I leant away from her as far as humanly possible and nodded. "Yes, Lindy. I'm aware."

But she just kept on coming. She grabbed the front of my jumper. "And he knows your name."

I was *this close* to slapping her out of whatever crazy land she'd fallen into. Maybe she'd found Narnia after all… I was a little jealous.

"Okay. Did we take our meds today?" I asked, trying to pull her hands off me. There was a momentary pause in my head as I stopped to remember if I'd taken mine.

"Ella's sister!" Milly snapped and I whirled around.

"That is me!" I yelped, still trying to dislodge Lindy. I finally got her death grip off my jumper and cleared my throat. "Yes?" I squeaked, throwing Lindy one more look to check she wasn't about to grab hold of me again.

"If the two of you are quite finished?"

"Oh, I wish…" I muttered and I was sure I heard Govi laugh.

I looked up at him but my eyes found Elijah instead. Not that Elijah was looking at me, because I was so far beneath Elijah Sweet's notice that it was unnecessary. Which was good. Because by all accounts, if you were in his notice, then you were getting your heart broken. Not that I'd give him anything to notice knowing my luck. But my brain still melted into a puddle on the floor and I was sure I blushed just thinking about the possibility of having to talk to him.

Well, this is a great start… I thought to myself as Milly droned on about the expectations on our time.

The Ass in Assistant

"No. No, Norb. You stay, buddy. I'll see you later," I said to the white and brown ball of floof desperate to come with me as I locked up the house and hoiked the bag up my shoulder.

"Chloe!" Ella screeched and I rolled my eyes.

"Coming. Coming!" I answered as I hurried around to the car and slid into the back seat.

Mum was already in the front with Ella.

"Your father will pick you up from Dance and drop you off at Piano, then I'll get you from there, and we'll go to the hairdresser. What time's the party?" Mum asked as she backed out of the garage.

Ella looked over her planner with a huff. "It starts at seven–"

"So by the time we're fashionably late to make an entrance… That will make it eight." You wonder where Ella learnt how to treat people so well? Just take a look at our mother. "Your father and I need to be at dinner with the Petersons by half-seven, so Chloe will take you–"

"Actually," I interjected, leaning forward, "Chloe has plans."

Mum waved away my trivial concerns, like I was interrupting her speech to NATO, or I was a particularly annoying fly or something. I was starkly reminded of Ruby Rhod from *Fifth Element*. And her outfit wasn't helping the image either.

"Chloe will take you, then wait for you to let her know when you're ready to come home. I have to put my face mask on tonight and your father's getting up early in the morning for golf with Hector."

I flopped back in the seat, knowing it was pointless to argue. I could – of course I could – and I had been known to on many occasions. But today I did not have the energy for the guilt trip speech; "but, the things we do for you, Chloe!" "Your sister is very good to you, Chloe." "It's the least you could do, Chloe." At least they remembered my name…most days. It was all just easier and life went quicker when I just went along with the madness.

Less than twelve months. Big neon lights. I reminded myself like a mantra.

Because in less than twelve months I would finally be eighteen. I could do what I wanted, when I wanted and I was counting down the days like my birthday would be water to my previously parched existence. Not long now. I'd lived like this for over seventeen years, I'd been the understudy to my sister's life for seventeen years. What was one more? One more and I'd be free; the idea alone made it all worth it. It made anything worth–

"Chloe, stop daydreaming!" Mum practically shrieked.

I jumped. "Sorry. What did you say?"

"You need to run to the pharmacy for me while your sister and I are at the hairdresser. We *just* won't have time to get there."

I nodded as I looked out the window. "Sure, Mum. No worries."

I ignored them for the rest of the trip, with thankfully no more screeching of my name at dog-attuned heights, with my nose stuck in my book. Well, one of the eBooks on my phone because then I wouldn't have to hear about how nerdy I was.

We finally pulled into the dance school carpark and I dropped out of the car, waving to Akira as I dragged the bags after me. As Ella passed, she held her hand out and I seamlessly put her bag into it with the three seconds I had to do so; practise makes perfect, and I was a well-practised assistant.

I fell into step with Akira as Mum tooted to Ella, who was flouncing up the stairs like she owned the place.

"How was your week?" Akira asked.

I shrugged. "It went. I'm on the formal committee now apparently."

Akira looked at me in surprise. "Oh good, because you don't have enough to do with your life."

I shrugged. "You know me. Give, give, give."

"You are a paragon of charity."

We both snorted. "Yep, that's totally me."

We went in and stretched while the previous class was finishing up. Ella was, as usual, the centre of attention and I was quite happy totally out of the spotlight. A couple of people tried to get my attention before realising I was in fact not Ella Cowan, then went running over to join the Evil Queen's groupies.

Akira chuckled. "I'm looking forward to the day people realise they've been fawning over the wrong Cowan sister all these years."

I grinned ruefully and blew my hair out of my face. "That day will never come, Akira. I am perfectly happy fading into obscurity as soon as I turn eighteen. I'll be one of those cold cases. In thirty years, the world will still wonder what happened to Chloe Cowan."

She sighed, but it was only fake annoyance. "But you're such a good dancer."

I shrugged. "Tough."

We shared a grin.

"Tell me about your week," I said as we changed positions.

She shrugged. "It was a week. Graham sat next to me in German."

I smiled. "Oh, progress!"

Her face went a slight tinge of pink as she shook her head. "He just forgot his book, so the teacher said he should share with someone."

"Yeah, but he picked you!" I said, nudging her with my foot.

"I'm sure it was just–"

"All right, guys," Miss Tara said as she clapped her hands. I gave Akira a supportive eyebrow waggle and she laughed. "We warm?"

"But nothing. Progress." I smiled to Akira and we helped each other off the floor to get in position.

Dance class went much the same as it did every week; we practised our choreographed pieces and we added to the ones we were still learning. As usual, Ella took front and centre, parading around and acting like a queen. I shared a few humoured smirks with Akira, the only person in class to see through Ella – Akira and I had been friends at my old school, before Ella and I had moved to Winters, after we'd found ourselves in the same extra-curricular dance class. Although, that had been back before we were in the same class as Ella.

Dad was there waiting when the class was let out in his flashy Merc. Unlike Mum, he didn't try to plan every second of our lives to the nanosecond. Instead, his Bluetooth earpiece was in and he was talking shop with someone in what I thought might have been Greek – the literal kind here.

As we drove to our piano tutor's house, Ella sat scrolling through her phone or taking stupid selfies and I got a few minutes of blessed peace where I could put my headphones in and imagined what it would have been like to be an only child. Again, there almost wasn't quite enough time to pull out my book, but I took every second I could and a few pages were better than nothing.

I would have been happy to give up all the extra-curriculars when we got into Winters – I already spent too many hours during the week dancing and practising music, I didn't need to do it on my Saturday too. But the one time I'd felt brave enough to subtlety mention that maybe it would be better if I dropped dancing and piano, I was told in no uncertain terms I should feel privileged that I did the things I did.

Sitting in our piano lesson, I made sure I hit a few too many wrong notes so as not to show Ella up – not that I got all that much time at the piano. Because my sister might have walked around like she was God's gift, but she wasn't nearly as skilled at anything as she should have been for the amount of flattering people did around her.

Was I bitter about that?

Sometimes.

Most of the time, I was just amused by the proof that if you walked the walk then people didn't really stop to care if you talked the talk. (Or, was that the other way around?) Mind you, she *did* do a lot of talking…

From Piano, I was dragged to Mum's and Ella's hairdresser. When I got back after my run to the pharmacy and I'd not forgotten anything on the three page list, I sat down and waited for them. I distinctly heard Ella say, "I don't know, can you just make it look more, like, natural?" as I swung around in my chair and read my book. Because, you know, strawberry blonde – I'd inherited all the strawberry and none of the blonde – isn't actually a natural colour. But the blonde highlights and darker red shades through strawberry blonde? Totes natural.

Anyway!

On I was dragged.

Back home; where I was required to run around after Ella while she lounged in the bath and Norbert and I made faces behind her back. Well I made faces at Norbert and I chose to believe he was smiling back at me. I ferried drinks and food back and forth, I found Ella's new razor, I got her the *soft* face washer, I found a way to charge her phone without electrocuting her, and I put her hair in the warm curlers while she nattered about Elijah's dreamy eyes and how he'd talked to her the day before.

Needless to say, by the time I was back to an empty house after dropping her off, I was looking forward to some me, my book and Norbert time. Ella even managed to get herself a ride home from some poor, unfortunate guy – quite possibly even *the* Elijah himself – and didn't deign to speak to me on her return.

So I actually had a pretty good Saturday night for once.

****

The door burst open on Sunday afternoon and the Super-G was waiting with her arms wide open. "My loves! How are we?" she cried, beaming.

She was wearing a bright purple and green poncho, which matched wonderfully with her orange glasses, and pale yellow shorts. Her feet were bare as they usually were when she was home and she had a smudge of dirt on her cheek the way she usually did after a day in the garden.

"Hey, Grandma," I said with a smile and let her wrap me up in her warm embrace.

"Hi, Mum," Dad said as I walked in and he deigned to let his mother hug him.

"Aunt Bow?" I called as Norbert barked and I let go of his collar.

He went running off towards the back garden so I followed him as the rest of the family trooped into the house behind us. I could hear Ella prattling on about all her 'accomplishments' for that week and her plans for the next. The garden, like Grandma, was a mess of colour and excitement; everywhere you looked was something new and different, a muddle of plants both edible and decorative coming together to form something truly amazing.

"Hiya, Norbie! Gin?" I heard Aunt Bow call and found her peeking out from among the holly hocks. She grinned at me widely.

Like Grandma, Aunt Bow was a free spirit, evidenced by the eclectic ensemble I couldn't even begin to break down. I knew for a fact that Aunt Bow had probably made everything she had on, or adapted it from op shop finds.

Aunt Bow clambered out of the garden and gave me a hug, neither of us caring if she got dirt all over me. Because, unlike my dad who had somehow managed to get a rod lodged so far up his arse he couldn't see the parts of life worth living anymore, Aunt Bow and the Super-G were more like me – if I'd been as creative; they were original and they were themselves, completely comfortable in their own skin in a way I knew I'd get to be someday too.

"How are you, my gorgeous Gin?" she said happily as she squeezed me then pushed me to arm's length and looked over my fairly standard outfit. "No-nonsense bun, plain pale top, boring jeans, peach Converse." Her eyes whipped up with endearing criticism. "My love, stop hiding away!" She let go of me a twirled around the garden.

I got that weird giggly grin I always got around Aunt Bow. She had the ability to treat me like a misbehaving five-year-old and an adult all at the same time. It was a wonderful feeling, and one everyone needed more of in their lives.

"We need some colour," she laughed then leant towards me as she whirled past. "We need some men in our lives." She gave me a wink and pulled me into her dance.

"A couple of Toms for a Sunday afternoon?" I asked her.

She gave me a cheeky grin.

"Rainbow!" I heard Dad's stern voice cut through our laughter.

I never understood why he bothered trying to reprimand her with her full name. How authoritative can you make saying the name 'Rainbow' anyway?

"Arlo," Aunt Bow sang, a little breathless after our shenanigans.

"I would appreciate it if you would keep *some* decorum around my children."

"Of course. We wouldn't want them having any fun now, would we?" She winked at me again and I hid a snigger.

"Mum is making drinks." He turned on his finely polished heel and went back inside.

Aunt Bow leant her arm on my shoulder. "So pleased he's still as stiff and boring as always," she huffed, only half sarcastically.

I put my arm around her waist and we headed inside.

"Now, tell me all about your week. Anything exciting?"

"I'm on the formal committee."

Aunt Bow stopped, forcing me to as well. "Boring. Also, what?"

I nodded. "It is *literally* my only news."

She turned me to face her, the blue eyes and bright ginger hair so like mine. "Honey, why?"

"Ella needed me to go."

I could tell Aunt Bow was having a mini tantrum in her head – her nose always twitched and her eyebrows narrowed for a few seconds. "Ella *needed* you to go to her committee?"

"It's not actually *her* committee…"

Aunt Bow frowned for real this time. "Wasn't she saying last week something about her committee?"

I shrugged. "I try not to listen to the majority of what falls out of her mouth."

Aunt Bow tried hard to keep her smile under wraps. "How does that usually go?"

"Fine."

And failed. "Lucky you. I'm sure she told Super-G she was running some committee for the dance?"

I snorted. "That would require her showing up."

"Do I want to know why that means you have to go?"

I grinned and waggled my eyebrows, and Aunt Bow settled into her gossip face.

"Right. Ella's got a date to the formal," I said conspiratorially.

Aunt Bow raised her eyebrows in surprise. "Really? And who might her date be?"

"That guy who fronts that semi-famous band at school? Quicksilver?"

"Elijah Sweet?" Aunt Bow went from conspiring aunt to semi-fan girl.

I frowned in humoured confusion. "How do you know who Elijah Sweet is?"

Aunt Bow grinned. "Honey, I'm older, not old."

"You read the newsletter, don't you?"

She nodded. "I read the newsletter. Religiously. There are surprisingly few mentions of my favourite niece."

"But plenty of the other."

"Too much of the other and not enough of it worthy."

I rolled my eyes. "Not this again."

"Gin, you have more talent in your whole body than Ella has in her little finger."

"Way to be original," I muttered.

"The cliché doesn't make it any less true. You could star in every play. You could open any concert. You could beat Quicksilver to international stardom. And what do you do with all that?"

"Nothing–"

"Nothing. You do nothing with all that. You hide in books and maths." She shuddered; Aunt Bow hated anything restrictive and structured.

"I'm good at books and maths. I don't want people to know my name. I just want to live quietly and contentedly. I love you, Aunt Bow. But I'm not you."

28

She sighed and pulled me into a hug. "I know, Gingernut. I know. I'm sorry. I just get so annoyed that Ella can sound like she's running over a cat and gets mountains of praise, when you're sitting over there with a perfect concerto and no one gives two hoots unless Ella's busy."

I smiled and gave her a squeeze, deciding not to pull her up on her hyperbole. "You and Super-G and Rica do. That's all I need."

"I'm sorry my big brother's such a shithead, honey."

I gave a short laugh. "It's okay. Soon, I'll get to live my own life. One day, I'll be the star."

"Oh, baby," she sighed. "You're already my star."

We gave each other one more squeeze, then swung to continue heading inside.

"Ah, girlies. Lovely!" the Super-G cooed. "Your boys will get drunk if you don't hurry up." She winked and jiggled her glass towards us as she swept away with a sashay of her hips.

"You know, most grandmas don't try to get their granddaughters drunk…"

"Most grandmas aren't my mum." Aunt Bow tipped her head.

We laughed and went inside to find Ella going on about what she was doing in the coming weeks; the committee,

dance recitals, piano recitals, her part in her drama class'
little performance...

And I tuned out with familiar taste of my one Sunday
Tom Collins on my lips.

Little Drummer Boy

I liked dance and I liked music, I hadn't been doing these things for nearly my entire life only to hate them. But they weren't my favourite subjects. I was just lucky that a lifetime of practise had made me decent at both.

"Uh… You…" Miss Felicia called on Monday afternoon, waving at me.

"Yes?" I replied, looking up at her and realising she'd forgotten who I was. "Uh, Chloe."

"What was it you do again?"

"What did you want me to do?"

She looked at me like she was trying to remember who I was and what instruments I played. As she frowned, her glasses slid down her nose. "Are you related to Ella?"

I sighed and nodded. "Have been for over seventeen years."

"And you've been at Winters for…?"

"Three and a half years."

The rest of the class was, not surprisingly, wondering when she'd get to her point and how much longer she was going to focus on Ella Cowan's little nobody of a sister. The mutterings of boredom began.

"And you play…?"

"Piano and guitar."

She brightened somewhat. "Like Ella. She plays the piano beautifully."

I nodded. If beautiful here meant half the time she sounded like she was strangling a particularly melodious cat – to quote Aunt Bow.

"Well, hop on up then and we'll see how you do," she said as though it was my first time in front of the keys.

I pulled myself off the floor and went up to the piano. I wasn't going to be a concert pianist like my father could have been – no matter what Aunt Bow liked to think – but I wasn't exactly bad at it after something like eleven years. Still, anything that drew the least amount of attention to me was great. So I played her a relatively simple piece and even threw a wrong note in there for good measure. When I was done, she looked at me like she was surprised I was as good as I was.

"Well, very nice…work…" And she'd already forgotten my name again.

I nodded and went back to my spot while Miss Felicia called on the next student. Honestly, sometimes I wasn't sure my grades were actually based on how well I did or on how guilty the teachers felt about forgetting who I was in the shadow of the great Ella Cowan. But it could have been worse; they could have assumed I didn't turn up and failed me.

Winters School of Fine Arts was, obviously, a school dedicated to the arts. But we also did things like Maths and Sciences as well. And those teachers tended to remember who I was, especially compared to Ella who was rubbish at all those things.

When the bell rang, I picked up my stuff and wandered to the auditorium for the Formal Committee meeting.

"Hey, you!"

I smiled and didn't look at her. "Hey, yourself."

"Where are you going? Freedom is that-a-way." Rica pointed like I might have forgotten my way around the school.

I nodded. "Committee meeting."

"But you're not actually on the committee. The committee is for Year Twelves…"

I shrugged. "I told Ella I'd go."

"Gin, come on! Let Her Lowness go to her own committee meeting."

"I told Milly I'd be there, too."

"Why the hell did you do that?"

I looked up from my feet. "Well… I committed."

"God, I love your loyalty. But you leave none for yourself." She held her hands up like she was strangling me.

I shrugged again. "Eh, I'm nothing if not consistent."

"That's the beaten down spirit we know and love," Rica said encouragingly, pumping her fist through the air across her body.

I smirked. "I'll see you tomorrow."

"All right. Woo good! Woo well! Whatever! Go woo!"

I nodded. "Yep, sure. Because I can put two words together in front of him."

"Practise makes what, Chloe Cowan?" she asked in the perfect annoyed imitation of my mother.

"Perfect," I laughed.

"Exactly. Now, go practise."

I shook my head and waved my arm at her as we parted ways and I found my way back to the auditorium. It was one of the smaller ones, with a stage and retractable seating. It was never booked for productions in Term Three because the formal committee took it over and the formal would be held there. As I walked in, I tried to envision what it would look like all set up; I'd never had any other reason to be anywhere near formal preparations before, not that I was thrilled by the prospect at that moment either.

The place had trestle tables set up and boxes and stacks of poster board and paper. It looked like the formal committee had put the five closest Officeworks out of business.

"Well, at least you weren't late today," Lindy huffed and I frowned at her.

"I just couldn't wait to see your beautiful face, Lindy!" I gushed and I felt the sarcasm was somewhat lost on her when I saw her smile.

"Good, good… You! Ella's sister!" Milly called as she hurried over to me.

I saluted her. "Chloe, reporting for duty."

Over Milly's shoulder, I saw Govi smirk.

"Good. I need you at that table," Milly said, staring at her clipboard and pointing to a table behind her, "and I need you to get a start on posters. We need them all done by the end of the week so they're up for at least a week before tickets go on sale."

"Come help poor unfortunate me," Govi called enthusiastically and I felt myself grin.

Lindy pressed against me and flicked her hair. "Shall I help them, too?" she asked Milly.

Milly was still staring at her clipboard. "No. I need you cutting tickets, Lindy."

And then she was off to direct someone else to wherever they needed to be. I smiled at Lindy, so glad I wouldn't be stuck at a table for two hours with her drooling in my terrible artwork over the Quicksilver drummer who was waving at me enthusiastically. I watched Lindy shuffle off to her designated area and went over to Govi.

"Hey," he said with a smile and I'm not sure why I blushed.

"Hey," I answered, looking down at the table with all the craft supplies.

"How are you?"

"I'm fine. How are you?"

"Totally wankered," he gave a rough chuckle. "Eli's on us about the set list and nothing we offer him seems good enough. The formal's a prac run for us, you know."

I nodded absently as I looked at the pieces of paper in front of us. "Is it? I did *not* know."

"Yep. We're opening at the Entertainment Centre in November."

I looked up sharply. "Holy shit. Really?"

He nodded, looking pleased as punch, and did an adorable little wriggle of excitement. "We are. First stop to proper international fame."

36

I couldn't help but smile at his enthusiasm. "Well, congrats. That's amazing."

"Thank you," he replied, brushing off his shoulders and I laughed. Then, he leant towards me. "So you obviously know what I do, then. What is it you do, Clo?"

I picked up the theme code and wrinkled my nose at him. "Enchanted forest?"

Govi snickered. "It sounds totally whack, but I reckon we can pull it off. Now, quit avoiding the question."

I grinned. "Yeah, maybe. Um, I dance and I music-a-little."

"You music-a-little? And what's music-a-little look like when it's at home?"

His humour was infectious and I couldn't stop smiling. "How are you at drawing?" I asked.

"Half-decent."

"Well, I'm awful. So draw me a big tree trunk on that." I patted the paper.

"That I can do." He nodded.

"Right. Music-a-little is I'm passable with a couple of instruments."

Govi picked up a pencil and leant over the poster board as we kept talking. "Passable? Passable at what?"

"Whatever I put my mind to," I answered teasingly, hunting around for tissue paper I was sure I'd seen earlier. I was surprised at the ease I felt around him, but Govi just exuded that sort of infectious calm.

"Really?"

I scoffed a laugh. "No. Two instruments passable. My lips were never flaccid enough for trumpet."

Govi snorted and threw me a humoured look. "Flaccid?"

I nodded to him as I started scrunching green tissue paper to make tree leaves. "I'm far too stiff, apparently." I puckered and pressed my lips together at him in perfect mockery of how not to play the trumpet.

Govi packed out laughing as he worked on the tree trunk. "Wow. And how long did you try trumpet?"

"Only a term a couple of years ago."

"Okay. So trumpet was a bust. What are you passable with?"

"I can play the triangle like you wouldn't believe. I'm like the *Mozart* of the triangle."

Govi snorted again. "Where the hell have you been all my life?"

I shrugged as I ripped up some more tissue paper. "Minding my own business."

"Oh well, please never do such a thing again. Although you still didn't really answer my question."

"You know my sister. Can't you guess?" I asked, taking a look at my leaves so far.

"I'm not asking about your sister. I'm asking about you."

I turned to look at him as he was busy with his tree, completely shocked that someone other than Rica, Super-G or Aunt Bow actually wanted to know anything about Chloe Cowan, not just the Ella understudy.

"Hey. No peeking 'til I'm done!" he said, covering the page with his body. "You play with your green stuff and tell me about you. What?" he asked as he looked at me and his smile fell. "You okay?"

I nodded. I was very okay. I was just super surprised.

"Uh, yeah. Um, I piano and I guitar."

"Hey, neat." Govi's infectious smile was back and he went back to his drawing.

"What are you down there? Picasso?" I scoffed and he laughed.

"Just you wait, Clo. Just you wait."

We chatted companionably about this and that while I started to colour in some letters with glittery paint to cut out and stick on the poster whenever he was finally done with his tree.

I looked up as I heard Govi huffing a laugh, then followed his gaze to where Milly was talking to Elijah across the room. I watched in fascination as I wasn't sure if they were fighting or flirting. I felt a hand on my head that lifted it out of the cocked position it seemed to have fallen in as Govi laughed.

"A fascinating breed aren't they?"

"Who?"

"Girls."

"Did you think I'm an alien or something?"

He laughed again and I found myself smiling. "No, 'course not. But I mean there are three types of girls at this school, right? Hell, in the whole world probably–"

"Really?"

He nodded. "Stay with me here. When it comes to Elijah Sweet, there definitely are. You've got the ones who just fall in a heap in front of him, desperate for his attention or his touch." Govi winked at me. "Then, you've got the ones with half a brain who know he wants nothing more than another notch in his bed post, but they can't help falling over him either. And finally, you've got the ones with a complete brain – see exhibit A across the room – who despise everything he stands for but still go a little ridiculous around him."

"You either think a lot of your friend or not a lot of the female population," I replied dryly.

He shrugged. "I can only work with what I've seen. And they, Clo, are the only three types of girl I've seen whenever Eli's in a room."

I snuck a look at him from my peripheral. "And what does that make me?"

Govi looked me up and down. "Well, you've got a complete brain. I'm just waiting for the little ridiculous."

I scoffed as I went back to my letters and he went back to the trunk. "I might pleasantly surprise you."

"I'm willing to bet you will."

I smiled to myself, then jumped as he stood up quickly and threw his arms out in triumph.

"I give you…a tree trunk!" he said, excitedly and I had to drag my eyes off his excited face and down to the poster board.

"Holy crap!" I laughed. "That is amazing!"

He'd not only drawn a totally beautiful tree trunk, but he'd given it an old wizened face, making it look exactly like something you'd find in an enchanted forest. Suddenly, the whole theme didn't seem quite as stupid to me after all.

"You like?" he asked.

"I like." I nodded. "I don't think my leaves will do it justice now.

He grinned. "They'll look great. Shall I do another?"

"Uh. If you want to, I would think that yes you should."

His grin widened. "Sweet." He shuffled his tree trunk over to me and pulled another piece of poster board to him and got started again.

"Do you think the 'E' should be blue or green?" I asked, looking at my conglomeration of letters so far.

"In my experience, they're red and filled with hearts," Govi chuckled.

I looked up at him and found him looking at me with humour. "We're talking about an enchanted forest, not a…vaguely enigmatic boy."

Govi snorted as though I'd completely surprised him. "Wait 'til Eli meets you," he said with a shake of his head.

Panic flooded me as he looked around like he was looking for Elijah right then.

"Ha! No. I don't need to meet anyone!" came out breathy and strangled. Although, how I was supposed to talk up Ella if I never talked to him… I'd work that out when I got to it.

Govi gave me a funny smile. "Nah, trust me. He's gonna want to meet you."

"Ah," I coughed awkwardly, "you know how we said I'd surprise you?" I said quickly, colouring my 'E' in blue.

"Ye-es…" he replied slowly like he expected my answer to be good.

"Put me down for a little ridiculous."

Govi sighed, but was grinning when I looked at him. "Not you too!"

I shrugged. "Sorry! I try very hard to not be affected by the arrogant sod, but…" I shrugged again. "Curse of the female hormones?"

He sniggered and sat down again. "The fifties called and they want their view of women back."

I snorted. "There is such a thing as tongue-in-cheek." In fact, it was the rule by which I lived my life.

He grinned. "But I guess I shouldn't be surprised. Although, I am a little bit hurt you haven't turned to drivelling mush around me."

"Oh! I almost did on Friday?" I said it like that should make him feel better.

He nodded, seemingly pleased. "I'll take that. What did I do? Just so I know for future reference. My panty-melter doesn't seem quite as good as Eli's, granted. But I can give it a red hot go?"

And in Govi's defence, the smouldering smirk he turned on me was enough to make my heart race and my cheeks burn.

I cleared my throat. "Yours is nicer."

"Nicer?" he chuckled. "Well, that'll have the girls leaving his door for mine."

"More effective," I clarified, my cheeks burning hot as I scratched the back of my head in the hopes my elbow would hide my face from him for a bit.

"Is this you going ridiculous? Because I have to say, it's kinda cute."

I dropped my arm to look at him incredulously.

"Strike that. Very cute." His eyes were warm and he really did have a nice smile.

"That is *not* a rave review, by all accounts!" I said, my indignation overruling any embarrassment or awkwardness.

"Some guys like cute," he answered defensively and I got the feeling Gabriel Costa was one of them. Didn't make me feel all that much better, though.

"Yeah, in a twelve year old sister. Not so much in potential girlfriends."

"Ooh! Who are we after?" he looked around quickly and conspiratorially like it could possibly be anyone in the room.

I couldn't help but laugh and I wondered what it was about Govi that made the girl who'd barely spoken to a guy ever so damned comfortable. And don't get me wrong, I wasn't a complete wallflower. But before Winters, I'd gone to an all-girls school for junior and then a co-ed school for one year. And anywhere outside of school I went I was shadowing Ella, so boys didn't really notice me and I didn't really have a chance to talk to them. I didn't mind by any stretch of the imagination, I busied myself with other things. It just made things kind of awkward now I was wanting to talk to boys. Especially after growing up with the expectation that boys were marvellous and different magical creatures from the way Ella went on about them. Logically I knew they weren't, but Ella had spent so much time fawning over them that my brain usually got all tangled up whenever I was faced with one.

"*I'm* not after anyone," I answered coolly.

"Oh, *shade*, sister," Govi laughed. "Okay, then. Keep your womanly secrets. I've got sisters, I know better than to pry."

"You've got sisters?" I asked.

"Oh, dude," I heard him chuckle under his breath and looked up from my 'S' to see Govi watching Elijah leaning in close to a girl who was giggling like mad. "Seriously. One of these days, he's going to regret this behaviour."

I doubted that very much. "Yeah, when? When he's a famous rockstar and girls know he's up for a no strings attached, crazy one-night stand?" I replied sarcastically.

"I was thinking more when he met the girl of his dreams."

I gave him a look that told him what I thought of that.

"You're a very cynical young woman, aren't you?" Govi huffed in amusement, looking me over. "What happened to you?"

"I was born," I said flatly, in a rare display of frankness.

The amusement still hovered around his lips, but his eyes had gone soft and calculating and I hoped he wasn't going to dig deeper into that comment. "Ouch. Well, I'm here now and I will fill your world with unicorn farts!"

I shook my head against a laugh. "Of course you will. Until you forget you even met me."

He shook his head with much more enthusiasm. "Nu-uh. I could have a thousand fans screaming my name, but I could never forget Chloe Cowan."

"You'll have forgotten me once this is all done."

And I sounded sorry for myself, but I wasn't. I had three constants in my life who didn't consider me the understudy, it was just how it was. Ella would pull her finger out at some point, get her wish, and have Elijah ask her to the formal, and Govi would never remember the stand-in he made posters with that one time.

When I looked back at him, he was shaking his head more gently. "Nah, I don't think I will."

I blushed at the sincerity in his voice, and blushed harder when he nudged my shoulder companionably.

"Come on, Clo, I need some more leaves."

I saluted him with an awkward chuckle. "Yes, sir."

We locked eyes for a moment and I wondered if maybe I wouldn't just be a stand-in to Govi after all.

The Stand-In Committee

Swinging into the art room, I looked for Rica at her easel. It was just like the art kids to keep working after the end of day bell. In many ways, they were the most dedicated of the lot of us. That or the most easily immersed.

"Hi. Can I help you?" the art teacher asked sweetly, like I'd just wandered in off the street and had no idea what I was doing.

"Uh, yeah, yep. I'm looking for Ri– Erica…"

The teacher smiled at me like I was a simpleton, or perhaps just a nervous five-year-old. "Of course. She's over there."

I nodded and bounced my way over to her, making sure not to brush up against anyone's wet projects or get in the way of their light – I'd been accused of that before and it wasn't pretty.

"Well, I thought it was you darkening my doorway."

I dropped my pleasant face. "Cut with the theatrics, Rica. I need a favour."

She looked me over quickly. "Straight to the point. Testy. Hair in a bun. Jeepers. Sure, I'll do it."

"You don't know what it is yet," I said, surprised.

She rolled her eyes at me while she mixed some colours. "No, but I've seen this," she waved her arm to indicate all of me without actually needing to look at me again, "and I know you need me. So of course I'll do it."

"Uh, great thanks… Auditorium, as soon as you can."

She glared at me, completely unaware that she was striking a pose that would have made photographers desperate for her picture. Stupid tall, beautiful, talented, wonderful best friend of mine…

"Fine. Do I need to bring anything?"

"We're making posters?"

She nodded. "All right. Fine."

"Thank you!"

"Great. I will see you there soon, just let me finish…" she indicated at her canvas with almost as much enthusiasm as she'd indicated at me just before, "this…" She waved her hand, effectively dismissing me. But when Rica did it, I knew she still loved me and I didn't really care.

"Bye!" I sang, threw a smile to the teacher and waltzed out.

49

I was in a terrible mood and, when in a terrible mood, I tended to get flouncy. Call it a defence mechanism, call it insane; when I got testy, I overcompensated with flounce because what in the world did Chloe Cowan have to be unhappy about and how dare she take *that* tone with anyone!

That'll happen when Ella corners you and tells you Lindy's 'busy' that afternoon so someone will have to go to the Formal Committee meeting for her – of course, I was still supposed to go for Ella, no thanks needed. Not that I was really convinced that Lindy had done an awful lot on Monday…? But still, my poster work hadn't come close to Govi's and I could do with an art student in my arsenal. So, enter Rica.

I dragged myself into the auditorium and looked around. I was, strangely, one of the first kids there.

"Hey. You're Ella's sister, right?"

Oh, I froze. I froze so bad. "Yep," I squeaked then winced, glad he was behind me.

"Cool. Look, I was wondering if she was coming today or…?"

I shook my head. "Nope."

"Okay…" he said slowly. "Oh, hey man!"

I blinked and saw Govi walking towards us.

"Hey, hey! You met my girl!" Govi laughed loudly. As he reached me, he put an arm around my shoulder and spun

50

me to face (gasp) Elijah Sweet – like I didn't know! I felt like a pebble between mountains, both in relation to their height and personalities. "Eli my man, meet Chloe. Chloe here thinks you're an enigmatic little boy," he scoffed and I watched Elijah's eyebrow rise with interest.

I shook my head. "No…" I swallowed and tried again. "No…" I breathed not much more successfully than the first time.

Govi chuckled and gave my shoulder a squeeze. "Ridiculous, huh?"

"Shut up," I shot back at him, then cleared my throat. "Elijah, nice to…meet you."

"Call me Eli," he said with that sinful smirk and I was amazed that my brain only softened and stuttered a little around the edges.

After watching him all Monday afternoon with the girls around the room, I had a sneaking suspicion he was attempting (and succeeding) to use seduction to get out of doing any real work. And that was something I could hang onto and use to fuel my brain's continued functionality. If there was one thing I hated, it was people who took all the credit and did none of the work.

Cough, Ella, cough.

"Eli…" I squeaked, nodding.

"You're Year Eleven, yeah?" Eli asked.

I nodded "Yep."

"You a dancer, too?"

"Kinda."

"Artist?"

"Oh no," Govi chuckled. "I've seen her skills with a texta and it is *nothing* to write home about."

I shook my head and my breathy "No…" seemed unnecessary after Govi's announcement.

"Theatre?"

I snorted, full of nervous giggles threatening to erupt. The idea of me acting was absurd. "No."

Was I sweating? I felt like I was sweating. Great rivulets of sweat cascading down my body and flooding the whole damned room. My brain had managed not to melt for once – in fact, it was running at an unusually crazy fast pace – but apparently I still couldn't really string much in the way of words together.

"Gin's multidisciplinary," I heard Rica say and we all turned to see the paint-splattered lovable freak walk through the door. She was, as usual, wearing a baggy t-shirt under a baggier pair of overalls with her button up shirt tied around her waist. All she needed now was glasses and a pony tail…

God, she even had paint streaked through her mess of dark blonde hair. Actually, on closer inspection, it looked like she might have put that there on purpose... Why was I not surprised?

"Gin?" Govi asked, looking down at me with a humoured smirk on his quite frankly adorable face and I elbowed him playfully in the side.

"Short for Gingernut," Rica answered, tapping the side of her head. Which I knew meant she was referring to my hair colour, I wasn't so sure the others did though.

The two boys looked at her, then me, and back again.

"It's a family thing." She shrugged, seemingly completely unfazed by the boys beside me. "Where do you want me?"

I looked around for Milly, shoving Govi's arm off me as I threw him a smile. "Dunno, we were at that table yesterday," I pointed to it, "but Lindy was on ticket cutting. Why don't you and Govi get started and I'll see what Milly wants me doing?"

"What? And I'll miss your wit-acious quips?"

"Wit-acious is not a word, and Rica's lovely. Oh. Rica, Govi. Govi, Rica."

"And. Eli." Govi kicked his head towards him, looking amused I'd forgotten his friend – although, forgotten was not the word I'd use – and I nodded.

"Yep. And Eli." I nodded again as I refused to look at him. "Yep." I popped the 'P' and looked anywhere but Eli Sweet.

Govi chuckled but mercifully said nothing about that. "Come on then, Rica. Let's get started while Clo finds her place in the world." He started walking away. "Parting is such sweet sorrow."

"Shut up!" I laughed at him then realised I was left standing next to Eli by myself and my laughter flat-lined quickly. I nodded at him and gave a weird grimace-smile in response to his questioning look, then hurried off to where Milly was thankfully across the other side of the room.

"Ah…you…" she said as I approached her, her face falling into the confusion most people feel when they realise they should remember my name but don't.

"Yes, me. I've swapped out my poster station, so I wondered where else you needed me?"

She looked me over like I was going up for auction. "Why are you here, again?"

I sighed. "Because Ella sent me. I can go if you really don't want me?"

Milly looked down at her clip board and sighed. "Look, you're only Year Eleven and I don't know you, but we're already short-handed. Add to that Ella's lack of show?" She huffed and I was reminded there was no love lost there. "If you don't mind helping…?"

I shrugged. "I said I would and a Cowan signed up, so a Cowan should really be here."

Honestly, I couldn't go even if Milly wanted me to; Ella expected me to keep an eye on Eli so I was going to have to stay and do that – though the how still eluded me. There was also a huge part of me that was driven by a need to make sure that someone lived up to Ella's commitments if she wasn't going to. She'd signed up for the committee so someone had to be there and do the work in her place. Who better than her understudy to stand-in for the leading lady when she didn't deign to show up? That was why I'd been born after all.

Milly was still looking me up and down like I must have some ulterior motive. And I guess in a way I did. But honestly, I just wanted to make posters, or sew drapes, or cut tickets, or untangle fairy lights, or any other number of odd jobs that needed doing, then go home and do my own thing, maybe finish one of my books.

Finally, she nodded like I'd finally met approval. "Okay, thanks." She looked back down at her list. "What are you good at?"

I blinked. "Whatever. I fetch, I carry–"

"Do you sew?"

I shrugged. "Depends what you want done."

"Handle money?"

"Better than some." *Cough, Ella, cough.*

"Right. I'll put you down for ticket sales shifts. It'll be lunch times from Monday week eight. Don't worry, you won't get every lunch."

I shrugged again. "Whatever suits."

"You were on posters on Monday?"

I nodded. "Govi was picking up a fair bit of my slack. We got about three done I think?"

A ghost of a smile lit her face. "You're not arty?"

"I'm more interior decorator arty, at best. I can't make anything, but I can put it all together in some semblance of decent."

Milly gave me that assessing look again, then nodded. "Okay. Well if you managed to keep Gabriel on task, then you can stick with that for now. I'll let you know if I need– BRENDA!" Milly suddenly shrieked and I winced. "Brenda! Get that material off the floor!"

"Uh, well… If you don't need me for anything else then…" I said, starting to back away slowly.

Milly's gaze fixed back on me before it flickered down to her clipboard. "I'll let you know, but posters are the priority right now."

I nodded in agreement, like I knew about these things.

"Do you have the specs sheet?"

I paused. "Uh, we did on Monday… Although I think Govi made an aeroplane out of it…" I grimaced in apology.

Milly just rolled her eyes and shuffled her papers before holding one out to me. "Here. Try to keep him occupied with less important documents, yeah?"

I nodded quickly. "Sure. I'll see what I can do."

"Thanks." Her eyes slid behind me again. "BRENDA!"

I turned and rushed over to Govi and Rica. "Well, that was fun."

Rica was in her element, totally lost to creation and Govi was staring at her in wonder.

"She's amazing," he whispered harshly at me as I plonked onto the chair next to him and we both just kind of sat and watched her for a little while.

"Eh, she's all right," I answered with a shrug.

Govi chuckled and the corner of Rica's mouth turned up.

"I've spent years working on my craft," she said as she stepped back to look at what she had so far and running her paint brush over her fingers absently. "Much the same as you've spent years on music. What I do is no better just because it's different."

"Uh, yeah. What you do is totally better," Govi said, sounding in complete awe.

Rica looked up at him through her fringe and gave him a shy smile the likes of which I'd never seen on her face before. I looked between the two of them with interest for a moment as they just looked at each other, a smile growing on my own face. I didn't know if there'd been some words exchanged while I was gone, or if Rica had just had a moment to realise that Govi was super cute and seemed to have that kind of personality that makes you simultaneously crush on him hard and divulge your deepest secrets like you're already best friends.

Finally, Rica pointed to Govi's posters with the end of her paint brush. "I like your trees."

Govi grinned winningly. "They look like shit compared to yours."

Was that an actual blush I saw on Miss Erica Gorman's face?

"That's not true," she said, looking down like she was embarrassed and going back to her poster while she smoothed her fringe.

"Well I'm going to keep colouring in pretty glittery letters because that's about all I'm good for," I interjected.

"You're good for plenty. Stop fishing for compliments," Rica said with faux exasperation as she was doubled over her poster and I heard the smile in her voice.

"I'm not fishing for compliments. I just happen to know every one of my extensive deficiencies. But I am willing to give anything a go."

"Anything, eh?" Govi chuckled and winked when I looked at him.

"Down boy." I shook my head.

"Your only extensive deficiency is not living for yourself," Rica snapped and I knew my flippant whining was annoying her. But she knew I wasn't being serious, she just hated when I put myself down because it was what most people seemed to do. "Unless Govi is likely to consider your extreme nerdiness a deficiency."

"Well, that all depends on what kind of nerd she is. The academic kind or the fandom kind?" Govi asked as he pulled open the glue pot.

"Both," Rica said simply, then stood up again to look over her work, which looked like it was going to be an amazing dark forest scene with mysterious eyes in the shadows. She looked up at Govi, then I noticed how her eyes slid off him like she was going to get ridiculous if she looked at him for too long. "Gin – appallingly to some people – wants a career outside the arts and spends more time mooning over *Doctor Who*, the *Marvel Universe*, or her latest book, or whatever other nerdy thing she's into than she does contemplating her audition pieces. Not," here, she glared at me accusingly, "that she doesn't get accepted to every damn thing she auditions for."

"Like what?" Govi challenged.

I shrugged. "She's exaggerating. I've auditioned for two things in my life and happened to get into them."

"Two for two, that's one hundred percent," Rica pointed out.

"Thank you. Yes, I do math."

"You ace math."

"Shut up."

"Okay, okay," Govi interrupted us, his hands up. "So what did she audition for?"

I glared at Rica, daring her to tell him. The way she grinned at me, I knew she fully planned to.

"Well, Winters doesn't count. But she auditioned for Merriman's and a spot on Got Talent."

I waved her words away.

"No shit! How did you do?"

"She turned them both down," Rica said with annoyance.

"I had to audition, but I couldn't accept when Ella didn't get through."

Govi leant towards me. "Sorry. You didn't take up Got Talent or Merriman's because your sister didn't get an offer?"

"If she was your sister, you'd understand," I said solemnly.

"That's what she keeps telling *me*," Rica told him in her most resigned voice.

I looked up to say something but saw she was frowning. I turned to see what she was looking at and saw Milly talking to Eli. Only today, there was more of a flirt vibe going on. I looked back to Rica and gave her a panicked look, to which she just laughed and I frowned.

"So, Govi. What's the story with Milly and Eli?" Rica asked, busy with her poster.

Govi turned around for a moment, then went back to sticking my tissue paper leaves to his tree trunks. "As far as I'm aware, nothing. But then I'd say that about Eli and any girl."

"Out of concern for his privacy?" I teased and Govi smirked knowingly.

"Even if he's hooked up with them?" Rica asked.

"Especially if he's hooked up with them!" Govi chuckled roughly. "Don't you know his reputation?"

Rica shrugged. "There are a lot of rumours running around this school. I choose not to listen to them."

"Cool." Govi nodded approvingly. "Well when it comes to Eli, rumours are more likely true. You get his interest and you're done for. He'll wear you down eventually, then a few kisses, and the one and done treatment."

"Uh, no thanks." I shuddered.

"You speak that highly of all your friends?" Rica's eyebrow rose along with the corner of her lips.

Govi sighed and turned back to look at Eli again. "Eli would hate for me to be purporting false rumours and, look, I love the guy like a brother. But I wouldn't let him near any decent girl."

Rica barked a laugh. "Well, Ella's in then."

I gave her my best 'shut up' look.

"Yeah, I don't think he's hooked up with Ella… Not that I tend to keep a running tally."

"You're not on guard detail to keep away jilted lovers?" I asked.

Govi snorted. "Nah, that's more Lake's job."

"He's your bassist, right?" Rica asked.

"Oh, you follow us, do you?" Govi joked as he elbowed me playfully.

"Like every other person in this school, we have been known to enjoy your musical talents," I answered, swatting his arm away gently.

"And your faces," Rica said almost absently, then looked to me in complete shock as though she couldn't believe she'd said such a thing.

I also couldn't believe she'd said such a thing.

Govi chuckled. "We've been told we're quite pretty," he said, running a hand through his hair mock-arrogantly.

I scoffed. "Who on earth would have lied so outrageously to you?"

"Oi," he laughed, "weren't you telling me on Monday how pretty I was."

"I was assuring you that your smoulder was on point, Govi. That doesn't mean *I* think you're pretty."

"Oh, but you think Eli's pretty?" He sounded indignant.

"Gin thinks Eli's the kind of pretty that needs a good punch to the nose."

Govi looked between us, clearly confused. "What?"

"In her words 'nothing that good looking should be such a twat'. I'm inclined to agree."

"Shit, does that make me a twat?" Govi asked, looking genuinely concerned for a moment.

"No, Govi. You're pretty and not a twat."

"So frankly, I should get more girls than him?"

I snorted. "Mr Insecure, aren't you? Or are *you* fishing for compliments?"

Govi grinned and wriggled adorably in his seat. "Of course not."

"If you don't believe me, show Rica your smoulder," I said as I went back to my glittery letters. "I guarantee she

63

will tell you the truth. Girl couldn't lie if her life literally depended on it."

I heard Rica breath out heavily and looked up to find her completely swooning. And to be fair, Govi was giving her a smoulder that was giving Hell a run for its money.

"Yeah, I'd say you're good," she said, sounding rather breathless and I just laughed.

Which earnt me a glare from Rica and a cheeky grin from Govi.

The Errand Girl

We pushed our way through the milling students. I had no idea if Lindy was making her appearance at the meeting, but Govi had talked Rica into coming back on Friday to finish the posters and help put them up.

"There you are!" the voice of my nightmares called harshly.

I flinched and Rica touched my arm in stoic support.

"Hey." I turned to Ella with a half-hearted smile.

"Elijah Sweet is yet to talk to me about anything, Chloe. But, he seems mighty cosy with Milly Wallis... Are you even doing your job?"

"*Your* job?" I clarified and her eyes narrowed dangerously. "Yes, I am." *No, I'm not...* "Everything's fine. He and Milly barely talk to each other. If you were that worried, why don't you just go to the meetings yourself?"

Ella swished her hair over her shoulder and scoffed. "I'm busy. Something you'd know nothing about. Just keep that lecherous little theatre freak away from him and make sure he asks me to the formal."

"And how do you propose I do that, Ella?" I asked, my annoyance flaring into uncharacteristic rebuttal.

She glared at me like I'd tried to kill her. "Get it done." And with that, she shoved her way through the students in the hallways and went off to do whatever it is that Ella Cowan does when she's busy.

"Your sister's a bitch, FYI."

"Thanks, hadn't noticed." I muttered.

"What's more important than flirting with Eli herself?"

I shrugged. "Probably has to tend her flying monkeys?"

Rica snorted. "Wicked Bitch of the West, indeed."

I smacked her lightly. "Come on. Wouldn't want to keep Govi waiting," I said with a sing-song voice.

"Shut up."

"You think he's cute," I teased.

"Of course I do, I have eyes! You can't tell me you don't think he's cute?"

"He's super cute, but *I* don't have a crush on him."

"Neither do I!"

I nodded as I started for the auditorium. "No, of course you don't."

"I don't!" Rica said quickly.

And she spent the rest of the walk trying so hard to convince me she didn't have a crush on him that I was pretty sure she did. At least it was a distraction from the foul and panicky mood Ella had put me in.

"Gin!" she hissed. "I do not–"

"Do not what?" Govi asked as we walked up to our table and I slid my bag over my head. "If you tell me you forgot your blutack then I shall rescind your invitation!" he teased dramatically.

Rica did actually blush and I looked away to hide my smile. "Nothing," she said softly, then cleared her throat. "Nothing. Women's things."

Govi nodded knowledgably. "That time of the month," he said with a wink and tapping his finger to his nose.

"No!" she gasped as I snorted.

"Nothing wrong with it. Normal. Healthy." Govi's smile faded as he looked thoughtful. "Well, no. Nothing should bleed that long and not die. BUT! That just makes you women even more amazing."

"Whose preferably-not-bleeding pants are you trying to flatter your way into?" I asked as I sat down and pulled our posters together.

Govi chuckled, sounding very pleased with himself. "Doing well, am I?"

"Well, you…" I stuttered to a stop as Eli walked into the room, with his typical arrogant swagger and a sexy smirk for any girl in the vicinity.

My heart rate spiked, but it was more in anger and a nervous tick than it was real proper panic and anxiety. So that was something. I had no idea how I was supposed to go about stringing enough words in a sentence around him to ensure he asked my sister to the formal. But I was going to have to come up with something or Ella was going to have words to say about it, I was sure.

I watched as he nodded to someone as he walked in like he was going in slow motion.

And it had to be said, the boy was fine.

He wore skinny jeans and a slouched black t-shirt, his ever present guitar strapped to his back. He pointed to someone else as he ran his hand through his shaggy dark blond hair and gave them a smile that I bet could have made the Statue of Liberty's legs feel a little wobbly. The guy oozed sex appeal and I was dangerously close to swooning.

"Oh for God's sake," I heard Rica mutter and I jumped, hoping I hadn't been drooling. I was seriously worried I might have been. "Govi, is Eli taking anyone to the formal?"

"No. Why? Does Clo want him to ask?" I wasn't sure why he sounded quite so insultingly disappointed.

"No!" I yelled far too loudly so that every person in the room – even Eli – turned around to look at us.

I went bright red as my eyes locked with Eli's and spun around so fast I nearly fell off my chair. I cleared my throat. "No, I certainly don't. God, Ree. I can't do this." I leant forward and stared at her pleadingly.

She shrugged. "Then don't."

"I have to!"

"You don't actually."

"I shouldn't be here."

"Then go?" Govi said, sounding like he was trying to be helpful but was actually just confused.

"She can't." Rica sighed resignedly. She'd try to persuade me to do things for me, but she knew what I needed just then was encouragement not a way out.

I glared at Rica and shook my head slowly.

"If you turn around and tell me you *do* want him to ask you, I am going to lose all respect for you, Chloe," Govi warned. And I noticed only a slight hint of teasing in his voice, like it was only there so I didn't get angry with him for telling me what to do.

I shook my head at both of them.

"It's the Wicked Bitch who expects him to ask," Rica said, giving me a look like it served me right.

"Sorry. What?" Govi looked between us and I dropped my head to the table.

I sighed. "Ella sent me to apparently woo Eli into asking her to the formal. I'm meant to keep him away from Milly, talk her up, and make sure he asks Ella."

Govi didn't say anything for a moment, until he breathed, "Does she see how *mental* that is?"

"I would say not."

Govi snorted and I looked up at him.

"What?"

"Well…" He looked between us. "I mean, that's hilarious. Does she actually think you're going to keep Milly off him and he'll ask her?"

I frowned at him and dropped my head back down.

Rica answered for me. "Unfortunately, yes. You're lucky. You see the congenial side to Ella. Chloe gets pushed around and she just does what she's told."

"I've told you a hundred million times, Ree, it's easier," I mumbled into the table.

"I know, Gin…" she said softly.

"There is a slight flaw in Ella's plan, is there not?" Govi pointed out.

"Please say he's taking someone else!" Rica cried excitedly.

"Uh, no. Chloe can barely say two words to him without going ridiculous, although she adamantly promised me she tries not to."

I heard Rica scoff. "Oh, trust me, she does. It is a source of constant amusement to me and annoyance to her that she lusts after a guy she hates."

I raised my hand up. "Firstly, I don't lust after anyone, especially not arrogant self-entitled wanker rock-jerks. Secondly, I don't know him well enough to hate him."

"You just hate everything he stands for and every rumour that circulates," Rica clarified.

"He just *sounds* like a dick," I muttered.

"Well, he is a dick," Govi agreed. "But he's got some good points... Granted, none of them have anything to do with his interactions with the female species, so I doubt you'll ever see them. But I promise they are there."

"Ugh, how am I supposed to talk Ella up to a guy I can't talk to?"

"How are you supposed to talk Ella up when she's a raging bitch?" Rica asked and I looked up to glare at her.

"How about we go put some posters up and I'm going to pretend you didn't say that?" I replied.

Rica's eyes narrowed dangerously. "You don't have to do her dirty work *and* stick up for her."

"You know what? I'm sure you'll be fine," Govi broke in, trying to keep the peace. "I mean, you managed five words to him on Wednesday and you only almost fell off your chair once today. So you know, as far as embarrassing yourself goes…?" He shrugged unhelpfully.

I sighed and pushed myself to standing. "Thanks, but I'm going to have to think of something. I'm quite partial to my skin."

I whirled around and came face to chest with a familiar black t-shirt. His hand went to my arm and he actually had the audacity to brush a stray strand of hair from my face as I looked up at him in panic. Which was a terrible plan in hindsight. My heart pounded and I reminded myself that he wasn't as hot as my brain was telling me he was. Even when he was looking down at me with nothing but mischief in his eyes and a gorgeous half-pout to his lips.

"My bad…" I said quickly.

"Two words!" Rica cheered and my cheeks burst heat and my eyes widened in humiliation.

Govi's snort didn't help anything, nor did the smile Eli was obviously trying to hide.

"You okay there?" he asked me as if he actually cared.

"I…" I nodded. "Fine. Good. Going. Posters."

"Four words! Not a sentence!" Rica yelled enthusiastically and Govi spluttered a laugh.

Oh, I was going to kill her. I loved her, but I was going to kill her.

I let out a deep breath, "Excuse me... I need to... Ree, bring the blutack."

I swiped the posters off the table and only just managed to not trip over my own feet as I hurried out of the auditorium, though it was a near thing.

"Gin, wait up!" I heard Rica laugh, but she didn't follow yet.

"Clo," Govi said as he jogged up behind me.

My face felt tomato red. "Oh my God, one word out of you and I think I'll implode from embarrassment."

"It'll almost be more than you managed."

I threw him a glare so fast, I did trip on my own feet and he had to catch me so I didn't land on my arse. "Yes, thank you. Because I am not humiliated enough."

His face softened as he looked down at me. "Don't stress, Gin, 'kay? Eli has girls embarrass themselves in front of him far worse than a little brain fart, yeah? Honestly, that is tame compared to some of the stuff we've dealt with."

"Govi, those girls want one thing from him, two if they're lucky. I want no things from him! None!" I hissed.

He looked at me apologetically and his hands on my shoulders gave me a gentle, reassuring squeeze. "Not quite true."

73

"Govi, I swear I am not interested in him."

"You *are* interested in getting him to ask your sister to the formal, though."

I sighed and threw back my head. "Okay, yes. I want one thing from him. But I'm not going to get that because my brain decides to go on vacation to Hawaii every time he walks into a room."

"There are worse places it could go."

I glared at him.

Govi grinned. "It's fine. Just keep practising."

I frowned heavily. "Yes, because practise makes perfect…" I mumbled sarcastically.

He looked at me calculatingly. "It does, but it doesn't sound like a good thing when you say it like that."

I shrugged and turned to start looking for bare patches of wall to hang our posters. "Because usually I'm practising to be perfect at things I don't even want to be mediocre at," I admitted.

"Blutack at your service!" Rica huffed as she arrived. "Milly was guarding this stuff with her life!"

I turned and saw her and Govi exchanging a look but I had no idea what it could have been about. It was definitely not flirting, that was for sure.

"Come on. Let's see where we can put these." Govi smiled and I gave him my best smile back.

74

We headed through the school. There were still a few kids milling around. There were some after school lessons, and some kids used the time to book studios for practice or to work on assignments. Recorded music wafted from some rooms and live music flowed from others. Some kids were dancers, some were musicians, a few rooms had art students, a couple had theatre kids running lines or painting sets.

As we shifted some other posters around to make space for ours, 'Shut Up and Dance' started playing from down the hall and Govi started singing along. He wasn't a main singer for *Quicksilver* and, for the life of me, I couldn't work out why. He had an excellent voice and he pulled Rica and I to dancing while he sang. And the boy could move. I mean he wasn't going to be a principal or anything, but he could very easily get by.

When the song was finished, Govi went to grab some more blutack and we found we'd run out.

"I'll head back and get some more. Stay here. I'll be right back." He grinned, then jogged off.

"That boy has far too much enthusiasm," Rica laughed.

"Yeah, but you *like* him," I said, nudging her with my shoulder.

She gave a small, shy smile. "He's nice, he's cute, he's funny. But he's not really my type, is he?"

75

I shrugged. "I wasn't aware you had a type. And if you did, anyone in this school would probably cover it."

She huffed and nodded as there was a giggle from up the hallway.

We both turned to see Eli and a girl stumble into the hall in a somewhat flirtatious embrace. She was clearly saying something seductive to him and he was smiling widely at her as he cupped her cheeks. Her hands were on his waist and they were walking awkwardly towards us. Not that we even existed to them.

"He looks like a total tool," Rica said flatly.

"A complete jerk," I agreed, because he did. "But I mean, he can't help his face."

Rica packed out laughing. Doubled over and everything, it was entirely unsophisticated. I was a little surprised Eli and his girl didn't turn around.

Govi appeared beside us, brandishing blutack. "What's up with her?"

Rica stood up quickly, her laughter magically dissolved. "Nothing."

"We were just complimenting Eli's face," I said, trying to hold back my smile.

"Oh, he'll be pleased." Govi nodded with a wry glint to his eyes.

"Yeah. I mean he can't help that his face looks like a jerk."

Govi snorted and, no matter how much Rica liked him, nothing could stem her laughter this time.

"That he'll like less," Govi said with a smile as Eli put his arm around the girl's shoulders as he saw us and headed over.

"Well you look like you're having fun," he said, looking over the three of us.

"We were just complimenting your face, mate," Govi chuckled and Rica sniggered.

Eli smirked. "Why do I feel like that's not quite a compliment?" He turned his honey eyes to me. "Want to let me in on the joke?"

I opened my mouth and my amusement was suddenly gone in a complete mental blank. "Uh...no, we just... I mean you can't help your face," exploded out of my mouth in very much not the manner in which it was intended.

"I can't help my face?" He looked me up and down slowly and I wanted to kick myself.

I flushed and the girl next to him laughed at me.

"Come on, ladies. These posters won't hang themselves," Govi said and it sounded an awful lot like he was siding with us in whatever battle of wills was playing out here. I wondered what the hell we'd done to earn that.

"Have you looked over the new set list?" Eli asked him.

"I'll look at it tonight. I have trees to deal with," Govi said proudly, holding up our last poster.

Eli looked it over and I could tell he wasn't doing much to hide his disdain. "Arts and crafts now?"

Govi shrugged. "What can I say, man? It's kinda fun. Plus work goes faster when we all pitch in."

"That a message, mate?"

Govi shrugged. "I gotta help Clo and Rica. You play safe, mate."

He gently laid a hand on my arm and we followed Rica down the hallway.

"See, jerk," Rica said.

"See, unable to make with the words good." I slouched and groaned. "I am never going to get Eli to ask Ella to the formal."

"Okay. How about I take pity on your ridiculousness and help you out?" Govi asked.

"Yeah and how do you propose to do that?" I asked, throwing him a look that I was sure told him every pitiful thing that was running through my frazzled brain.

Govi shrugged. "I'll work it out."

"You'll work it out?" Rica asked with humour. "What are you? The Godfather now?"

Govi chuckled and threw an arm around my shoulder companionably. "I'll talk to him, yeah?"

"Talk to him?" I asked.

"Yeah. I'll talk to him for you. I'll talk up Ella, tell him she's interested, get the ball rolling kinda thing."

"He did ask about her the other day... What kind of ground work are you working with?"

I felt Govi shrug. "Don't really know. He flirts with anything with tits, so naturally I've seen them flirting. She's in music with us," he took his arm off my shoulder and ran his hand through his hair, "but I've never really seen them talk. Eli's not the kind of guy to *like* anyone so I'm not promising anything, but I'll see what I can do."

He looked so apologetic, but I didn't care. In a rare move from me, I rushed forward and threw my arms around him. He chuckled and hugged me back.

"Thank you, thank you, thank you!" I cried.

"If playing Good Samaritan gets me more hugs like this, I should try it more often."

He laughed as I pulled away and swatted him playfully.

"Or you know, it's called being a decent human being," I replied.

"Or you know, in Gin's case it's called being a slave," Rica commented.

"I swear if I didn't love you, I'd hit you," I muttered as I bumped her hip with mine.

Govi smiled at us and shook his head. "Right. Where shall we put our final masterpiece?" he asked, holding it up.

Chinese Whispers

I walked in to the auditorium on Monday, my nose buried in my book as I wandered towards the table that I'd been at the week before. I dropped into one of the seats as I put my bag by my feet and ran my hand through my hair.

Rica had told me in no uncertain terms that she was so not going to come to any more meetings. I didn't know if Lindy was going to start turning up again or whether Milly would be a man down now. If that was the case, I knew that would sign me up for twice as much work. I wished I could have convinced Rica to come. We needed to get a start on the decorations and I could have used her artistic ability. I was pretty sure Govi and I weren't going to be producing anything of note if I was involved.

A body leant against the table next to me.

"I feel like we're going to be on trees again," I said as I picked up my phone to scroll through the pictures of enchanted forests I'd opened earlier. "Do you think we can make some of those faces of yours 3D? That might look pretty cool."

Govi didn't say anything for a moment and I didn't look up. Govi wasn't known for sitting still and listening for long periods of time, but it wasn't entirely unheard of for him to not say anything when he thought I was on a roll.

"What if we make a forest?" I asked. "For the walk way maybe? I guess we'll have to talk to Milly about what she wants done. Do you think we're going to have to make little models first?" I laughed.

"I don't know much about trees, but models…I do…"

The hand with the book in it dropped to my lap and my thumb paused mid-scroll as a chill entered my veins.

That very sultry, seductive voice did not belong to Gabriel Costa.

I slid my eyes sideways and realised those were not Govi's legs wrapped in dark grey jeans, one crossed over the other and going on for ever – honestly, whose legs were actually that long? My eyes roamed up. That wasn't Govi's slouched white t-shirt with black shirt over it. That wasn't Govi's cuff or Govi's rings. That wasn't Govi's trademark sword and angel wing cross pendant – it looked like a bone whale tail on a leather strap. And that certainly wasn't Govi's sexy smirk, those honey eyes were totally not Govi's nut brown ones, and the dark blond hair was far too light and missing any sign of green streak.

Then I realised I was staring into Eli's face and I quickly looked down again, hoping my cheeks weren't as red as they felt. I cleared my throat.

"I'll bet... Sure... Yep," was apparently what came out of my mouth and I mentally rolled my eyes at myself.

"It's Chloe, right?" he asked casually, leaning towards me.

I had no idea what to do. "Uh, yeah."

"You're the multidisciplinary one who thinks I'm an enigmatic little boy?" He sounded like he might be amused by that, but I wasn't sure if he really was.

I started nodding, then stopped and I was sure my cheeks were as red as they felt – stupid red-head tendencies – especially when he chuckled. I cleared my throat again, totally not succeeding in sounding like I knew what I was doing. I made the mistake of looking up and found him watching me carefully.

"No. I mean, I..." I cleared my throat again. "You seem..."

I'd been intending to say 'nice', but I realised at the last minute that wasn't strictly true. I mean he looked nice, but nothing I'd heard or witnessed about him made me think he was nice. He was arrogant, shallow and expected girls to fall at his feet, but he wasn't nice.

"You look nice...?" I finished lamely.

His eyes widened and that smirk played at his lips. "You complimenting my face again? I feel like every time you do that, it's not really a compliment." He grinned and my brain would have told my heart to stop pounding if it had still been working.

Why does he have to be so goddamn attractive? I wondered.

"Well I can't compliment what I don't know," I said quickly, standing up and surprising myself with the number of words I'd managed.

Eli stood up as well and I felt like he towered over me quite unnecessarily while my brain stuttered and my stomach churned. He took a step towards me and I took a hurried step back, my legs hitting the chair I'd just been sitting in.

"I'd be quite happy to fix that," he drawled, looking me over like he was undressing me with his eyes.

"Uh..." I took another alarmed step backwards and tripped over my bag but managed to keep my feet. "I'm sure that's... I mean... Not... Okay, I've got to... Milly!" I called, finally spotting her and figuring that would be the easiest way to get out of whatever situation I'd found myself in.

Milly waltzed over, quite obviously waiting for Eli to look at her. "Yes?" she asked, still looking at Eli.

"I, uh, just wanted to ask…" I snuck a look at Eli from the corner of my eye, wondering why the hell he was still standing there just smirking at me. "What do you want me doing now? I was thinking…maybe…"

My train of thought just fizzled out as Eli stretched and a section of his stomach appeared between his t-shirt and his jeans. I was glad Milly seemed to have noticed as well because then she was probably not noticing me perving on him. I righted the tilt my head seemed to have taken without my consent.

"Chloe was thinking of making up a forest for the walkway," Eli finished for me and I blinked, wondering what he was doing.

I'm sure he's just waiting for Govi, I told myself as I looked around for Govi myself.

"Govi and I were going to help."

My eyes darted straight to his in a surprise that overruled every sensible brain function telling me to look away.

"Oh, that's a great idea," Milly giggled. "It will look so…enchanting…" she breathed and I wondered if she was envisioning Eli wandering among the trees like some highly sexual faerie looking for a lady to woo. And she totally hoped that lady was her.

"Great. We'll get right on it. I hear Chloe's great with leaves."

My cheeks flushed exuberantly *again* and I desperately wished Govi would arrive.

"Good. Well I will expect to see some good progress. With tickets on sale next week, we need to get a wriggle on." Milly looked me over and flounced away.

"Now that we're alone…" Eli said with a sinful smirk as he took another step towards me.

This time, all coordination went out the door as I tripped over my bag again. But this time I couldn't save myself and I ended up on my arse on the floor.

"Ow," I breathed out heavily.

Eli's eyes widened with surprise and I could see him trying to stifle a smile, although only just. He held his hands out to me.

"Thanks. I'm fine," I said, marvelling again at how many words I was managing with him, especially when my brain was spluttering.

"Clo, what are you doing down there?" I heard Govi ask and I turned to look at him.

And there was the Govi I knew and was coming to love, the guy who looked like he'd fallen out of a 90's teen movie;

maroon Doc Martins, baggy jeans with the ripped knees, Nirvana t-shirt and baggier flannel checked shirt. After the unexpected sight of Eli, Govi was much too pleasant on the eyes.

I widened my eyes at him and kicked them in Eli's direction, giving him a panicked, quizzical look. Govi looked between us like it was normal for me to be on the floor with Eli standing over me.

"Hey, man." He nodded. "What's up?"

"I'm helping you and Chloe with your trees."

"Helping? Our trees?" Govi asked, looking at me for an answer.

When Govi held his hands out to me, I freed one hand to take them and let him haul me off the floor. My eyes slid to Eli of their own volition and I noticed him looking between Govi and me with amused interest.

"Trees, Gin?" Govi pressed, giving my hand a squeeze before he let go.

I coughed and dragged my eyes up to his. "Yes. Trees. Walkway. Forest. Pretty."

I looked at him, pleading for him to make it stop, for him to help me, and preferably for him not to laugh at me. But that last one wasn't happening and his eyes told me he wasn't really all that sorry about it.

"Of course," he chuckled. "Where do we start?"

I looked around. "A base. Wait…how many should we make?" I looked around, ignoring Eli so my brain didn't fall out again. "We can probably get more card if we need, but this should be good to start. How long is the walkway going to be?"

Govi and I looked towards the door, leaning shoulder to shoulder.

"I'm thinking we're going to want two or three deep on each side," Govi said.

"About five or ten long?" I asked.

"Start with five and set them out?" he replied.

I nodded and we both turned back to the table to find Eli flirting with some girl. I rolled my eyes and picked up some sheets of brown card.

"So we want a base?" I started, quite happy to get on with things without Eli.

Govi grabbed a piece of card and made a cylinder out of it. "So if we want them, what? Trunks at least as tall as…" He looked between him and the slightly shorter Eli. "Me or him?"

I looked between them, but it was hard to tell with Eli busy trying to get in that chick's pants. I shrugged like Govi should really get his friend under control and Govi gave me an exasperated grin.

"Yo, Mr Helpful! Your *help* is needed," he called to Eli.

Eli said something in the girl's ear that made her blush and I shared a knowing look with Govi. When Eli finally turned around, Govi grabbed him and pulled him next to him.

"What do you think?" Govi asked.

"Is this some kind of appraisal? Because you know the ladies like me better, mate," Eli said with an unnecessary smirk and wink in my direction.

I really felt like telling him not all ladies, but my brain and mouth connection seemed to have broken temporarily. I walked up between them and looked from one to the other. Not only did I feel totally tiny – again – but totally out of place; the two of them oozed rock star and me in my boring pale blue jeans and pale pink and white sweater just felt so…plain.

"You can pick me, Chloe. Govi really won't mind," Eli said, his voice low and sexy.

I flushed and looked at Govi, who was giving me a sympathetic smile tinged with humour.

"Go on. Put him out of his misery," Govi chuckled. "He won't be helpful until you do. Who'd you pick?"

"You," I told Govi, then hurried on. "Well, we're going to want some decent height. So bit taller than you I think. I might need a ladder… How about the drama blocks as a base?"

Govi looked thoughtful. "Could work. How many of those little ones are there?"

"Hang on," Eli said, holding a hand up between us. "Did she really just pick you?"

"Deal with it, mate," Govi huffed a laugh as he started following me back stage.

"Where do they keep most of the blocks?" I asked, hoping that if I kept ignoring Eli and anything he had to say, my brain might stay functional.

We got backstage and found a pile of grey and black drama blocks. Mind you I'm not sure if that's what they were really called, but it seemed an apt description.

Govi picked up a couple of the small ones and headed back out to the table.

As I was reaching up to try to get some from towards the top of the pile, I felt a body against my back, a hand on the bare skin of my waist where my sweater had ridden up and an arm reached past me. I whirled around and found myself far too close to Elijah Sweet. Brain functionality was zero, leg stability was draining steadily, and everything stuttered so fast I felt like I was going to vibrate through the floor Barry Allen style – *I'm an equal opportunity superhero fan.*

He smiled down at me. "Hey."

Oh. My. God.

He smelled like…

God. I didn't know what it was, but I'd take a bath in it any day.

No. Bad brain.

I blinked. "Uh, hi…"

"Let me help with that." He kicked his head, indicating behind me.

"I… Uh…" I began intelligibly.

But he just kept on smiling down at me as he leant towards me. I didn't know what he was planning, but my hand hit his chest just before he was close enough for my knees to completely give out.

"I. Can. Blocks. Table." I said, mentally rolling my eyes at myself.

The corner of his mouth tilted in a way that made you want to touch it. I got control over my hand just before it came into his view. I hoped.

"Sure. How many do you want?" he asked, everything about him a tantalising smoulder.

"Many," was all I was capable of saying.

He licked his lip slowly and, embarrassingly, I felt myself do the same. I snapped my mouth closed as I watched his eyes follow the movement.

"Dude, you right?" Govi called and Eli stepped away from me.

"Fine. Just helping Chloe with these blocks."

Govi's eyebrow rose at me in question and I nodded quickly. Eli grabbed a few of the blocks down and headed to the auditorium.

"What. Happened?" I hissed at Govi.

He blinked in surprise. "What do you mean?"

"Why is he flirting with *me*?" My voice was a pitiful excuse of a stage whisper. But in fairness, my heart was beating a million miles a minute and I was sure it was going to explode.

Govi shrugged. "I don't know. I was telling him about your sister and... I don't know? Guy spaced out like he does?"

"Govi...you *did* tell him it was Ella that was interested, right?"

Govi nodded. "Yeah, totally."

I gave him a look that told him I didn't quite believe him.

"We talked about you. But I told him it was Ella who was interested," he said persuasively.

But, it seemed like maybe Eli hadn't quite grasped the difference between Ella and Chloe (much like the rest of the world). He spent the rest of the afternoon winking at me or smirking at me or finding excuses to brush past me. Thankfully, there was little talking going on. He obviously realised talking to me was a waste of his time.

We were testing out our first tree, with the card around the bottom of the drama block, then another layer, and the three of us were trying to attach the third layer of cardboard cylinder to the top. I held the card up while Govi stapled it and found he'd run out of staples. The tree was a little bit tall for me, granted. But I wasn't entirely convinced it warranted Eli's next action.

I was standing on tip toes while I held the card in place and Govi wrestled a new string of staples in the stapler, and I almost over-balanced. But then hands were on my waist and lips were by my ear.

"Need some help?" There was nothing innocent going on in that head with that tone of voice, I can tell you.

I pulled away so fast, I did over-balance and ended up falling through our tree so far. I crushed the top of the trunk under me and my legs got caught on the drama block as I toppled over it and took it with me. I was pretty sure my whole body went red and I wrapped my arms around my head. I was going to have a lovely bruise on my leg.

"Gin, you right?" Govi asked suddenly, sounding concerned.

"Sure, Gove. Fine," I mumbled.

I snuck a look at Eli and saw nothing but teasing flirtation on his face. He knew the effect he had on me and he wasn't shy about using it to his full potential.

Rotten, no good–

"Elijah?" I heard Milly call.

He gave me a wink and sauntered away in a manner than I was sure was supposed to make me appreciate his arse. I was ridiculous enough that I did.

Govi crouched beside me. "You good?"

"I don't think he got the right message, Gabriel," I said through gritted teeth, looking to him for an explanation.

Govi paled and his eyes went soft. "Uh, yeah. I'm sensing that, too. I'm sorry, Gin…"

I sighed, any annoyance I felt at Govi disappearing. You just couldn't stay mad at those sweet nut brown eyes and that boyish charm.

"It's fine. I mean it's not fine. But I'm not angry with you or anything. I get the feeling Elijah Sweet will only do whatever Elijah Sweet wants to do."

Govi huffed and we both looked towards Mr Flirt. "*I* get the feeling you understand him far better than he'd like." Govi stood up and held his hands out to me, then pulled me to standing. "Look, I'll see what I can do. In the meantime, just hold firm."

"What? You think I'm going to fall for that wank?" I asked.

Govi smiled, but there was a hint of sadness in his eyes. "I haven't met a girl yet who could withstand his flirting."

94

"Well, you hadn't met me."

Govi's eyes warmed. "True. If anyone can manage it, it's you." He brushed my hair off my face. "I'll talk to him. Get him to ease off. He'll probably get bored in a day or two. Don't be offended by it, it's just his way."

I looked into his eyes and smiled. "How are you two such good friends but so different?" I asked.

Govi shrugged. "Don't get me wrong, I can be exactly the same as him."

"Then why aren't you?"

His smile softened, became somewhat tender. "Dunno. There's something about you, Chloe Cowan, unfortunate name or not. I can't be fake around you, I can't be that shallow prick." He shrugged again. "Guess I just like you."

"I like you, too." I smiled.

"As much as you like *Eli*?" he teased.

I shoved him. "Shut up, or maybe I'll prefer the shallow prick."

"Eli will be pleased," Govi snorted.

"How did *Quicksilver* get together?" popped out.

Govi smiled and talked while we straightened up the scrunched tree. "Well, we met in Year Eight in music. Eli was always the confident ringleader and Lake, Ramsey and I were just drawn to him. We started hanging out and got talking music, then we realised we had the perfect makings

95

of a band. So we started playing other people's stuff and eventually started writing our own."

"Do you still play other people's stuff?" I asked.

He nodded. "Yeah. We play other stuff for fun and at some gigs, it fleshes our stuff out and crowds like to hear songs they know from bands they don't. The gig in November will just be our stuff, though."

"And the formal?"

"Bit of both I think. We're not playing all that long, it's just a bit of practise and we wanted to hang out with our mates for at least some of our last formal, but I don't know if we have enough polished songs to play just our own. We probably do, but we've got a few more in the works to be ready for November. Although," Govi huffed a sardonic laugh, "we're about to get into the all-night rehearsals if our esteemed front-man has anything to say about it."

"What? You mean he actually puts hard work in?" I asked, surprised.

Govi nodded. "Totally. I know he doesn't look it, but when something really matters, he'll move heaven and earth for it."

I snuck yet another look at Eli as I held the card up for Govi. He was certainly not looking anything like the sort of guy who knew anything about hard work. And to be honest, I didn't want to know that he was. My brain already went to

96

mush around him, I didn't need to risk my heart doing the same.

"I think we need to look at different bases," I said to take my mind off Eli.

"Any ideas?"

I nodded. "Yeah, I'm working on it."

My mind was successfully off Eli, but my eyes weren't.

Needy McNerdleton

"…money just ruins it." Rica said as we narrowly avoided being run over by some Year Nines on the way to morning break on Tuesday.

We were discussing our aspirations. Again. It was a debate we had regularly. Neither of us were trying to change the other's mind – it was impossible anyway – and the debate was pretty well always the same, but our friendship seemed to thrive on irrelevant disagreements.

"Money also helps you pay bills and buy food," I reminded her.

"Buying food sort of goes against the whole starving artist aesthetic," she commented as she popped an M&M into her mouth with a cheeky grin.

"Oh no. Wouldn't want to ruin the aesthetic. It's not like Byron had money to spare or anything."

"It only counts as money if you make it from your craft."

I shook my head as I threw myself against the wall out of someone's way. "No I think it goes to show you can still be a brooding, melodramatic wanker even with shit tonnes of money."

"Poets are different."

I laughed. "Poets aren't different. They do what you do, but with words not pictures. Dancers do it with movement. Musicians with sound. You all have the fundamental same qualities, you just use a different medium. And I refuse to believe that a lack of money will make you better for it."

"Well it's a lack of money or some horribly traumatising experience. Take your pick."

"How are you so talented and yet so stupid?" I asked her. I didn't need to smile so she knew I was teasing, but I did.

She snorted. "I like to think I'm in the young and naïve portion of my career."

"Exactly. A fancier way of saying stupid."

She nudged me with her hip as she laughed. "No. Hopeful yet despairing, cautious but reckless, confident yet doubtful."

I nodded, thoughtfully. "Maybe I am cut out for the artistic life after all."

"Because you're also standing at a crossroads, knowing you have your all to give and praying it will be enough?"

"Because I'm also mentally unhinged."

We burst into laughter and it wasn't the first time I was glad that Rica understood my self-deprecating humour. I was comfortable in who I was and, even though some people didn't understand it, I could laugh about it. After all, when it was a choice between laughing and crying, laughing felt more like I was in control, it felt more assertive, it felt like I was the master and not the slave.

"You could be worse," Rica said and I nodded.

"I could. In five years' time I could be you, poor and in a loft surrounded by my unbought paintings while I eat my third pot noodle of the day."

"Unlike actual you who will be lost under six of my paintings eating your fifth pot noodle of the day?" she teased.

I nodded. "Yes. Because what else is a starving artist without a dependant?"

Rica snorted. "Of course. Why would you go and get a job with that Commerce degree so we can have a two bedroom apartment, when you can live off my incredible lack of wages?"

I shrugged. "It just makes more sense."

"It really does."

"Chloe!" wafted to us and I turned without thinking.

I didn't think about the fact that only one person ever called my name in the corridors of Winters and she was standing right next to me. I didn't think about the fact that the voice was masculine. I didn't think about the fact that I was in the middle of laughing nigh uncontrollably, completely at the mercy of everything that was Chloe Cowan and not the cultivated outside I reserved for everyone but Rica, Super-G and Aunt Bow.

I turned, an unbashful smile on my face, and unintentionally locked eyes with Eli.

There was a split-second moment where it felt like I'd caught him off-guard or something, a rare moment where the real Chloe had been seen and not found wanting. But that was stupid because it was Elijah Sweet and I neither wanted nor was he capable of seeing any version of me, real or otherwise.

My smile went from possibly insane to very much bashful and rather annoyed as he gave me that stupid half-smirk.

"Are you two having fun without me?" I heard Govi's voice again and dragged my eyes off Eli to look at him.

"Us?" Rica asked innocently. "No. Definitely not. We wouldn't dare."

"The lady doth protest too much, methinks," Govi said, pointing at her.

Rica frowned as she cocked her head to the side. "What is that from?"

I sighed heavily. "Please don't tell me we have to do 'Hamlet' next year."

"Of course you know," Rica said as Govi nodded once.

"Okay. I won't." He looked between Rica and me. "On an unrelated note, for reasons unknown I will have a spare copy of 'Hamlet' for anyone who *might* require it next year…" A pause. "Just sayin'…"

"Can I chose not to do English next year?" Rica asked.

Govi thought about it. "No…?"

"Not at Winters," Eli said. "I tried."

It was like him speaking seemed to break some spell and suddenly I wasn't the only one who was hyper aware that Eli Sweet and Govi Costa were talking to two veritable nobodies in the school corridor. Out of the corner of my eye, I could see everyone who walked past us looked at us in question – some of them, I was sure, were wondering who we were and if we even belonged in Winters and, if we did, why they hadn't noticed us before.

"Hi Eli," one girl said as she walked by, batting her eyes and pouting at him.

"Hey," he responded, kicking his chin towards her, raising his eyebrow, and giving that sexy half-smirk. Then, as though we hadn't all just watched him making eyes at another girl, he turned it all on me.

"No shame, mate. No freaking shame," Govi chuckled under his breath and I wasn't sure if he was chastising Eli or praising him. I had a feeling it was a little of both.

I pulled my eyes off Eli's smoulder before the use of my legs followed my brain to Hawaii, and remembered Govi had called my name before.

"Did you want something?" I asked him.

Govi blinked, looking adorably confused. "When?"

"Just now. When you called out. Did you want something?"

He looked at Rica for a moment as though he didn't understand the question and she might have the answer. "No. I don't think so."

Now I was confused. "Oh. Then why did you call out?"

"To say hi."

"Why?"

Rica whacked me, which was our terribly original code for 'shut up, you're being weird and not in a good way'. "Hi." She smiled widely at him and he gave her a warm smile in return.

"Are you guys heading to lessons now or...?" Govi petered off and looked between us as he waited for an answer.

I didn't really hear Rica's reply as my eyes shifted to Eli, who was watching me with a combination of arrogant humour and cocky confusion, and who seemed uncharacteristically quiet.

Not that I actually knew what his character was like. I was relying solely on rumour and assumptions I made based on nothing but his appearance. But everything I'd heard and assumed suggested Elijah Sweet was not a guy who sat back and let his drummer do all the talking. It suggested he was an overly confident, casual young man who liked to make every situation about him. So why was he just standing there and watching me as my cheeks went hotter and hotter?

And I was fully aware that I was also standing there and watching him while his cheeks remained a perfectly normal, unemotional colour. But I couldn't help myself. He was hot and, like many creatures on our planet, I liked to look at attractive things even when they infuriatingly knew they were attractive. It brought me joy. Which, in hindsight, sucked because then Eli would definitely pass the Marie Kondo test.

Just as I was about to win the struggle to pull my eyes off him, he leant towards me.

"I'm not just for looking at. You can touch, if you like," he said quietly as Rica and Govi chatted about their art teacher.

I blinked. "I… You… What?" was all I managed, despite my internal outrage – at both his audacity and my idiocy.

Eli's honey eyes burned brightly as he searched my face and I swallowed hard. There was a battle of wills playing out here and I had come very much unprepared. Eli had wills in spades by the look of it and he knew it. He knew it and he was perfectly happy to use it on whoever he needed to get whatever he wanted, deserved or not.

Like Ella.

That was familiar. That I could contend with.

I felt some of my confidence returning, along with some of my brain function.

"No touchey," I answered. The fact I managed to keep a straight face and superior, determined tone through such a pitiful response was exceptional. Especially when Eli failed to hold back his laughter.

But he did pull away, nodding as he said, "Sometimes even I believe you." He was all suave sophistication as though one word from him would topple my known universe. "But do you?"

I frowned. "Excuse me?" I huffed.

"Oh shit…" Rica muttered, obviously hearing my tone.

"What?" Govi asked.

From the corner of my eye, I saw Rica shake her head. But my eyes were focussed on Eli. My head to mouth connection might have been spotty, but I was going to attempt to put the smarmy twat in his place.

"Gin…" Rica said slowly, plucking at my elbow.

"No," I said firmly.

Eli's eyebrow rose in humour. "No?" he chuckled.

"No," I repeated pointing at him. "You don't get what you want just because you want it."

He gave me a look of mock-surprise. "Oh really?" he asked and I nodded. He gave me a single nod, then looked around the corridor. "Hailey!" he called.

"Hi Eli," a girl in the year below me giggled back at him.

He kicked his chin at her and winked and she giggled again. "You want to go out this weekend?"

Hailey pulled her books to her chest as she bit her lip, looking at him through her eyelashes. "I don't know how Jack will feel about that…"

Eli rolled his eyes. "Baby, I promise you won't even remember Jack by the end of the night."

She giggled again and I felt all hope for the universe dissolving.

"Eli…" Govi hissed at him, all warning this time.

Eli waved a surreptitious hand to Govi, acting to Hailey as though all his attention was on her. But I saw his eyes slide to me with a cocky look of victory.

"What do you say, Hails?" Eli cooed and she grinned.

"Okay."

He nodded. "Great. We'll talk later."

She nodded. "Okay." She gave him another smile, then headed off.

Eli turned back to me, his arms out to his side in a clear display he wanted kudos.

"No," I said forcefully. "What did…? Are you…? Ugh!"

Eli sighed. "I so thought we'd made it to full sentences. But I suppose jealousy can be an odd beast."

"Jealousy?" I spluttered.

Eli nodded and I had the singular impression that him asking out Hailey was supposed to have done more than just proven his point that he could indeed have anything he wanted when he wanted it. It was also supposed to have made me jealous.

"Jealous?" I repeated. "The only thing I feel after seeing that is disgust."

He was genuinely surprised by that. "Why?"

"Eli…" Govi muttered as Rica mirrored but with my name.

But neither Eli nor I seemed inclined to listen to them. "Because you just actively encouraged her to cheat on Jack."

"You don't know that they're dating."

I blinked, taken aback for a moment. "You don't know they're not."

Eli shrugged. "True."

"And yet you suggested she go out with you anyway?"

"It's not for me to put labels on another person's relationship. If she wants to go out with me while she might be with someone else, that's their business."

On one hand, I agreed with him – the only person to blame for cheating was the person who did it, not the person they did it with. Not really. But on the other hand, I couldn't help arguing with him.

"You could still be a decent human being and not…con her into cheating on her boyfriend."

"Who we don't even know she has."

"Not the point."

"Well what is the point?" Why was he angry? He had no reason to be angry. "Because all I see here is jealousy."

I huffed, my eyebrows feeling like they were so close they were creating one epic monobrow. "You see whatever suits your arrogance. You believe whatever suits–"

"Okay!" Govi slid a hand between us as well as half his body and laughed awkwardly. "So this has been fun…" He shot me a semi-awed look like he had no idea where I'd come from and he wasn't sure if he wanted me to go back or stay forever. "But I'm going to take Eli away–"

"Chloe does need a moment to calm down," Eli interrupted and I glared at him.

"I was thinking more for your safety, actually."

Eli scoffed. "You think she could hurt me?"

Govi nodded hastily. "Uh. Yes. And if you don't shut your damned mouth, I'm going to give her full access to you. I might even hold you for her."

Eli's cocky arrogance slipped and he looked at Govi. "What?"

Govi shot me another look then whispered to Eli so quietly I was sure I wasn't supposed to have heard, but I did. "You're being a fucking dick. Worse than usual. It's not cute this time, man. Do not ruin this shit, okay? I will mess you up."

Eli's nose scrunched and his lip rose in a snarl for a moment. "Fine. Fine," he huffed back to Govi. Eli shook himself out. "We need to get to class anyway."

"Eli!"

My reaction to that voice was visceral and, while Govi missed it, Eli didn't. He had one moment to look at me in what was almost concern before my sister pushed her way in front of me.

"Elijah. Hi," she said, full of pep and superiority.

"Ella." He nodded. "Heading to Music?"

She nodded. "Of course, dummy. Walk me?"

Eli's eyes slid to me for a moment, then he nodded. "Sure." He tapped Govi on the chest. "Coming, man?"

Govi nodded. "Yeah. See you around." He looked at me and I felt like I was being told to behave as well as he was checking I was okay. "Gin."

"See you later, Govi."

At the sound of my family nickname, Ella turned her deep green eyes on me with a furious glare. She looked to Lindy, snapped her fingers, then dragged Eli away. Govi gave us one more look, then went after them. But Lindy hung behind.

"Why is Gabriel Costa talking to you?" Lindy asked me.

I blinked. "Excuse me?"

"You heard." She shifted her weight to her other foot as she looked me over like there was no way in hell anyone would choose to talk to me.

"I… I don't know, Lindy. We've got to know each other through the formal committee, I guess. He was just saying hi."

"With his hands all over you?"

I wasn't sure when that had happened, but arguing with her would be pointless. "He and Eli were just talking to us," I said, my hands up in my defence.

Lindy smiled at the mention of Eli. "Elijah's so nice like that. Always sparing time for those less fortunate, the needy, the little people."

Rica and I shared a glance of disbelief.

"Yes. Eli's *very* nice," I said, but once again the sarcasm was lost on Lindy.

"He so is though. Ella's so lucky."

"Lindy!" the Wicked Bitch in question shrieked back down the corridor.

"Stick to your own kind," Lindy said, looking down her nose at me.

"I am also here," Rica said and Lindy glared at her. The ever stoic Rica quailed a little. "But I will also stick to my own kind…"

Lindy gave us each a parting glare, as though that would keep us in our places, then walked away.

"…when I work out who that is…" Rica finished quietly, then looked at me. "Well, I think that qualifies as well more than five words to him. How do you feel?" Rica asked as we watched Lindy hurry to catch up with Ella.

"Mortified."

"What for?"

"Because fighting with me is unlikely to make him want to take the harpy to the formal."

"Okay. Maybe not. But look! They're talking now so maybe she'll do her own wooing now?"

"That is *not* going to spare me from having to do it."

Rica clucked her tongue. "True. But this…" she indicated to all of me, "is not just because of that."

111

I huffed. "I'm not the confrontational type, Ree. I stick in my corner and wait semi-patiently for my time."

"So?"

"I don't know what came over me back there."

Rica was weirdly silent, so I looked up to find her with an odd look on her face.

"What?" I asked her.

She shrugged coquettishly. "No. Nothing."

I frowned. "What?"

She shrugged again, but I knew it was only for my benefit. "Maybe you feel you can project your cooped up feelings about your family onto Eli because there are no perceived ramifications. You can't put Ella in her place, so Eli's your substitute."

I nodded. "Yeah. Maybe. That makes sense."

"Or maybe...you *like* him?" she teased as she took hold of my arm and shook me.

I rolled my eyes. "I am not interested in Elijah Sweet."

Prince Slightly Charming

As I walked to the Willis Theatre on Wednesday afternoon, I promised myself I wasn't going to react to Eli. I wasn't going to let his annoying arrogance get under my skin. I wasn't going to let myself get confrontational again. I was going in there like a normal person capable of normal interactions with people of all types.

"Hey you." Govi bumped into me as his arm went around my shoulder and I nearly lost my balance in the corridor.

I laughed as he helped me keep my footing and my book in my hand. "Hi. You make it a habit of trying to run people off the road?"

"Only the ones I *really* like," he chuckled.

I nodded. "Oh. So pleased."

He nudged me companionably, and less enthusiastically than before. I looked up at him to find him smiling warmly and it gave me a feeling I only had with three other people.

My heart warmed and I had trouble fighting the smile on my face.

Govi grinned as though he could read my mind. "Don't fight it, Gin. Just feel it."

"You sound like Rica," I told him.

He gave me another grin. "Yeah? So she and I have a few things in common then?"

I laughed. "It seems so."

He pulled a little bit ahead of me, and turned to face me, walking backwards. "Not least of which, we both like you."

I nodded. "If you say so."

"I do say so. And no amount of self-deprecation on your part can convince me otherwise."

I laughed. "Okay. You win. I'll even allow it."

Still walking backwards, he flung his arms up in triumph and three things happened.

The first being he collided with Milly and Eli. The second being, on its way up, one of his hands connected with the clipboard in Milly's hands and sent it flying. The third being his other fist crashed into Eli's cheek and knocked Eli to the floor. Milly managed to stay on her feet, but she smacked Govi in the arm.

"Gabriel! The clipboard!" she cried, glaring at him and pointing at the clipboard on the floor. She'd paused for so long, I actually almost thought she was waiting for him to pick it up for her.

But Govi gave her his adorable little smile. "Sorry, Mill. My bad." And she actually softened.

Even with her all-important clipboard not in her arms, she softened. It was a sight to behold.

"Just watch where you're going," Milly said quickly, then turned to pick the clipboard up.

"And I'll just stay here, will I?" Eli drawled from his spot on the floor.

"If you're suddenly too old and decrepit to pick yourself up, yes," Govi answered, but he held his hands out to help Eli off the floor.

I watched as, in true Govi form, he let go of Eli's hands while they were halfway there and Eli fell back down again. Govi sniggered and even Milly smiled as Eli glared at his drummer.

"Dude. Uncool."

Govi shrugged. "Was it though?" he asked in perfect imitation of Thor as he looked at me.

I managed to stifle my smile, but I shook my head.

"Consensus. Was that cool or uncool, Gin?" he asked me, goading me to side with him. He really needn't have bothered.

"Cool," I answered.

"Cool?" Eli spluttered, but when I slid my eyes to him he was smiling. "Fine. I guess I might have done at least *one* thing that deserved that," he said as he pulled himself off the floor, waving away Govi's proffered assistance.

"One?" Govi cried. "One? Mate, you've done plenty of things to deserve that."

"Name a single one," Eli said. "One. I dare you."

The two boys headed over to where we'd started building our trees on Monday, still arguing but the way friends argue over insignificant things.

"You…uh…." Milly started.

"Chloe?" I offered.

She nodded. "Chloe. You okay with those two?" she asked.

I looked over at them, shoving each other. "I think so. At least, I can handle Govi."

"And Govi can handle Eli," Milly said knowingly.

I looked at her. "You…know them well?"

She shrugged. "Ramsey, second guitarist for *Quicksilver*, is my cousin. Our families are close. So I know them…pretty well."

"And still…" I mused, then froze in embarrassment.

Milly and I turned to look at each other, me in horror but she was smiling.

"Still." She nodded and looked back to Eli. "Every sensible part of my brain tells me to run in the opposite direction, but Eli's...Eli." She shrugged and the soft and sweet Milly disappeared under the officious formal committee head. She pulled her clipboard to her tighter. "I'd like as many trees as you three can get done."

"We can set up the blocks and see what will look best?" I asked.

"Good plan." She nodded once more, then her eyes slid behind me. "BRENDA!" she yelled before she hurried away and I made my way over to the boys.

They were still scrapping over something, all huge arm gestures and goofy smiles. Both of them were laughing so hard they were crying by the time I reached them.

Govi made what sounded like attempted words through his laughter at me, then waved his head and his hand and that set Eli off harder. Their laughter was infectious and I found myself smiling.

"I don't think I want to know," I told Govi ruefully. "I'm going to get another block. Milly wants as many trees as we can make."

"I help," Govi panted, failing to get any control over his laughter.

I shook my head. "You work on standing up straight, then start taking the blocks we have over to the main door."

117

He nodded as he fought to control himself and I headed backstage.

Obviously quicker at recovering, although only just, Eli hurried to fall into step with me.

I studiously ignored him while my heart raced and my mind crashed around trying not to think of incredibly stupid things I could say like how his face still looked nice. But it seemed an affliction I only suffered when we were alone, or without Govi at least, because it took it appearing for me it realise I hadn't felt it just before.

"About yesterday…" Eli started as I climbed up the stairs to the stage.

"It was Tuesday," I said. Although, I wasn't sure if I was trying to be sassy or if I'd just had a brain fart.

"Oh, see. That was the problem!"

I paused and turned to look at him. It was a terrible place to have stopped because we were hidden from the view of everyone in the theatre behind the curtains of the wings. My stomach felt like I was zip-lining though the jungle as I looked up at him. Unlike with Govi, I didn't get the warmed heart, I got the fretting and the panicking and the sweaty palms.

"Tuesday was the problem?" I asked him stiltedly.

He nodded. "Yes."

"How…? Why?"

118

He nodded, a hint of that cocky wanker about him. "Because my foot-mouth disease tends to be worse on a Tuesday. Something about Tuesdays just makes my arrogant conceit flair up wildly."

Was that... Was that an apology? A weird sort of apology. But it sounded apologetic at the very least. A small part of me wanted to argue with him, to not let him off so easily. But I shushed it because I didn't want to disturb the very fragile foundation upon which my easy future rested. Twelve months. Neon lights. One wrong move and the whole circuit blew.

So I nodded. "I hear you can get something for that."

He huffed and gave me a small smile. "Yeah. I have a cream, but I forgot it."

Thinking this might actually be one step closer to getting my job done, I said, "You...and Ella...after our...?"

"Attempted negotiation of the nuance of language?" he offered and I frowned, knowing that phrase well.

"You have Tom for English? And you actually listen to him?" I asked and he smiled.

"What is song but poetry, only–"

"–far less melodious," I finished for him.

Our English teacher was fond of perpetuating the old duddery philosopher image, his over-the-top metaphors and long-winded language (not always technically correct and even then by a stretch) most often a way to remind us that you can often achieve a better result with much more simplicity.

"That's what I'm told on a near daily basis, yes," Eli said with a nod.

"Uh…" I started then stopped. "Blocks." I pointed at them.

"Are we back to incomplete sentences?" Eli whispered as he leant closer.

I shook my head, but said, "Yes," as I picked up a block and took it out to where Govi was arranging our half constructed trees.

Eli said nothing as he followed me out.

Govi had his hand up and was looking at it like he was using it to measure. "What do you think?" he called. "Three centimetres to the left? I quite liked seven millimetres to the right, but now I'm torn."

I heard Eli's soft laugh. It was the sort of laugh you could call affectionate. It was also the sort of laugh you could say was not supposed to be overheard. So I just took my block over to Govi and then stepped back to see how our progress was going.

Eli dropped his block with mine. "Another?"

"Not yet. But Govi looks like he's running out of card," I said before going back over to Govi, picking up a new line of staples on my way.

"Have you managed full sentences today?" Govi teased as I took the cardboard from his hand.

I nodded. "Yes."

"But without wanting to rip his arms off and beat him with the soggy ends?"

I laughed. "Yes. He seems...different today."

Govi looked over to Eli, then back to his stapling. "Eli's not a bad guy, Gin. Not really. He can be a totally arrogant arsehole–"

"I can?" Eli asked excitedly as he arrived and gave Govi another piece of card. "Aw, shucks. Thanks, mate." He looked at me and waggled his eyebrows. "I have permission now."

"That wasn't permission, dick," Govi muttered, fighting a smile. "I was telling Gin how you often are."

"I don't know, mate. I specifically heard the words 'he can'. That's permission."

"'You can', maybe."

I could see this had the potential to go on for a while. "How about we all behave ourselves and get some more of these trees done?"

Govi and Eli looked at each other.

"Are we going to let her call the shots?" Eli asked.

"You worried she's going to upstage you?"

"Should I be?"

Govi shrugged. "Well she is better looking than you…"

Eli nodded, stroking his chin thoughtfully. "True. And we all know the best looking person takes the lead."

"I mean, it's like unwritten law."

"It is."

"Although we broke it."

"What?"

"With you being lead."

Eli snorted, his expression saying he knew he should have seen that coming but he stuck with their bit. "Well yeah, because obviously it should be Chloe."

"Yeah. Chloe, then me, then Ramsey–"

"Then Lake, then me?" Eli finished with a grin and Govi grinned back.

"Obviously."

"If I hadn't left my pick in my other jeans, we could have had a ceremony."

"Don't be all sour just because Chloe's better looking than you, mate."

"Oh, I'm not. I just didn't think you'd be so shallow as to think looks were everything."

The way Govi snorted, I guessed they had these sorts of conversations all the time. I also guessed that I wasn't the only one thinking that Eli had a serious case of pot calling the kettle black syndrome.

"No. Of course," Govi chuckled. "But we're just fortunate that, with Gin, the insides match the outsides."

"The very pretty outsides?" Eli asked.

Govi nodded. "Yes. Those."

I snorted. "Well, we can call off the search for Brenda's missing magic mushrooms then."

"What?" Govi cried, totally affronted. "I resent the suggestion I would only think you're pretty if I was on something."

I looked at him with a smile. "Are you saying you like my face?"

Govi wrapped me up and whirled me around. "I'm saying I like all of you, Gin," he laughed as I tried to stop the giggles.

"Trees, Govi!" I hissed and he finally put me down.

"Fine. Trees. What next?"

I looked around at our impressive display of what I imagined deforestation looked like. "Ah... A lot, Govi. A lot is next. Anyone thought about how we're going to make the branches?"

"Ah..." Govi breathed. "No."

We went back to the drawing board, looking around the room and trying to decide what we could make the branches out of. Through the jokes and flirting, we decided on scrunching up newspaper and then papier-mâché to make it smooth. It was going to be time consuming so someone had to check with Milly it was what she wanted or if there was a better use of our time.

"Eli," Govi said quickly, pointing at him like they'd just been asked who farted.

"What?" Eli asked. "Why me?"

"Because Milly hates me," Govi said.

"So why can't Chloe go?"

"Because I actually like her and would like to keep her on this planet a little longer. You on the other hand…"

Eli sighed. "Fine. Fine. I'm going."

Govi and I leant against the table and watched as Eli walked over to Milly who was, as usual, yelling at Brenda. This time it was about something to do with a popcorn machine.

"He complains and yet…" Govi said, then pointed as Eli as the *Quicksilver* front man fell into his stride.

Eli leant a hand on the table next to where Milly was standing and turned his already not insignificant charm up to full. Milly smiled and batted her eyes at him as he talked to her. Milly nodded and waved her hands around a bit, then Eli gave her a wink and headed back over to us.

"It's just natural for him, isn't it?"

"What?" Govi asked.

"Flirting."

I felt Govi shrug. "Yeah. I guess it's like his natural state or whatever."

"And we tend to be *very* good at our natural state," I said quietly, not intending for him to hear me.

"That's why you're so good at self-deprecation and lurking in the shadows," Govi teased and I nudged him with my elbow.

"Something like that."

"Oh! And the triangle," Govi laughed and I nudged him a little more forcefully.

"The triangle?" Eli asked as he stopped in front of us.

I nodded. "Really good," I said.

"Like, the freaking Mozart of the triangle," Govi added.

"Just so good," I finished, then Govi and I burst into laughter.

Eli nodded slowly. "I am going to leave that where it is for fear of sticking my foot in my mouth again, and just tell you that yes Milly wants all the trees with all the work."

Govi dragged himself off the table. "Although undoubtedly more eloquently?"

"Oh, for sure," Eli replied.

"Right," I sighed. "Newspaper."

I pulled a stack towards me and started scrunching, and the boys followed suit.

An hour later, we'd moved to the floor and, after trying to scrub the worst of the newsprint off our hands, we were having a break. Eli and I were sitting among our branches and Govi was stapling more cardboard.

"Gin! Gin, look!" Govi called and I looked over to see him standing precariously on one of the blocks, one leg and both arms stuck out. "I'm a tree."

We all burst into laughter again. I hid my face behind a bit of newspaper I'd been fiddling with.

"None of that!" Govi called.

A hand gently pulled the newspaper from my face and I looked into Eli's smiling eyes. "He's right. You can't let him miss you laughing."

"Yes. He can't miss the tomato cheeks, the runny eyes or the snotty nose."

"Well…as you once said to me," he said as he leant back on his hands again, "you can't help your face."

"Are you complimenting my face, Eli?" I teased with a grin.

"I can see why Govi's partial to it." He shrugged.

"But just Govi."

Eli nodded. "Definitely just Govi."

He slid me a look that heavily implied it wasn't just Govi and I felt myself flush again. I cleared my throat and pulled myself to standing so I could go and help Govi struggle with the stapler some more.

Before I could walk away, a hand slipped into mine. I looked down quickly and was sure I imagined the look on Eli's face. Because within a blink, it had gone from something that could have been mistaken for sincere to his usual confidence.

"Oh. You're not helping me up?" he asked.

I felt my cheeks heat even more. "Why not?" I asked myself, turning to offer him my other hand and brace myself to take his weight.

I ignored the tingle I felt at his touch, telling myself it was nothing. I ignored the way my heart beat when he smiled at me, telling myself it was stupid. I ignored the way me getting angry with him the day before had seemed to mean I could talk to him almost properly. I ignored the way he seemed just a little bit less haughty than before I'd got angry with him.

"You're amazing," Eli said softly and I frowned in confusion. He blinked quickly. "Amazing. With Govi. Amazing with Govi. He can be an intense guy with a weird sense of humour. Not everyone gets him. And that's if they've given him time to grown on them."

I nodded. "Yeah. We have that in common. The weird sense of humour anyway."

Eli nodded knowingly. "I knew there was a reason I liked you so much."

I cleared my throat softly. "Because I'm basically a second Govi?"

Eli looked down at me. "You're second to none, Chloe."

It was then I realised that we were still holding hands. I cleared my throat again and gently extricated my hands from his. He seemed almost unwilling to let go, which made me almost unwilling to keep pulling. But this was Eli and no amount of flirting was going to make me fall for him – mainly because me falling for him would guarantee one of two outcomes; broken heart, or broken head when Ella found out.

We kept up our work for a little while longer, then I managed to find a moment alone with Govi as everyone was leaving. "You need to do something," I hissed.

He frowned. "I will have you know that my glutes are killing me after the amount of climbing up and down that ladder I did."

I blinked in confusion for a second, then shook my head. "No. Not on the trees. You're doing far better than the rest of us with those. No. With Eli."

"What do I need to do with Eli? Is he back on the whole Spartan thing again? Because I already told him I had no problem with Lake and Ramsey but I wasn't touching him with all the Aqium in the world."

"What?" I breathed, not even sure where to go with that. "No. How you guys foster loyalty is totally up to you. I mean the flirting."

Govi nodded. "Right. Yeah. Okay. I'll try to talk to him again. It's only been a couple of days though, he'll get bored soon. I promise."

I frowned. "He told me I was second to none."

Govi's eyes went wide and I missed half the expressions that crossed his face. "Shit. I rescind all promises previously made. But I do promise I'll fix it. We'll turn his attention to the right Cowan sister…"

I didn't like the way he petered off. "What?" I asked.

"If that's still what you want?"

I crossed my arms. "I am not even going to dignify that with an answer."

"The lady doth protest–"

"Don't even start with me, Gabriel."

He started backing away slowly towards the door. "…the lady doth protest–"

"Gabriel!" I said, starting towards him.

"Too much, methinks! I'm sorry!" he yelled quickly as he ran out.

I shook my head and followed him at a more stately pace out to the car.

Cast the Lead

Rica batted me as I ran my hand over my plait again on Friday.

"Seriously, stop that," she hissed.

"Stop what?" I asked, my eyes scanning the hallway from our perch under the stairs.

"The nervous fidgeting. Step one is achieved."

"What was step one?"

"Be able to talk to Eli like a normal person."

I rolled my eyes. "Yeah and it only took me two weeks."

"Progress, Gin."

I sighed. "At the rate I'm going, Eli will ask Ella to the formal around...our Maths exam."

"*Your* Maths exam."

I glared at her. "Yes. My Maths exam." I blew out a heavy breath, trying to calm the nervous thudding and fluttering pattern my heart seemed to have taken up.

"Oh my God," Rica laughed. "He's really affecting you isn't he?"

"Shut up," I tried to snap but it came out more of a pathetic breath. "He's...hot and flirty and my brain inexplicably goes to mush every time I'm around him. It's ridiculous."

"It's natural."

"How is it natural?"

She shrugged. "I dunno. But I'm pretty sure it's totally natural that people go a little ridiculous around people they're attracted to."

I huffed at her. "Firstly I'm not attracted to him. Secondly who thought that was a good plan? Like well done, evolution! The human race needs to procreate to continue but the fundamental starting point towards procreation is awkwardness. You proud? What is this? Survival of the most confident? Because we need more self-entitled wankers in the world."

"Okay, who dosed your tea with Red Bull this morning?" Rica looked at me like I'd gone mental and I didn't really blame her.

"No one."

"Then what is..." she indicated all of me, "this?"

I took a deep breath. "I don't know."

I didn't know for sure, but I had an inkling and voicing it out loud was just going to be embarrassing.

I had a suspicion that all this nervous fidgeting had to do with the fact that Eli had been…smiling at me the past two days. It was that knowing, cocky half-smirk that made my insides go all wibbly, my brain take a vacation, and give me the sudden need to sit down like it was still Regency England and Eli had ten thousand pounds a year. It was the kind of smirk that put him in slow motion as he passed me in the corridor and made me stare at it so long I ran into things. It was the kind of smirk that made me rather urgent to get him to ask Ella to the formal already.

But telling Rica all that would have been…more than embarrassing.

"I don't know," I repeated. "I'm just not very good at this and Ella's going to start getting testy at some point."

"How about you let Eli ask you to the formal and hope it's the poison that makes the Wicked Bitch shrivel up?"

I rolled my eyes at her. "I'd like to think, if that was what I wanted, I could be allowed to ask him. It is the twentieth century, thank you."

Rica nodded. "Oh, for sure. But it is also you and you've only just managed full sentences without letting loose seventeen years of pent-up anger. So…you know." She shrugged. "Power to you and all, but my bet's on incapable."

"Damn you for knowing me so well," I grumbled and she laughed.

"Right," she said as she slid off our perch. "I should be off or I'll miss the bus."

I grabbed her arm. "Then you can help us with trees!"

She threw her head back and cackled, then fixed me with a fierce stare. "Yeah, no. I will see you tomorrow."

I nodded. "All right. Fine. Be that way."

"I will." She blew me a raspberry and a kiss as she flounced off down the corridor.

I sat and kicked my legs around for a while, my eyes still scanning the corridor but I didn't know what for. I took a few more deep breaths, knowing I should be able to do this – whatever 'this' was. I was a confident, modern young woman…when it was just my small cheer squad… I just had to remind myself there was nothing actually special about Eli except what his ego had him believe. He was just a guy. A guy I could talk to.

I hopped down and headed for the auditorium again, wistfully watching everyone who was heading out to a weekend of freedom. I didn't see Ella, which wasn't surprising as I usually did everything in my power to avoid seeing her. I did see Lindy ahead of me in the crowd, heading in the direction of the auditorium, but I successfully avoided her as well.

I was still trying to come up with a bunch of ways to just tell Eli that Ella wanted him to ask her to the formal, so I didn't see Govi until he was practically on top of me.

"Oh, hey!" I laughed, instinctively throwing my arms around him to keep my footing.

"Hey," he said with a grin. "Going my way?"

I snorted and elbowed him. "You're really running with this road theme."

"I am nothing if not consistent," he said with a nod.

We walked in silence for a few moments, then Govi broke it with a big sigh.

"So… I had a chat with Eli yesterday…" Govi said slowly.

"Yeah? What about now?" I asked. "Which girl would chip the next notch in his guitar neck? Or which pair of jeans makes his arse look best?"

Govi chuckled. "Yeah. Fair. No. Actually it was about…him flirting with you…"

My step faltered and he paused so I didn't fall behind. "Right. Go on."

"I think my interference had the opposite of the desired effect…"

"In what way?" I asked, trepidation filling me.

135

"Ah…well… This is all speculation, mind."

"An educated presumption based on your many years of friendship?"

"Yeah. That." Govi sighed. "I think you're going to have to be the one to tell him."

I sighed as well. "Well, this is going to go swimmingly."

"Buck up, soldier. One more push and we'll put that Gerry in his place."

I snorted. "Your parents watch Blackadder, do they?"

Govi fidgeted comically. "My parents…yes…"

We walked into the auditorium laughing.

"But yeah. My parents got me into it. We used to watch it after dinner on a Friday when I was little. You?"

I nodded. "Not my parents. My Aunt Bow and Gran. I used to stay with them back when there was something Ella did that I didn't…yet. They'd show me all their favourite old comedies. I think that might have been where I get my sense of humour."

"Well, I certainly appreciate the years they spent cultivating it. Aunt Bow is an interesting name, though."

I nodded again as I dropped my bag by our table. "Short for Rainbow. Gran was – still is actually – a real flower child. Aunt Bow's just the same and my father seems to have rebelled by being ridiculously straight-laced."

Govi's face scrunched up. "Bugger."

136

I shrugged. "It is what it is. I just have to wait until I'm eighteen and I can be who I want to be."

"I guess that makes sense... Shame though."

I gave him a small smile and looked at the table to see what we needed to start with.

"Hey, man," I heard Govi say.

"Hey," came Eli's deep voice and I resisted the urge to turn around just to look at him.

"What are we up to?"' Govi asked. "Should we try to get at least one full tree done?"

I nodded. "That sounds good. We're going to need some more card and way more glue though. And some plain paper."

"The art room should have all that if Milly doesn't," Govi said. "Want me to get it?"

I shook my head. "Can you finish putting the trunks together and maybe look at putting the first lot of branches on and I'll grab it?"

Govi nodded. "Can do. Man, can you give her a hand?" he asked Eli.

"Oh, no... I can..."

Govi grinned as I came to a stop. "Use full sentences?"

"Apparently not," I muttered.

"I think you'll find I'm very good at lifting," Eli said with a hint of a smile in his voice.

"I think art supplies weigh a little less than your usual hook-up," Govi stated and I choked on my spit in surprise.

"So if I can carry a girl, I can carry some glue and paper."

I blinked, having absolutely no idea what to say to that. Instead, I pointed towards the art rooms. "I'm going… If you want… Help…" I shook my head and started walking away. "Back soon."

Eli easily fell into step beside me as we left the laughing Govi behind.

Lindy very not surreptitiously caught my eye on the way out and gave me a huge thumbs up and a wide smile. I nodded at her and motioned for her to play it cool, but she just winked super obviously and made a show of turning around. I sighed as I heard Eli chuckle under his breath.

"She's not…" I started then cleared my throat. "That's not… I'm not…" The words did not want to come. I clenched my teeth and groaned.

Eli laughed again, but it seemed more good-natured than teasing. "Are you trying to tell me you're not interested and that wasn't what it looked like?"

I nodded. "Yes. That."

He didn't say anything more as we walked to the art room and I found I was actually far less uncomfortable during the awkward silence than I was when I was trying to talk to him. But that all went out the window when we got to the art supplies cupboard and he swung himself around rather expertly to box me against the shelf.

My heart tried to escape out my throat and my mouth went dry as he looked down at me. The smoulder was strong with this one and I was very nearly going to fall for it. But as I'd said to Govi, I was quite partial to my skin. And that wasn't even taking into account the fact that I actually wasn't interested in Eli at all.

"It's devastating," he said, his voice soft and deep, his face way too close to mine.

"What is?" I squeaked.

"If you're really not interested."

I swallowed hard but it did nothing for the dryness I was suffering. Based on how sweaty my hands felt, I knew where all the moisture had gone. "Well…I'm…not…" I stammered.

Now was as good a time as any. I just had to tell Eli that Ella was the interested Cowan, not me. I just had to reattach the connection between my mouth and brain, although the way he was looking down at me made that incredibly difficult. At least my hands – sweaty as they were – stayed well out of attempted touching range.

"I…" I cleared my throat and tried again. "I'm not interested, Eli. My sister, Ella–"

"I know who your sister is," he said slowly, a hint of humour playing at the corner of his actually quite kissable lips.

Focus! "Good. So, she's the…interested." *Oh my God, he's coming closer!*

Based on the wide smile that lit his face, I'd said that bit out loud. "Kissing you is a little hard from over here," he replied as he edged closer.

It took my hand far too long to move to his chest and halt his progress. I even looked down for good measure. "Eli…" I breathed out, willing myself to get some control. "I'm serious," I said softly.

I felt him take a step back and looked up to see he'd shoved his hands in his pockets. "I'd just like to point out that just because Ella's apparently interested, that doesn't mean you can't be."

I nodded, conceding that, then realised what he could infer from that. "No!" I said quickly. "No. I mean, you're technically correct in theory, but in practice no. Just Ella."

"And is there a reason why she's not the one I'm in a supplies cupboard with?"

I huffed. "Believe me, we'd all rather it be her than me."

"And if I don't?"

I frowned at him for a moment. "Look, Ella wants you to ask her to the formal–"

"If she wants to go with me, why doesn't she just ask me?"

Stupid, obstinate, headstrong butthole! "I don't ask questions, Eli. I just do as I'm told–"

"That's a dangerous way to live, Chloe. And if I told you to kiss me now?"

My frown was a little more long-lived this time. "I... You could try."

The corner of his lip tipped up. "I just did and you stopped me."

I groaned in annoyance. "The point is that I am only here to...encourage you to ask Ella to the formal."

"In this particular cupboard?" he asked sceptically. "Does it have magic powers? You make a request and it comes true?" He looked around in faux-excitement.

I crossed my arms so I didn't feel inclined to hit him. "Unlikely. Just... I'm not interested, okay? So you can stop with the..." I petered to a stop as he turned that honey gaze on me again. My heart didn't just thud, it skipped, but not in a way that felt like a good thing.

"Is there something wrong with her?" he asked.

"With who?" I breathed.

"Ella."

"Why?"

"If she's sent you, then I'm going to assume there's something wrong with her. I mean, she looks normal and all. But…is there like something under her dress or something?"

I frowned. Again. "Not that I'm aware of."

"So why did she send you?"

I sighed, trying not to lose my shit with him again. "Because she did."

"Is she just really good at hiding how nervous I make her?"

"Look. No offense, but her ego rivals yours. So, no. The both of you are too arrogant for anything to make you nervous."

"That is so not true. I get nervous."

"Pfft. Yeah. Sure."

"Are we going to have another attempted negotiation?" he asked and we shared a split-second smile.

"No," I told him firmly. "I've got a job to do."

"You still haven't actually explained why it's your job to what…woo me for your older sister," he pointed out.

I threw my arms in the air. "Because that's my life, Eli. Okay? Ella does what Ella wants. Ella gets what Ella wants. But she never does any actual work for it because she has me to do it for her. So can you just do me this one favour and lay off flirting with me and just…I dunno, focus on her or whatever."

He looked at me for what felt like the longest time, but was probably in actuality only a couple of heart beats. I felt totally naked under that deep, searching gaze. He was looking at me like he'd never seen me before. I'd expected to see teasing on his face, humoured disbelief at the least because outside a storybook who lives the sort of life I do? But there was none of that. He just watched me like he was trying to fit together a puzzle with some of the pieces missing.

My heart started thudding again and I had to break that awkwardness. "What?" I asked him.

"I'm just… Look. I was kinda taking the piss before. I'll admit. Watching the way you reacted to me was…fun. But you're serious about this Ella thing aren't you?"

I nodded, feeling exposed and on the brink of humiliation. "Yes. I just… She's interested. Very interested. Me? I'm…very not. I'm just the vanguard making sure it's…safe or whatever for the princess. I'm the…opening act, priming for the main event. I'm the stand-in for the leading lady."

Eli looked me over again and there still wasn't any sign of teasing. "You really believe that?"

I nodded. "It's my life, Eli."

"I'll make you a deal."

My brows furrowed, not sure where this was going. "What kind of deal?"

"I won't flirt with you…on purpose, if you tell me why you're not interested."

I swallowed. "Because Ella is."

He looked down as he shook his head with a sad smile. "Please don't tell me that's the only reason."

I frowned. "Why not?"

He looked up at me through his lashes. "Because a guy could get all sorts of hopes up if that was the only reason."

I took a deep breath and managed to stop my mouth blurting out that he could hope all the hopes he wanted, because that was definitely not the only reason. Was it?

"You're just not my type," I told him.

"Which is either code for you're a total snob or there is no other reason." He grinned.

"You're a serial flirt and don't care what kind of heartbreak or mess you leave in your wake."

He tipped his head to the side. "On the surface, maybe."

"Because you've got a soft gooey centre?"

"You said it, not me."

"What about Hailey?" I asked, suspiciously.

He shrugged. "I…suggested to her that if she was still with Jack then it would be better we didn't go out."

I crossed my arms, not believing it. "Really?"

He nodded. "She said they could not be going out…"

"And?" I pressed when he didn't continue.

"I told her anything she had with Jack was worth more than I could give her."

"Because all you want are one night stands?"

"I thought you weren't going to get argumentative?"

I deflated. "Sorry."

He blinked. "Why are you apologising?"

"Because I did say that. And I meant it too. You just…"

He gave me that crooked smile. "I just what?"

I huffed. "Nothing."

"Look, for what it's worth, I'm not going to lie and say the idea of one night stands don't have a certain appeal. I'm a teenage boy who has the idea thrown at him from all angles on a daily basis. But there's a difference between a girl you want to hook-up with and a girl you want to be with…"

"If you tell me you haven't met the right girl yet, I might throw up," I warned him.

He laughed. "I'd have no idea if I have."

"But there's a caveat on that statement."

He nodded. "Sure there is."

"Are you going to tell me what it is?"

He shrugged. "Maybe I'm not the right guy for the right girl yet."

"Are you suggesting you have the power of growth and change within you?" I teased.

"And I don't think I'm the only one."

"I'm fine just the way I am. Thank you."

"Are you?"

That felt far too poignant. We were delving into his insufficiencies, not mine. I shook myself out and looked around. "We should get back to Govi."

"Yes," Eli said almost sullenly. "We couldn't possibly leave Govi waiting."

I looked at him for a moment, wondering what that tone was. But I chose to let it go.

"Just find the card and a ream of printer paper."

He saluted me. "Aye, aye, captain."

I grabbed some glue, a couple of old ice cream containers, and some paintbrushes while Eli got the other things, then we headed back to Govi and our trees.

Govi had managed to get one trunk finished and was in the process of attaching the branches. He smiled as we walked over.

"I thought you guys had got lost," he said.

I smiled back. "Nope. All good. We–"

"Had trouble finding the glue," Eli finished and I looked at him quizzically.

"I'm surprised it wasn't locked away to stop us degenerates huffing it," Govi chuckled.

I snorted. "It would probably go well with Brenda's magic mushrooms."

Govi barked a loud laugh. "That it would. Here, give us a hand, would you? I need to grab some more tape."

I climbed the ladder to take the branch from him and he ran off. I turned to see where he was going and my foot slipped. But Eli was there with a hand on me to steady me. I looked down at him and he swallowed.

"I… That wasn't meant to be…"

I bit my lip in an effort not to smile. "An incomplete sentence?" I finished for him.

He gave me that half-smirk but, even though it was just as hot, it was a lot less cocky now. "I was going to say I wasn't trying to… You know."

I nodded. "I appreciate that. Thanks."

He nodded as well. "I'd like to point out this is very unnatural for me, though."

I laughed. "You want props for being a decent guy now?"

He sniffed and looked away to hide a smile. "Fair point."

"Hey!" Govi cried excitedly as he came back. "There is physical contact occurring and Gin appears fully functional!"

I went bright red and flaming hot as Eli failed to stifle a laugh and I muttered, "Thanks, Govi…"

We all laughed together and went back to work.

It had to be said that the three of us worked well as a team. The boys were both tall so I took over possession of the ladder and they helped me with holding a branch, passing me paper, or holding up the container of papier-mâché mix. We talked about very little of interest, but we had fun and joked around as we came closer and closer to finishing our first tree. I felt more natural and less weird around Eli with Govi there and without the heavy flirtation Eli had aimed my way before.

So it was all going well until I misjudged my placement and dropped a soggy piece of paper on Eli's head.

Govi and I looked at each other and then back at Eli, who had one eye closed against the glue that was dripping into his eye as the other glared at me in humoured annoyance.

"Gin…?" Govi said slowly.

"Yeah…?" I replied in kind.

"Is it just me or has Eli got a little…"

He didn't get to finish his sentence as Eli uttered an 'Oi,' in protest and flung the soggy paper at his friend, who ducked but failed to avoid the projectile.

Govi scooped up a ball of newspaper and threw it back at Eli, who laughed and managed to duck out of the way. As he was lording it over Govi, the soggy piece of paper landed on his chest. Laughter cut short he looked down at it.

"Gin, little help?" Govi called in mock fear.

I shook my head. "Nope. I'm staying out of th–"

I looked down at my hip where the soggy piece of paper was now sitting, then back up to Eli. "Really?"

He nodded unapologetically. "Um. Yep. It seems so."

The papier-mâché mix was sitting on the top of the ladder so I dipped my hand into it and flicked it at him. Govi packed out laughing as Eli looked at me in a poor attempt at angry.

"Is that how it's going to be?" Eli laughed.

"Gin! Dump it!" Govi giggled and I looked at the container then at Eli.

"No! No! No!" Eli said as he reached to pull the container out of my reach.

I lunged for it at the same time and the ladder wobbled alarmingly. Eli tried to right it, but ended up pulling it the wrong way. We locked eyes for a second, then him, me, the ladder and the papier-mâché mix fell in a pile of laughter, added to by Govi.

"Oh, that was gold!" Govi hooted as I looked Eli and me over.

Papier-mâché mix had gone everywhere. On our clothes, the floor, the ladder.

"It's a good thing we put down the extra newspaper," Eli said, a smile in his voice.

I looked at him and realised just how close we were. "Yeah."

"You okay?"

I nodded. "Yep."

"Come on then," Govi said, coming over and holding his hands out to me. "Let's get you cleaned up."

I disentangled myself from Eli, with much cheek heating, and let Govi pull me up.

"Of course, we could just let it dry and peel it off?" Govi asked. His eyes suggested he was laughing at my predicament, but he wasn't going to say anything about it.

We packed up as best we could, then headed for the bathrooms.

"Can we not forget the short meeting on Sunday please, people?" Milly called as we left. "I want to make sure everything's ready for Monday! That goes for the rest of you, too."

Quicksilver and Sweetness

I pulled into the school carpark on Sunday in a foul mood.

I'd tried to politely suggest to Ella that she could take an hour out of her day to go to the committee meeting, but she'd assured me that she just *had* to run through her lines for the play. My mother had then stepped in and 'reminded' me that it was a privilege to be part of something that no other Year Eleven was part of. I'd had the audacity to mutter that was because it wasn't their jobs and been called ungrateful for all the opportunities I was given in my life.

So really, foul didn't properly cover it.

I was indulging in a bit of a wallow, my music turned up loud while I was locked in my car before I went inside. I was lost enough in 'Something Just Like This' that it took me a moment to realise that the extra thudding wasn't coming from Spotify, but on the car.

I stopped singing and opened my eyes. And what I saw made me smile.

Govi was tapping on the bonnet along to the beat like it was a drum and grinning while he sang along. When he saw me watching him he threw out his arms and took a bow. I turned the volume down and just heard his muffled shout of, "Chloe Cowan!"

I turned off the car, grabbed my stuff and got out.

"Something just like…this?" he asked cheekily and I laughed.

Nodding, I answered, "Definitely."

"Oi, Slacks McGee!" someone called and I looked over to see two guys at a station wagon closer to the school building, with a third hunched over in the boot.

The someone who'd called out was a dark blond haired someone I recognised but didn't know. Same with the black haired guy he was with. But when the one in the boot stuck his head out, it was Eli.

"Hold your damned horses!" Govi called back.

"That's the way it's gonna be, little darlin'!" the blond sang.

"We'll be riding on the horses, yeah," Eli joined in.

"Way up in the sky, little darlin'," the guy with the black hair joined far less enthusiastically.

"And if you fall, I'll pick you up," Govi joined and did just that to me, ignoring my yelp of surprise.

153

"Pick you up!" they all finished while I was trying to keep hold of my book and my bag.

"Oh my God," I laughed as I dangled in Govi's very capable arms. "That song is *so* old!"

"It is *the* Aussie pub song," the blond said.

"It's not," the other guy said as Govi and Eli sighed, "Lake!" exasperatedly.

Lake shrugged. "What? It is!"

The guy with the black hair – who had to be Ramsey – frowned. "Do you want a repeat of me kicking your arse?"

Govi sniggered as he put me down. "Sorry boys, we don't have three hours for Lake to fix his hair after."

"Sorry," Lake said, sparing a quick glare for Govi. "Who beat whose arse?"

"I distinctly remember…"

Govi swayed towards me and drowned out Lake and Ramsey's argument. "I promise we love each other," he assured me.

I nodded. "Of course you do."

Govi leant his cheek on my head. "We're like brothers. Hence, we fight like brothers. Sometimes I think the closer you are with someone the more often you fight with them. But the true test of that ironclad bond is…" He seemed to be waiting for something and I looked back at Lake and Ramsey.

After a few more moments of fighting, Ramsey pointed at Lake with a scoff and they both burst out laughing. Eli laughed with them, his smile becoming softer for a moment as he looked at me. Then Lake patted Ramsey's arm and they both turned to help Eli get one of the big boxes out of the boot.

I watched them in confusion. "Is what?" I asked Govi.

"Is that when it's over, nothing's changed. Like you and Rica." Govi touched his hand to my arm for a moment then went to help the boys.

I thought about that for a moment. I might not have known that in a familial sense, but he was right. Rica and I squabbled over things all the time – expressing differences of opinions and sometimes just for the sake of it – but I always considered them insignificant. We could argue over religion or sport or musicians or books and, no matter how heated or that – on closer inspection – we were actually discussing fundamental differences in life beliefs, we still thought the world of each other.

There was something really nice in that revelation and it made everything that had happened that morning pale into less significance. I smiled at Govi, thankful in one way for once that Ella had left her responsibilities to me yet again.

As Lake and Ramsey carried the box inside, they still seemed to be arguing over which song was *the* Aussie pub song.

"Farnham, all the way," Ramsey said.

Lake scrunched his face. "No. Braithwaite."

I couldn't help myself asking, "Did you guys just watch that beer ad or do you actually like those songs?"

All four boys froze and looked between each other before looking at me.

"Uh... We did... We didn't..." Ramsey stuttered.

"What he's trying to say is we most definitely not just see that ad. We came up with the argument ourselves," Lake offered.

Eli chuckled. "Oh, for sure."

"Oh! Lake. Ramsey. This is Chloe," Govi said happily. "Gin. Lake and Ramsey."

"I guessed," I said with a smile, nodding to them.

Lake was cool as the proverbial cucumber, standing there in his pastel blue jumper with the sleeves pushed up and his dusky chinos and his hair swept back perfectly. It was a far cry from the more indie rocker look he sported on stage, but it was the Lake I was more familiar with at a distance in the corridors of Winters.

Meanwhile, Ramsey looked the same as he always did. He was the token punk boy with the dyed black hair, leather cuffs and all black clothes. But he always seemed nice enough from what I saw – again, at a distance.

"I don't really think hot does her justice, Govi," Lake said and I could see he was just as suavely casual as Eli.

I cleared my throat and gave up hoping my cheeks weren't as red as they felt. "You told them I was hot?"

Govi shrugged. "What? You are hot."

"Classically beautiful fits far better," Lake said, giving me a wink.

I looked down to hide my shy smile. "Shall we get these things inside?" I asked, assuming that was their aim and wanting to shift the conversation from any talk about me.

"Chloe's right," Eli said loudly, pushing his way between me and the box Lake and Ramsey were carrying with a box of his own.

Lake and Ramsey snorted as they looked at Eli's retreating back, gave me a nod, and followed him inside.

"Need any help?" I asked Govi.

He shook his head as he closed the boot. "Nah. We're good. You just hang around and look pretty." He winked and I laughed.

When we got inside, the boys were pulling bits out of the boxes while Milly seemed to be checking things off her list and arguing with Ramsey as though it was second-nature for them.

I dropped my bag by our trees and went to check the papier-mâché. It had dried nice and hard and the tree seemed pretty sturdy.

"These look good," Lake said, tapping one as he stopped beside me.

I nodded. "Thanks. Most of it's Govi to be honest."

Lake smirked. "He's trying to impress you."

I blinked quickly and looked over at Govi. "No," I laughed awkwardly. "No. He's not."

Lake nodded. "He is."

"But why would he…?"

Lake shrugged. "No idea. There seems to be something about you, Chloe Cowan."

My snort was almost hysterical. "There isn't, I promise."

Lake looked at me. "So why do those two only talk about you and the set list?"

My heart thundered. "I…don't know."

Lake laughed and patted my back. "Sorry. I'm teasing. I mean, it's true but I'm just playing. I get it."

Govi called him over to them and Lake left me standing there wondering what it was he got and how I could get him to un-get it…

"Stop distracting them!" I heard Milly cry and looked up to see her frowning at Ramsey. "Seriously, if you're going to be here you can be helpful at least."

The boys of *Quicksilver* all grinned at each other before breaking out in an a Capella version of the Beatles' 'Help'. Milly tried to keep a straight face, but she finally broke into a wide smile.

"Fine," she huffed. "Just don't be distracting."

Lake segued them into 'With a Little Help From My Friends' and Milly threw her hands up in defeat before walking away and calling everyone else to gather around. Govi winked at me as they sang and I shook my head with a smile as I went over to Milly.

"Right, people," she started then clicked her fingers at Lauren. "Focus please. Ignore them. Ticket sales start tomorrow and I need to make sure we've got floats, tickets, schedules, and posters ready." Milly looked down at her clipboard. "Lindy, Anna and Claire, how are the tickets? Are we all ready?"

Anna nodded. "They're all cut out and we've put them in a box with the float."

"And the float has been counted and locked with this key?" Milly asked, holding up the key attached to the clipboard.

Really, there was no safer place for it since I had never seen the clipboard out of her sight.

Claire nodded. "The spreadsheet's all ready and so is the app."

Milly nodded and ticked something off on her list. "And everyone's familiar with how to use the app?"

I was the only one who nodded when Milly looked up and she sighed. In the background, the boys had finally stopped singing.

"For the rest of the class, Chloe, can you tell us how to use the app?" Milly asked.

"Uh…" I looked at them all. "Sure. So just open it on the tablet, select the library, click on 'Formal 2019 tickets', input however many tickets the person wants, click 'add' up in the top right corner, then click 'charge' at the top. If they're paying by card, you swipe it. If not, you select cash and put how much they give you, then you give them any necessary change and if they want email or text for the receipt."

Everyone looked at me blankly.

"How did you remember all that?" Lindy accused.

"Um…" I cleared my throat. "Good memory I guess."

I wasn't going to tell anyone I was so terrified of messing up, I'd spent the last week trying to memorise the sequence.

"At least someone's putting in the effort," Milly sighed. "Thanks, Chloe. Now, schedule. I would prefer two volunteers for…"

She stopped as music started up and we all turned to see the *Quicksilver* boys up on the stage with instruments playing the opening bars to one of their songs, 'One More Time'. It was probably their most popular song and I was sure it wasn't lost on Milly that her command of the crowd was waning.

She clapped her hand against the back of her clipboard a couple of times. "Focussing, please." She waited until everyone was looking at her again. "Thank you. Now as I was saying, I'd prefer two volunteers for lunchtime tomorrow, but I will choose if necessary."

It was obvious no one wanted to volunteer and I felt very 'Hunger Games' for a moment, but managed to stop myself volunteering as tribute. I did, however, volunteer.

"I'll do it," I said, putting my hand up.

Milly looked me over and, when it was painfully obvious no one was going to offer as well, she nodded and turned to the band.

"Who wants to volunteer for ticket sales with Chloe for lunchtime tomorrow?" Milly called to them.

Eli broke from the song only long enough to nod and raise his hand to her.

"Thank you...Eli," Milly said, sounding surprised, before she turned back to the rest of us. "Right. If no one else wants to volunteer for any shifts, I'll make up the roster and hand it out at the meeting tomorrow afternoon. I would like to say I am a little disappointed, though." She looked

161

pointedly at poor Brenda, who flushed and looked at the floor. "Okay, now I want to do a quick rundown of where everything's at before we go," was met with a round of heavy sighing.

Milly looked at me and I spared her a sympathetic smile. I knew Milly and Ella hated each other – the why I didn't know – and she was a task master with formal preparations, but as far as I could tell it was only because she wanted it to be perfect. And honestly, without her breathing down everyone's necks, I was pretty sure we'd all get distracted and not get a lot done. So while I couldn't say I *liked* Milly, I certainly didn't dislike her. I felt like I understood her and at heart she wasn't a bad person.

Which was probably why Ella hated her. And the fact Milly hated Ella was not a mystery to me at all.

Milly went around the circle and had us give her a progress update on all the different aspects of the preparations while the band played us a weird assortment of songs – both theirs and covers – between arguing over what to play next. When it came to my turn, I really wished that Govi hadn't left me to do all the talking.

I pointed a little pathetically at our finished tree. "So, we're on trees for the walkway and we have one done so far. It doesn't look like a lot, I know. But now we know what we're doing, it should all be a much faster process."

162

Milly nodded as she made notes.

"They look really good so far," Phil said.

Taken aback, I had to remind myself to smile. "Oh, thanks."

There was a general consensus of nodding and smiling and I felt like that was one little win. Which was more than could be said for Brenda and her magic mushrooms.

"I'm almost at twice what I had before..." she started hesitantly, looking to Milly.

"Before you lost them," Milly finished for her.

Brenda nodded, pushing her glasses up her nose. "Yes. Um...We have one for the middle of each table now and we're just working on the...the smaller ones."

Milly nodded. "Good work."

Brenda smiled happily and I returned it when our eyes caught for a moment.

There were a few other updates needed – the disco ball, the linen, the tulle and fairy lights for the ceiling – then we were told to make sure that we had everything sorted and dismissed.

The band was still playing, so I wandered over to our finished tree to look over it again. As I'd said to Milly, now we knew what we were doing, we could probably be working on one each at the same time and get it done much faster. We'd ended up sticking with the drama blocks because it had been easiest after all. But it was pretty well hidden and passed a cursory nudge test.

After listening to everyone's updates, I was starting to be able to picture what the formal was going to look like when they were all finished. I looked around the room, imagining the dappled light streaming through the tulle and the 2D trees Milly had planned. Someone was in charge of little forest and fantasy creatures to be peeking out from corners and tables. It was going to look amazing.

But the band suddenly playing a very upbeat, punk-like version of Toto's 'Africa' sort of spoiled it all. Which was probably good, because there was little use in me dreaming about something I was never going to experience.

For some reason, as I thought that, my eyes drifted to Eli. He smiled and gave me a wave from the stage, and it was a very surreal moment.

They might have been playing to a maximum of thirty people, but all four of them looked completely in their element. They looked like they were in the place they were meant to be. They looked like they'd found their purpose.

For one brief moment, I was a little jealous. I let myself have a tiny moment where I imagined being up there on the stage in front of thousands of people and playing music, but nothing about it felt right. That wasn't my life. That was

Ella's life apparently, and one I was being prepared for in case she failed or she'd died tragically young or something.

When the boys finished their song, they put the instruments down and pulled together to talk.

Instead of leaving, I pulled some more paper to me and started making more branches.

"You can go if you want," Milly said from behind me.

I smiled. "Thanks." Reluctantly, I put down the branch.

"I applaud the work ethic, though," Milly said in that stilted way she had and I was starting to think she just wasn't used to letting people in.

She and I had that in common though, so I had no right to judge.

"Thanks," I said again.

Milly nodded and moved off to check on whatever else needed checking.

"Are you free this afternoon, Gin?" Govi asked, dropping onto the table next to me.

I smiled. "I'm not unfortunately. I'm due at my gran's."

Govi groaned dramatically. "Curses!" He looked at me and chuckled. "No worries. Next time?"

I nodded and, despite having no idea what next time would involve, I said, "Sure."

Govi fist-pumped the air. "Sweet."

"Did we get everything out of the car?" Lake called from the stage.

"Yeah. I think so," Govi called back.

"I'll see you tomorrow, Gove," I said to him.

He looked at me and smiled. "Wild horses couldn't keep me away," he said with a wink. Then pushed off the table and walked back to the boys, his arms spread wide, shouting more than singing, "That's the way it's gonna be, little darlin'!"

Lake and Eli joined in while Ramsey cried, "Not again!" then tried drowning them out with 'The Voice'.

Needless to say, three to one was not a fair fight and I managed to slip out unnoticed while they play fought between themselves.

Ticket to Flirt

"That's the fourth person in twenty minutes," Eli commented and I nodded as I sat back down.

"Yep."

He dropped into the chair beside me, fiddling with the lid of his Peach Coke bottle. "I don't get it."

"Don't get what?" I asked, watching the people continue to walk by out little alcove in the hallway.

Some of them flirted with Eli, who felt no qualms about flirting back, and some got all shy when he smiled at them. And some – read most – of them thought I was Ella and the audible sigh of disappointment was I presumed what had Eli confused now.

"How do they think she's you?" He paused. "You're her?" He frowned like he wasn't sure what he was saying.

"You don't have to like a person for the family resemblance to be strong," I replied resignedly.

"But you…" He breathed out heavily, shook his head, and sat back further in his chair.

"I what, Eli?" I asked as I smiled politely at the person who walked up to the table.

"Two please," she asked and I nodded as I put it through the app.

"Grace," Eli said, sitting forward quickly and slamming his Coke on the table.

"Hey Eli," she said with a rueful smirk.

"Hey yourself," he answered. "This. Is this Ella?" He pointed both his arms at me.

Grace looked me over and I felt very exposed under that deep brown gaze. Finally she frowned and shook her head. "Am I supposed to say yes?" she asked slowly.

Eli leant on his knees. "Did you at any point today think that this was Ella?"

Grace looked at me again. "Well yeah. On first glance, she looks like Ella." Grace shrugged. "But if she's Ella, she's Ella with some concept of dignity."

Eli snorted, trying to hide it too late behind his fist. He nodded. "Okay," he said, still with his fist in front of his face.

"Cash or card?" I asked Grace, wishing Eli would just let it be. I decided not to say it in case that led to an impromptu concert after the day before.

168

"Cash," Grace said, handing it over.

I took it, gave her the change, and looked back at her. "Receipt?"

Grace nodded. "Thanks. Gdiamond at Winters."

I nodded and input it into the tablet.

"Oh, Gracey baby. Born rockstar with that name," Eli sighed appreciatively, crossing his arms.

Grace snorted. "Says you, Mr Sweet." She shook her head at him. "Behave yourself."

"I make no promises," he answered.

Grace looked at me with a smile. "Good luck with this one."

I smiled back. "Thanks. I need it."

Grace looked between us and a weird smile passed over her face. "Yes, you do."

She walked away and Eli was shaking his head, his smile just showing behind the fist back in front of his face again.

"Here I thought it impossible for you to be friends with a girl," I quipped.

Eli's grin widened. "Not impossible at all."

"Is she gay?" I asked. It seemed just like Eli to only be able to be friends with a girl he had no chances with.

"Sexist!" Eli cried then grinned again. "But no. I don't blame you for thinking it, though. Nah, Grace is just good people."

"Which makes the girls you flirt with…?" I asked him.

He looked at me and I could see he was about to say something less than complimentary but stopped himself just in time. His self-satisfied smirk dropped. He drummed on the table for a moment as he looked at me and I patiently waited for his response.

"Is it Tuesday?" he asked slowly, his face wrinkling hopefully.

I shook my head. "Not last I checked."

"That foot in mouth seems to be spreading."

I looked away to hide my smile. "That's what you're going with?"

"I have no excuse. I'm a terrible human being."

I looked back at him. "That seems a little drastic."

He grinned infectiously. "Does that mean you like me?"

I scoffed. "I wouldn't go that far."

"Yeah, you…" he started.

I frowned. "Me? Me what?"

"Yeah, you." He looked around quickly, then shuffled his chair closer to mine and broke out into song. "I used to wanna be, living like there's only me…"

I hung my head, shaking it wearily as he went on. And on.

"…somebody to you." He finally paused and looked at me. "What?" he asked. "No?"

I looked at him. "You know there are other ways to flirt with people."

"Firstly I don't know what you mean. Secondly, if I did, I can't be flirting with you because I said I wouldn't."

"I believe the deal was you wouldn't on purpose."

He nodded. "Therefore I can't be blamed for singing to you."

I looked at him, hoping to convey all my exasperation with him, but it was difficult when I hadn't actually hated it. "Really?"

He nodded. "Really. Much like I can't help my face, I also can't help my love for song." He leant further towards me and whispered, "It's kind of my thing, you know."

"You don't say?"

"I really do, though. And I'm very good at it."

"Modest, too."

"Oh, very." He threw me a cheeky grin.

I pushed him away, but gently. "Well my thing is keeping my skin, so you stay over there with…your thing."

"That can't be your only thing," he said, resignedly shuffling his chair away again.

"Making sure I still have my skin to keep all my insides…inside?"

He nodded. "Yes."

We paused our conversation as some else came over to buy their tickets. The guy fist-bumped Eli, called me Ella, and said something about some concert before walking away again.

I pulled open my book, but Eli nabbed it out of my grasp.

"Excuse you," I told him with a frown, but he was wearing a cheeky half-smirk that made it difficult to remember I was upset with him.

"You're not getting out of it that easily."

"Out of what?" I asked, hoping if I pretended not to know for long enough I could distract him.

"Out of telling me more about you."

"There really isn't all that much to tell you," I said, lurching to get my book back, but he pulled it out of my reach and I had to put my hand on his knee to stop myself falling into him completely.

I looked up and found our noses were much too close. But I didn't move away just yet.

"My book, Eli." I left my hand on his knee and held my other palm up for him to put the book into.

He leant closer and turned his face so my lips were next to his ear. "What's the magic word, Chloe?" he asked.

I tried and failed to keep a straight face as I said, "Brenda's magic mushrooms."

He dissolved into laughter and I couldn't help but join him. He looked at me, his honey eyes alight with humour, and I had that thudding and fluttering in my chest. Our laughter seemed to die simultaneously on our lips as we just looked at each other.

"Chloe–" Eli started softly, but was interrupted by a much shriller shriek of my name.

I jumped and pulled away from Eli guiltily, turning to the harpy. "Ella." I nodded, then added quickly, "We were just talking about you." If there was anything that Ella liked it was people talking about her.

"We were?" Eli asked, then nodded when I kicked him under the table. "Yes. We were."

Ella looked down at me in every possible sense of the word, one hand on her hip, exposed even in the middle of winter, and the other up to keep her handbag in the crook of her arm. Lindy hovered next to her but a step behind like all good minions, glaring at me like Ella wasn't doing a great job of it already.

Eventually, Ella pulled her eyes off me and turned to Eli with a saccharine sweet smile. "Hi Elijah."

Eli nodded and I watched his body language change from comfortable and relaxed to smooth charmer. I hadn't even realised he had another setting until I watched it happen in front of me.

"Ella. Lindy. How are we this fine lunchtime?"

Ella batted her eyes at him and bit her lip. There was absolutely nothing subtle about her. People on the moon would be able to see she was flirting with him. "Fine. How are you?"

Eli leant an elbow on the table and smiled up at her. "Better for seeing you, gorgeous."

"That's very *sweet* of you, Elijah," she tittered. Yes the evil sister tittered. I partly wished I'd recorded it for Rica.

Eli masterfully let his smile widen just a touch to make the implication of his next words crystal clear. "I hear you don't have a date yet for the formal."

Ella nodded and pouted like she was some hard done by orphan in a Dickens novel. "No one's asked me yet."

I managed not to ask her why she thought that was.

Eli sat back in his chair. "Well, maybe that will change soon. Yeah…?"

While one part of me was busy trying not to gag, the other was starting to believe that I was going to get to keep my skin after all. Especially the way Ella gushed at his words.

"I hope so," she said, batting her eyes again.

Eli did his trademark chin kick towards her, his arms crossed nonchalantly. "I should probably finish up my shift. I'll see you in music, yeah?"

Ella licked her lip nauseatingly before she bit it. "Okay." She gave him a little nose wrinkle in a silent 'rawr' for good measure and sashayed away.

As soon as she was gone, I gave an involuntary, "Blergh," and Eli turned to me with a humoured laugh.

"What?"

I shook my head. "Nothing."

"Not nothing. What?"

I looked after my sister. "Just...her."

"You two really don't get along, do you?"

I looked at him sarcastically. "Oh, how did you guess?"

He nodded. "Was that appropriate?"

I frowned. "Nothing about what I just saw was appropriate. There are minors in the corridor, Elijah," I chastised.

He laughed. "No. I thought I was supposed to be purposefully flirting with her."

"Oh, you were flirting? I didn't notice," I said as I looked at my watch and saw it was two o'clock and the end of lunch. I pulled the float to me and started counting the takings.

"Is this a reaction to her or are you jealous I flirted back?" he asked teasingly.

I spared him a glare. "I'm not jealous, Eli."

175

I was actually surprised Govi didn't just pop up with his 'The lady doth,' nonsense.

"Wasn't I supposed to…turn my attention to Ella?"

I nodded. "Yes."

"So why are you in a shit?" he asked.

When I didn't answer, he took my arm gently and pulled me to face him.

"Clo? Are you angry with me? Because I'm sorry if I did the wrong thing or…?"

I shook my head. "No. I'm not angry with you. I just…" I sighed and flailed my hand in the direction Ella had gone. "Ella's nice – or the closest to nice she ever gets – to everyone but me." I huffed, partly in annoyance and partly in disbelief. "Oh my God, I sound like such a whiney bitch." I pulled away from him and went back to the float.

"She's your sister, I get that it sucks."

I huffed again, humourlessly this time. "I don't care. Not in the way I wish it was different anyway. I just… It pisses me off. Watching her be so false to people all the time like she thinks I'm too stupid to know better or something. Or maybe like she's daring me to try to call her out on it and see what it gets me." I shook my head. "I don't know."

Eli was silent for a while. When he finally spoke, all he said was, "You know, you're really selling this whole I should ask her to the formal thing."

176

I looked at him and couldn't help but laugh with relief. "It's my job to talk her up, keep you away from Milly and get you to ask her. She didn't explicitly say which of her...qualities I was meant to talk up."

Eli sniggered, spraying the Peach Coke he'd just tipped into his mouth everywhere. "Fair." He twisted the lid back on and tried to brush the majority of the liquid off himself. "I guess I appreciate the honesty?"

I nodded. "Good people probably don't rag all over their sisters, huh?" I asked.

"I dunno..." he said slowly. "Good people tend not to sugar-coat shit for their friends."

"Literal shit or...?"

He huffed a laugh. "Both. Either."

I nodded again. "Friends?" I looked at him askance.

"You wouldn't call us friends?"

"I thought you didn't flirt with friends?"

He leant on his knees and looked at me thoughtfully. "Have you seen me and Lake together?" he asked cheekily.

I smiled, but looked down to hide it. "Not enough obviously."

Eli reached over slowly and tipped my chin up with a gentle finger. He looked me over, his expression soft. A couple of times, he looked like he was going to say something but thought better of it. Finally, he pulled his hand back and said, "You never did tell me what your thing was."

I cleared my throat and tried to find something to busy myself with. "Uh, my thing?"

"Yeah. Like my thing is music, remember?"

I nodded. "I remember. I was hoping you didn't."

"Well that much is obvious," he chuckled.

I took a deep breath, but just as I was about to answer, he spoke again.

"You're in Winters, so I want to say something arty. No one gets in without being arty. But I haven't seen you do anything remotely arty except papier-mâché, so I'm going to have to guess not?"

I sighed. "I don't really have a thing."

"You must have a thing. Everyone has a thing."

I shrugged. "I guess not."

"A ha!" he cried. "Books! Almost every time I've seen you, you've had a book with you."

I grinned despite not wanting to encourage him. "I like reading, yeah."

"So you're a writer!" he guessed, obviously thinking he'd guessed right.

I frowned at him as I packed up the float. "No."

"What?"

"You think everyone who reads must write as well?"

He looked like he was thinking it through for a moment. "Well, I mean there's the literal ability to write, and then the crafting of novels…"

"I have zero skill in the latter."

"So not a writer, then."

I shook my head at him. "Decidedly not."

"But a reader," he clarified and I nodded. "Okay. So… How did you get into Winters?"

"The usual way."

"And yet you claim to have no things…?"

I looked up at him as I stood up. "I have no things. I have books and Rica, and now the formal committee," I amended. "Other than that, no things."

"What do you do for fun?"

"Read."

"When you're not reading?"

I thought about it. "Watch movies."

"Any hobbies that don't involve someone else's creations?"

I sighed as I thought some more. I made to nod, but then shook my head. "No."

"You don't do anything except read, watch movies and work on papier-mâché trees?"

"Okay, I have homework and my extra-curriculars."

"Ha! What extra-curriculars, then?"

"Nothing I choose to do."

He groaned. "Fine. What's your favourite subject then?"

"Maths."

He blinked at me. "What?"

I nodded. "I know," I sighed. "I'm the weirdo at the specialist arts school who'd rather be at a normal school and focussing on maths."

"No. Look, each to their own. I'm just surprised."

"Surprised a girl likes maths?"

"I didn't realise maths had a gender preference. But no. You just don't have that…maths vibe."

I turned to him. "And what vibe do I have?"

He looked me over and shook his head. "I don't know." He got up, picking up his half-drunk Coke. "But it's not maths."

"I don't know if that's a compliment or not," I told him.

He shrugged. "It wasn't intended as anything."

"Does this mean we can't be friends now?" I teased and he grinned.

"Well, look. At the very least, I'll have someone to help me with my budget when I'm rich and famous," he chuckled.

"Isn't the goal to be so disgustingly rich that you don't need to budget?"

"Oh, you're familiar with the rich and famous dream, then. Are you?" he joked.

"I know of it, yes."

His smile was more sincere now. "It's kind of hard not to in a place like this."

"Yeah, but there are the dreamers and then there's you, Govi, Lake and Ramsey, actually on the brink of stardom."

He shrugged, looking away almost like he was a little embarrassed. "There are unfortunately no guarantees in this life."

"Well if it doesn't work out, you can come and teach at my music school," I offered.

He smiled. "You're going to have a music school, are you?"

I nodded. "If the whole Commerce things flops."

He nodded thoughtfully. "Sensible to have a backup."

"Very."

"And you never know when someone will want to learn the triangle. And from a maestro, no less."

I snorted. "Very true. Although I did picture myself the old spinster piano ma'am."

Eli pointed at me. "Oh, I know that one. Everyone hates her and wonders who pissed in her coffee?"

I nodded. "The very same."

He put his hands in his pockets, cradling the Coke bottle under his arm. "You know what they say, aim for the moon and even if you miss you'll land among the stars."

I grinned, deciding not to inform him that the moon was in fact closer to earth than any star. "Exactly."

He nodded again. "Good plan."

"Yo, dude there you are!" Govi called, grinning as he came over to us. "We've got English and Old Tom told me to hurry your arse up."

Eli looked at me and I had a little trouble deciphering his expression. He almost looked like he didn't want to leave me, but I wasn't sure if he wanted to continue our conversation or if it was because he didn't want me thinking he was shirking his responsibilities.

I held up the float. "All good. I have a break, so I'll take this back for Milly."

He nodded. "Oh, okay."

"See you this afternoon, Gin!" Govi called as he grabbed Eli's collar and started dragging him away.

"Yep. See ya," I replied.

I stood in the hallway for a few moments longer, then pulled myself together and hurried off to the auditorium.

So not interested

On Wednesday, Lake and Ramsey decided to come to the committee meeting again, much to Milly's chagrin. I walked in to find all the *Quicksilver* boys on the stage again, playing while Milly was rushing around trying to keep everyone focussed on their tasks at hand and not breaking out into impromptu dance.

I gave the boys a return wave as I headed to our table and tried not to smile too hard at Govi's animated drumming. The guy just looked so happy, it was hard not to feel happy when you saw him. But then, Govi pretty well always looked so happy.

I dropped my bag and my jacket on a chair and rolled up my sleeves, unconsciously singing along as the band played 'Shut Up and Dance', before mixing up some more papier-mâché mix so I could get a start on the trees while Eli and Govi were practising. From what I'd gathered, there was still a lot of argument over the set list. With the formal being a run-through for them – not that they hadn't played gigs before – the nerves seemed to be setting in and making them feel like nothing was good enough.

With the papier-mâché mix all finished, I turned to get started and nearly ran into Lindy. If I'd been a faster sort of girl, I would have 'accidentally' spilled it down the front of her no doubt very expensive crop top and jeans combination.

"Argh," I yelped. "Lindy. Hi. Can I help you with anything?"

She looked me over suspiciously and I wondered what in the seven hells I was supposed to have done now. Or not done, maybe…

I could see why she might have been sent to get on my case.

"Elijah and Ella," she answered, confirming my presumptions.

I nodded. "What about them?"

"Why hasn't he asked her to the formal yet?"

I shrugged. "I don't know," I told her, my eyes sliding to look at Eli up on stage. "I've been talking her up, but I can't just be totally obvious about these things. Ella wants it to be Eli's idea, right?"

Lindy looked like she had no idea but, since I sounded so confident, then that must be right. "Of course she does."

"Exactly. She doesn't want him to ask her because he was told to, does she?" I said as though it was obvious.

"No," Lindy scoffed, then frowned as though she was trying to work out if that was right or not. "No?"

"No," I encouraged. "So let me work on it."

"He'd better ask her by the end of the week." I wasn't sure what the 'or else' was going to be, but I was going to try to avoid if it I could. Then surprisingly, Lindy leant into me and whispered, "People who don't get asked look pathetic. And Ella doesn't want to look…"

"Pathetic?" I offered when she didn't continue.

Lindy winked. "So you understand the mission?"

I blinked at her, wondering at the sense in reminding her I'd been 'on the mission' for coming up to three weeks now. But I was saved having to make a decision when Milly's voice floated over.

"Lindy, is there something else you should be doing?"

Lindy jumped then frowned. "Stupid Milly Wallis thinking she's in charge."

I kept my face as neutral as possible. "She… She is in charge, Lindy. She's…head of the committee…" I said slowly and as calmly as possible.

Lindy flicked her head back. "Until Ella arrives."

I didn't need to wonder if I should tell her that wasn't how it worked, I just asked politely, "And when will that be?"

Lindy scoffed. "Ella is *very* busy, you know."

I nodded. "Doing what exactly?"

Lindy visibly bristled. "Important things!"

Which was definitely code for either Lindy didn't think she was privileged enough to know what Ella got up to, or Lindy knew full well that Ella was just a lazy sod – although probably in more flattering terms.

"Lindy!" Milly called.

Lindy huffed. "I'll be watching you," she told me aggressively.

I nodded. "Of that I have no doubt."

She huffed again, then turned on her heel and stalked away to do whatever she was on now the tickets were being sold.

I shook my head and dragged the ladder over to the second tree to get started.

I had all the branches attached and was adding the second layer of papier-mâché when *Quicksilver* started playing something different.

The boys were playing a song that sounded like slightly modernised version of something from the 50's, but it was

186

catchy and I found myself smiling and bopping my head while I got papier-mâché more on my fingers than the tree.

When the song finished, they didn't start another one and they didn't seem to be arguing. I looked up to see Govi launch himself off the stage enthusiastically as the others were standing around, still with their guitars, like they were checking a chord or something.

"That one I liked," I laughed as he came over to me.

"Thank you," he said with his trademark wide smile.

"Did you write it?"

He scoffed and put his hand to his heart. "Did I...?" he spluttered.

"I'll take that as a no?" I asked uncertainly.

He shook his head. "Nah. That one's for my mum. It's from her favourite movie."

"Aw," I cooed. "Aren't you cute?"

He wriggled adorably. "I'm a mumma's boy, it's true."

I snorted. "That's no bad thing."

He leant towards me conspiratorially. "Not very hardcore rockstar though, eh?"

I couldn't help my eyes drifting to Eli. "Not everyone wants a hardcore rockstar, Gove."

He nudged me playfully. "Once more. This time like you believe it."

I pulled my eyes off Eli and looked at him. "Excuse me?"

Govi nodded towards Eli. "You heard me."

I scoffed and not very believably. "I'm not interested in any rockstars, hardcore or otherwise. Thank you."

"Aren't you though?" he cajoled, nudging my leg with his arm.

I nudged him right back with my foot and we both laughed as I said, "No. I have a very specific view for my future and it doesn't involve playboy rock-god wannabes."

"Is that so?" Govi said, as though he wasn't sure whether to believe me or if he should try to make me change my mind.

I nodded. "It is. I've got neon lights in my future, Gove. But unlike you and your friends, mine herald freedom and a more hermitic life."

"A hermitic life?" Govi asked. "For those of us more artistically inclined, exactly what is that?"

"Being one of those mad recluses, hiding from society, bah-humbugging the rest of you chasing stardom."

"Ah…" he said slowly. "You disapprove?"

I shook my head as he passed me some more paper. "Not at all. Each to their own. But stardom is not for me."

"And therefore anyone reaching for stardom is also…not for you?" His voice was so uncertain and hesitant that I looked down at him, being slightly shorter with me on the ladder.

"I… Well, that's not to say…" I faltered, not sure what was going through his mind.

If I'd completely missed him having some crush on me or something then I didn't want to put my foot in it. On the flipside, if he didn't have some crush on me and I looked like I thought he did, I also didn't want to put my foot in it. Either way, I could see my foot getting right up in the proverbial it in three…two…one…

"No. Anyone with dreams of stardom isn't…not for me." I stopped, my face scrunching while I tried to work out if that was right as I wiped my hands clean(ish) on a rag I'd found.

"So…you're not going to just disappear after the formal's over and your responsibilities are done, and I'll never see you again?" he asked.

Trying to lighten the mood, I joked, "No. I was planning on disappearing once Eli asked Ella."

Govi looked up at me quickly, but the panic on his face melted when he saw me grinning ruefully. He scoffed. "Very cute."

I nodded. "Thank you."

"I'm serious though, Gin. I don't want you to end up just being some song I sing myself after too much Johnny Walker."

I wrinkled my nose, this time as I questioned his drink of choice. "Aw, you're going to write a song about me?" I teased.

He smirked. "Maybe." He took hold of the ladder, his fingers fiddling with the label that was peeling off. "On a related note…"

"Ye-es…?" I asked slowly when he didn't continue.

"I know it's mates before dates and all…" I saw his face contort like he wasn't sure how to go on.

"Gove…what about mates before dates…?"

"How would you feel about me asking Rica to the formal?" It all came out in a rush before he looked up at me.

I couldn't stop the smile of both relief and support. "I'd feel fine," I told him.

His face dropped out of uncertainty and into a relieved happiness. "Really?"

"Of course. Why would you think I'd mind?"

He shrugged as he took hold of my hand and looked at it. "I didn't want it to make anything weird. What if Rica said no or she said yes and then we dated for a while but then we broke up and the break up was awful and then I'd lose you because of course you'd have to side with her because you were friends first and I'd be–"

"Woah!" I laughed, squeezing his hand. "Take a breath, dude."

190

He looked back up at me with a smile that was half apology and half self-deprecating. He breathed in deeply, then let it out. "Breathing again," he said.

I put my other hand on his shoulder. "You want to ask her, you ask her. We'll work out the rest as we go."

"I over thought that a little, huh?"

I nodded. "Just a little."

He nodded as well. "I don't have a lot of people I think of a close friends, Gin. I just don't want to lose the ones I do have."

I smiled softly as the hand on his shoulder moved to his cheek. "Right back at you."

There was a twanging crash and Govi and I turned around to see Eli hastily picking up the guitar he'd presumably just dropped.

"You right, mate?" Govi called.

Eli seemed to shake off a frown for his drummer and nodded. "Yeah. Fine."

"Butter fingers!" Govi laughed then turned back to me. "Which tree do you want me working on?"

"Which ever one looked less daunting," I answered.

Govi looked around. "Okay. And if they all look daunting?"

"Eeny meeny miny moe?" I offered.

He sniggered, "Helpful."

"If you start singing again…" I warned.

"Help!" he started and I left him to it while I went on with my tree.

Govi had made good headway on his tree when I finished mine. As I was climbing down the ladder, my foot slipped again but Eli was there to catch me. Again.

"Thanks," I smiled, letting him hold my arm as I found my way to the floor.

"Ah. No worries." He pointed at the tree. "Looks good."

"It's not too bad, hey? Govi's is looking better, though."

Eli followed my gaze over to Govi, then shrugged. "It's all right."

I frowned a little, wondering what was up with him. But I thought it might be better not to mention anything.

"Uh…" he started, looking around. "So the guys thought they might hang around and give us a hand?"

I smirked. "A semi-famous rockband are going to stoop to building decorations?" I teased.

There was a ghost of a smirk on his face. "Never let it be said we forget where we came from."

I snorted. "Sure."

"So where do you want us then?" Ramsey asked as he walked over, rolling up his sleeves.

"Can you be trusted to a tree of your own?" I asked him.

He looked up from his arm. "Can I...?" He looked at Eli, then back to me and grinned. "Yeah, I think I can manage."

"I wouldn't bet on it," Lake said as he strolled behind Ramsey, all elegance and nonchalance. "This one okay for me?"

I nodded. "Have at whatever you want."

Lake paused in his inspection of the tree to look at me, an eyebrow raised. "And If I want to have at you?"

I flushed bright red by the feel of my cheeks, but Eli answered before I had a chance to say anything.

"Then you are shit out of luck," he growled.

"Mr Aggression over there is not wrong!" Govi called, his tone chipper.

Lake smirked. "Message received and understood."

He gave Eli a look I couldn't decipher before he went to work.

Ramsey needed a little bit more direction and was less than thrilled to take it. Lake, on the other hand, was quite happy to let Govi show him a better way of doing things. And that was only when Govi wasn't charging ahead and getting shit done all on his own initiative. Eli was usually like Govi, but every now and then kept asking me questions. And they weren't just about the trees.

"Clo?"

"Yes, Eli?"

"What do you think? Lake reckons go from 'That Thing You Do' into 'One More Time', but Ramsey thinks 'Africa' first and finishing with 'High Hopes' is better."

I paused and looked around at the others, who also seemed confused as to why Eli was asking me.

"Um…" I stalled. "Which one is 'That Thing You Do'?"

"The one for my mum," Govi answered.

"And Panic! At the Disco?"

"That's the one."

I nodded. "Right. Um, well… I would have no idea, actually."

Eli sighed. "Your uneducated opinion, then?"

I looked at him, affronted. "How do you know my opinion would be uneducated?"

He did have the decency to look apologetic, but he teased, "Of course. You play piano. My bad. A knowledge of the classics will definitely give you a good grasp on modern set lists." He winked though so I remembered it was teasing. At least, I chose to think that was why he was winking.

"I never said I had a knowledge of the classics. I could be *the* authority on modern set lists," I laughed.

"Are you?" Govi asked, poking his head around his current tree.

I shook my head, managing to climb off the ladder all by myself, and headed over to our table. "Not at all."

"Okay," Eli said. "So what is your semi-qualified, maybe or maybe not educated opinion?"

I looked back at him with a smile. "'That Thing You Do' then 'One More Time', 'High Hopes' then 'Africa'. Should allow for a decent flow and build the atmosphere."

I heard Ramsey say something behind me, but was distracted because Eli appeared beside me.

"Good idea. You sure your thing isn't music?" he asked quietly and his body warmth suddenly felt very close.

I shook my head and held up my gluey hands. "It's quite clearly become papier-mâché."

He huffed a soft laugh. "I don't think you give yourself enough credit, Chloe Cowan."

"I think you might give me too much, Elijah Sweet," I replied

"Impossible," he breathed.

I looked up to find him looking down at me. There was an intense heat in his eyes, but it was different than the smoulder. There was something sexy about that hint of a half-smile, but it wasn't cocky arrogance. Everything about him was hot, but it was softer, more gentle. I didn't want to admit it was all unintentional on his part, but I definitely couldn't pull him up on doing it on purpose.

I cleared my throat as I looked back at the table and tried to remember what I'd gone over for. "There's no depths to explore here, Eli…"

"Govi was right, wasn't he?" he asked.

I uselessly moved some bits of cardboard around. "About what?"

"That you understand me far better than I'd like."

I looked up again and his honey gaze pinned me. "The understanding seems mutual," just popped out of me. I felt my cheeks flush and was more than grateful when Milly called out that we could go.

Govi arrived beside us, nattering away about something, which gave me a chance to compose myself. He and the other boys helped me pack things up. We were standing in the hallway when I realised I'd left my phone on the table among the cardboard.

"You coming, Gin?" Govi asked.

I shook my head. "I forgot my phone. I'll see you tomorrow."

"Cool, cool." Govi hugged me.

"See ya, Gin," Ramsey called as they all headed off and I nodded.

I let them get out of sight before hurrying back to find even Milly had left.

Thinking I had the auditorium all to myself, my eyes drifted up to the piano and thought, *to hell with it*. I climbed up on stage and sat down.

I'd never been the girl who wanted to play in front of adoring crowds; that was Ella, she who didn't care what she did as long as it was in front of adoring crowds. But maybe, just once, I wanted to see what it felt like to play on a stage. Sure the auditorium stage wasn't huge and there was going to be nothing but arts and crafts to hear me, but still.

My fingers hovered over the keys. I let them fall and waited to see what came out.

Unexpectedly, I played 'Let Me Be Myself' by 3 Doors Down.

And I accompanied myself with vocals.

But I went with it.

There was something that felt weirdly poignant about it, but I ignored that. It would be my time soon. I was *strategically* living as the understudy to someone else's life. Soon I could be my own person. It was planned.

When I got to the end of the song, I sat and stared at the piano for a moment.

"You know," a voice started and I jumped, "a person's song choice says a lot about them."

I turned to look at Eli, pretending my heart wasn't running a million miles a minute and for more than one reason. "Is that so?"

He nodded and hauled himself onto the stage. "It is."

"And what does that particular choice say about me?"

"That I was right before and you're a lot more talented than you give yourself credit for."

I shrugged. "Years of practise will do that to you."

He dropped onto the seat beside me. "The talent or the short-changing?"

"Both."

He nodded his head once. "I didn't know you played." His head dropped sideways before he amended, "I didn't realise you'd play so well."

My hands wrung in my lap. "I play."

He huffed a laugh. "I see that."

"I thought you were going."

"I...also left something behind..." he said cryptically.

We sat in silence for a while, both just staring at the keys in front of us. Eventually, Eli stated tinkering with the keys. He seemed to just be messing around, until I recognised 'Heart and Soul'. I kept my head down against a smile and joined him.

"Naw, are we duet-ing?" Eli cooed.

I nudged him as we kept playing. "That's not a word."

He nudged me back. "Is now."

"You're not famous enough to just make up words."

"Yet."

"Arrogant."

He laughed, "Yes," then started singing Train's 'Play That Song'.

So I joined him. We shared a few smiles as we sang and played together, and I didn't chastise myself for the way my heart fluttered at the easiness of it all. I chose to live in the moment and just enjoy myself. After all, two people could play piano and sing together without it meaning anyone was interested in anything more than friendship.

Douchebags gonna douche

Friday lunch, Eli and I were back on ticket sales. There were enough people on the committee that you'd think we might not have had to do it twice. But people were quite terrible at volunteering and, so when Milly asked me, I'd felt bad for her and said yes.

Rica and Govi were hanging out on the other side of the corridor from us, being generally unhelpful but keeping us entertained. Lake and Ramsey had needed to go and talk to their music teacher about something so had left only a few moments ago and Eli and I were watching Govi and Rica do what we assumed they thought was some kind of slapstick routine.

Eli leant towards me. "On a scale of one to ten, how likely is she to break his heart?"

I shrugged and leant back in my chair. "How likely is he to break hers?"

Eli cocked his head to the side. "Fair."

I snorted. "That's not an answer."

"At least I didn't answer with a question. And the same question I'd asked."

I smiled. "No. But Rica's not the semi-famous rockstar with a little bit of a reputation."

"Neither is Govi."

I looked at him in confusion.

"That would be me."

I smiled, but it was a cover for the way my heart dropped, before I looked away. "So I'm aware."

He laughed. "I can't help the ladies like me."

I nodded and kept up a smile, despite not feeling it at all. "You certainly can't help your face."

"That definitely didn't sound like a compliment..." he said slowly. "You okay?"

I nodded at him vaguely, pretending to be engrossed with Rica and Govi's impromptu dance routine that looked to be about two people who liked each other but neither had the courage to make the first move.

"Chloe..."

"Mm?"

He gently turned my face to look at him. "What's up?" An encouraging smile hinted at his lips. "You can't be worried I'll break Ella's heart."

I swallowed. "Even if I was, I'm expecting it."

He winced a little as he slowly took his hand back. "I want to tell you I'm not really that guy…"

I nodded and looked down.

"I'm the first to admit – embarrassingly – that I like the attention and I let it go to my head. I'm young and stupid and – yeah – I'm arrogant. I feel like I have to be a certain kind of guy to get where I want to go in life. But I'm trying to remember nothing's worth it if I lose the things I care about. I'm trying to be a better person."

I looked up with a frown. "Why?"

He scoffed, but it was humourless. "Because you…" He paused. "People like you can't really like that guy. And being scared the important people are going to leave is only going to make them leave…"

"Are you trying to tell me you're afraid to have your heart broken?" I asked him.

"Aren't we all? Friends, family…" He tipped my chin back up so I looked at him, "people who could be more."

"Yet you didn't really care when you broke all those other hearts?"

His eyes searched mine. "If I did, I didn't mean to."

"I could argue that makes it worse."

"Are you going to?"

My lips tipped up involuntarily, which made his. "Not this time," I told him.

My head was trying to remind me that he might have some pretty words, but that didn't change anything. And it didn't change the fact that Ella wanted him. So even if he wasn't the guy I assumed he was and I was interested in him, he still wasn't for the likes of me.

"I'll let you win, if it will make you feel better?"

I laughed. "Thanks, but I'm okay."

His smile was warm. "Okay."

Our somewhat serious moment dissipated naturally and we waited for the next person to come and buy their tickets, chatting with Govi and Rica across the corridor.

Sometimes we pretended we couldn't hear them, talking in stage-shouts. Other times the boys broke out into song. Usually it was Govi obviously trying to serenade Rica, and I could see it was totally working. He even pulled her into a dance at one point where they ended up hugging. To give them as much privacy as possible, I turned to face Eli.

"Sorry about him," Eli laughed, turning around as well.

I shook my head. "I'm not."

"I want to say he's not usually like this–"

"But we both know he is," I finished for him and he grinned.

"Govi's gonna Govi."

"And the world's a better place for it, too."

"So your perfect guy is someone like Govi then?" he teased and I smirked.

"Is that your unsubtle way of asking me who my perfect guy is?" I threw a ball of scrap paper at him and he caught it.

"Well, yeah. I wasn't intending to be subtle," he chuckled.

I nodded, sneaking a look at our friends as they were being all cute and mushy. "Okay. I'll share if you do."

He nodded. "Deal."

I sat back as I thought about it. "I guess my perfect guy would make me laugh like Govi does. But I don't know if I have the energy to keep up with his enthusiasm for life."

Eli nodded and waved his hand at me to continue as he took a sip of his Peach Coke.

I grinned. "I don't know," I laughed. "I haven't thought about it that much. I guess I want a guy who sees me. A guy who looks at me and doesn't see the Ella understudy. Someone who doesn't constantly compare me to her. He just likes me for who I am."

"Hm…" Eli mused as he put the lid back on his bottle. "Makes sense."

"That is not sharing."

He grinned. "My perfect girl is drop-dead gorgeous. Blonde of course. Big boobs. Tiny waist. Wide hips. Legs for days. Oh and a brain the size of a pea."

A snort escaped as I tried not to laugh. "I so hope you're joking."

"Of course I am."

"Thank God. I might have lost all respect for you."

"I didn't realise you had any to begin with."

"I have…a small amount of respect for you. Out of love for Govi, of course."

"Oh. Of course. I couldn't have possibly fostered any of that for myself."

I shook my head a little overzealously and I hoped he didn't notice.

Because it was plainly obvious that the respect I had for him had very little to do with Govi anymore. I wasn't going to fall for Eli, but I liked him. He had, under everything, the makings of a decent friend. When he wasn't being the rockstar wannabe. Those moments when he was properly relaxed, not performing, those were the moments I saw through what I sincerely hoped was a façade.

I cleared my throat, not trusting my voice to come out properly, then said, "You still haven't told me about your perfect girl."

He nodded, looking thoughtful. "She doesn't put up with my bullshit, for starters. Anyone who lets me get away with acting like a twat is not long-distance material–"

"Long-distance as in long-term, or literally because you'll be world-famous and always travelling?" I interrupted.

He looked at me. "Do you think you could do the long-distance thing?"

I shrugged. "I don't know. It would probably depend who was on the other end of the distance, wouldn't it?"

Eli looked down to the bottle in his hands. "He'd have to be something pretty damned special?" It wasn't really a question.

"I think they'd both have to be pretty special for it to work."

"You don't think you'd be worth it?"

I shrugged and looked down again. "I don't think I've proven I am."

"I think you're short-changing yourself again."

I smiled humourlessly. "I'm not. Right now, I'm a person I'm not interested in. How can I expect someone else to be interested in me?"

"How sure of that are you?"

I looked up quickly in surprise. "What?"

He shrugged almost self-consciously. "Well, how sure are you that someone couldn't be interested in you?"

I blinked as my heart skipped a painful beat in my chest. My throat went a little dry and my breath felt short. "I guess then I'd have to say that they're interested in someone I don't intend to be for long."

His eyes narrowed, like he was trying to find the right words. "What are you going to do if you're already the person you're meant to be?" he asked gently.

It was like he knew I'd take offence to it, but he was offering the suggestion as a comfort, as a compliment even if I thought it was the opposite.

"Eli…" I started, hoping this wasn't going where it felt like it was going. "I don't know what you think–"

"I think," he interrupted pointedly, "there *is* someone I want to ask to the formal."

I shook my head wildly and actually pushed my chair back with the force of my knee-jerk retreat. My heart hammered. It was a good hammering and a bad hammering. It was nervous excitement and panicked terror.

"Gin?" both Govi and Rica asked, pausing in whatever conversation they were having now.

I was still shaking my head. "No, Eli," I said firmly.

"Chloe–"

"No." I stood up.

"I didn't even finish–"

"You don't have to. My answer is still no."

"Why?"

I leant towards him in the hopes Govi, Rica and whoever else might have been in the corridor wouldn't hear me. "Because my sister's a vengeful bitch."

"Again the only reason you come up with?"

"What? No. It's not the only reason."

"Then give me one I'll not only believe, but accept."

"I don't want to go to the formal with you."

"Really? Because there is a definite vibe between us."

I felt my cheeks flush, but held my ground. "There really isn't."

"I'm not the only one feeling it."

I was very hot all of a sudden. "You must be."

"Are you really telling me you're not interested in me?"

"I'm really not interested in you." I made to turn away but felt rude, so I added a weird, "Thank you," I immediately regretted then started walking away.

"Gin?" Rica called.

I stopped again and looked to Govi. "Can you... Can you take over for me please? I need to... Bathroom."

"Sure." Govi nodded, concern strong on his adorably confused face.

But I had no time for that.

I needed to put as much distance between Eli and me as possible.

I took deep, shuddering breaths as I manoeuvred through the steady trickle of students in the corridor. I almost felt like my heart beat was under control until I felt a hand on my shoulder and I jumped in fright.

"Dude! Sorry," Rica said as I turned around. "I just wanted to see you were okay."

I nodded. "I'm fine." I wasn't fine. "I just need to… Breathing."

Rica looked at me and I knew she knew I wasn't fine. I also knew she knew what had happened. I just had to hope she wasn't going to try to make me talk about it.

And she didn't. Sort of.

She just nodded. "Is there anything you want to talk about?"

I almost nodded, but shook my head.

I didn't want to talk about what was going on in my head because that would make it more real than it was already starting to feel. And that was dangerous.

Because what felt real was that someone had picked me. They'd had Ella on as much of a silver platter as they were going to get her, but they'd picked me instead. And they weren't Rica or Super-G or Aunt Bow. They were an attractive young man who made me laugh and made me question if what I'd planned for myself was actually what I wanted, someone who made me question who I thought I was and who I thought I wanted to be.

"No," I told myself sternly.

"No, you don't want to talk? Or no, you're arguing with yourself in your head again and losing?" Rica asked uncertainly. "Again."

"Why did it have to be him, Ree?" I asked. "Of all the people who picked me, why did it have to be him?"

"And what am I now?" she huffed. "Figment of your imagination? Consolation prize?"

"Never. You know what I mean," I sighed.

Rica lost all her faux-bluster. "Yeah. I do. And I don't know, Gin. I don't know why it was him. But for what it's worth, I'm sorry."

I nodded and gave a humourless laugh. "I mean, it's not like I *am* interested. Of course. I just…" I shrugged, letting her work out whatever I might have been going to say.

"Sure." Rica wasn't convinced, but at least she didn't call me out on it.

I was about to say something, but a commotion back down the corridor distracted me.

"What the…?" Rica muttered as we both turned to look.

People were milling about and the sounds of muttering were almost drowning out a song being played. Something about it drew me closer, and Rica stuck behind me as I pushed through to the front of the gathered crowd. But what I saw made me wish I'd kept walking away.

Eli was standing in the middle of the corridor in front of a totally fake surprised Ella, strumming his guitar and singing some nonsense about her going to the formal with him. Ella made sure to look around to see how many people were watching rather than concentrating on the guy who was apparently throwing all his hopes at her feet, if the lyrics were to be believed. There was a noise beside me and I turned see Lindy was even there, filming the whole sham.

My stomach plummeted and my throat closed up for a second.

But then Ella found me and the smile of victory on her face just made me angry.

As usual there was no sign of thank you, there wasn't even an insincere modesty to the whole thing. She grinned like the cat who didn't just eat all the cream, but devoured every mouse as well. She may as well have been standing triumphant on the lifeless corpses of all the people she stepped on to get what she wanted in life.

"Dramatic much," I sighed, chastising myself.

I felt Rica shrug. "I dunno. I have to say I saw it coming. Like, way to be original, man." She shrugged again and I looked at her in annoyance.

"What?"

She pointed to Eli. "He's a rockstar, for all intents and purposes. So logically in this narrative, how else was he going to ask her?"

I opened and closed my mouth a few times, but didn't really know what to say to that.

Before I'd worked it out, Eli looked at me and I had trouble trying to work out what his expression was trying to convey. He seemed to want me to be proud of him. Proud of him for asking a girl out? Like he did all the time. Like he could probably do in his sleep by now.

I felt myself give him a sarcastic grin and turned to walk away.

But the tersely snapped, "Chloe," stopped me in my tracks.

I swung back around unenthusiastically to face my sister. Now that my mission was complete, I had zero inclination to pander to her absurd expectations.

"Ella," I said testily and felt Rica's elbow in my side.

I sighed, knowing Rica wasn't wrong; it was better and safer to play nice. Even with the corridor now emptying of students on their way to classes.

"So Eli asked you to the formal?" I said as though it was a surprise to me. It earnt me another elbow from Rica, but

Ella grimaced in the closest she could managed to a smile in my presence.

She batted her hair off her shoulder and I watched Lindy follow suit, her eyes on Ella adoringly.

"He did. I was surprised, of course. Who knew *the* Elijah Sweet could be interested in little old me," she gushed.

I fought very hard to keep my shit together.

Twelve months. Neon lights. Freedom, I reminded myself.

"You don't say," was all I could come up with that was remotely polite.

Ella looked me over, displeased I wasn't bowing and scraping and calling Eli the luckiest boy in the whole world to be taking Ella Cowan to the formal!

"Make sure Rica is free after school," Ella said scathingly. "If she's going to be at the formal, I need to approve her dress. I can't have her embarrassing me."

I had a great many things I wanted to say I response to that, but if I was physically holding Rica back now so she didn't do it, then I should probably keep my own mouth shut as well.

"I've got the formal committee," I reminded her.

Ella looked me over like less than the dirt on the bottom of her shoe. "I don't recall you being needed."

I looked at Rica whose expression told me in no uncertain terms that if I wasn't there, she'd lay a whole world of hurt on me.

I took a deep breath. "I'm sure Rica would like me to be there with her."

Ella sighed. "And she will. Next year. If anyone asks you to the formal." She looked at Rica. "Be in the carpark by four." And with that she left.

"I'm going to kill you," Rica breathed.

I nodded. "I do not blame you."

"Why couldn't you have said yes?" she asked, her voice still a harsh whisper.

"When?"

"When Eli made it very clear he wants to take you."

"He seems perfectly happy to be taking Ella."

Rica groaned through gritted teeth as she grabbed my arm and shook me. "Did you ever think he might be doing that for you?"

"He did not so enthusiastically ask her to the formal for me."

"How do you know?"

"Because that's ridiculous. He's just finally turned his attention where it's actually wanted."

"Sure. Even though he quite clearly didn't want to turn it there?"

"I was entertainment and now he's moving on to the next act."

"You *did* turn him down…"

I shrugged out of her grip on my arm. "Ella got what Ella wanted," I told her forcefully, hoping to end the conversation. "Everyone's happy."

"Except Chloe, who never gets what she wants."

I scoffed. "I don't want to go. And certainly not with Eli."

Rica had her 'I don't believe you' face on. "Mhm…"

I shook out my shoulders. "I don't."

Casting a shadow

Ella had been a total prat all weekend. All I heard about was Eli. How dreamy Eli was, how perfect, how famous he was going to be. It was sickening. So sickening I slipped out of dinner and into Super-G's back garden.

Aunt Bow found me a little later, sitting on a bench and staring up at the stars.

"You've been strangely quiet tonight, Gingernut," she said as she sat beside me. "Are you compensating for the extra waffle coming out of Ella's mouth? Or is something up?"

I huffed a small laugh. "What did you want to be at my age?"

She breathed out and looked up at the sky. "I wanted to be in a folk band and travel the world in my van."

"What changed?"

"Well, for starters, the rude reality that it is *very* difficult to drive to another country from Australia. Waterproofing a kombi van was going to cost a shit tonne and I wasn't convinced the old vdub was worth it."

I snorted and looked at her. "Seriously?"

She shook her head and settled us back, her arm around my shoulders. "Plans change, baby. People change." She kissed my hair. "Why do you ask?"

"I thought I knew what I wanted. I had it all planned out. But…what if I was wrong?"

I felt her shrug. "Then you were wrong."

"That's it?"

"Pretty much. I mean, I wouldn't call any aspiration *wrong*, but that doesn't make it right for you. Where's this all coming from?"

"You know how I was going to do Commerce?"

She nodded. "Generic and boring and safe Commerce?"

"Aunt Bow!"

"Sorry, that's what it was called in my day. They changed it to just Commerce now."

I snorted. "Well, what if I just wanted to do whatever I thought was the opposite of what Ella wanted to do?"

"Following Arlo's footsteps and rebelling, are you?"

The thought I was anything like my dad was scary, but might not have been wrong. "I don't know. Maybe. Is it possible?"

"Anything is possible."

"I mean… What do you think?"

Aunt Bow leant her cheek on my head. "I think you have a lot of talent for something you profess to have no interest in. I think you should take another look and see if you do want to go into the arts. But then I'm biased. I want the world to see you the way I do, but they will no matter what you choose to do."

"What should I do then?"

"Well, you need to work out what you really want."

"How do I do that?"

Aunt Bow laughed and hugged me tightly. "Oh baby, I'm thirty-eight and I still have no idea."

"Then what use are you?" I chuckled as she took exception to that and started tickling me.

She stopped and made me look at her. "I'm here to support any decision you make. Even if I think it's not the right one–"

"No! You're supposed to steer me in the right direction."

Aunt Bow smiled warmly. "That's all you, Gingernut. I'm just the wind in your sails, you're the rudder."

"And if I steer wrong and hit the rocks?"

"Then I'll be there to bail you out every time. Literally and metaphorically." She winked.

I frowned. "That's really unhelpful."

"Ice cream time, my girls!" we heard Super-G call.

"I'm also here to eat all your ice cream," Aunt Bow laughed as she jumped up and started running inside. "Gin said I can have hers!" she called back.

"Hey!" I yelled, following. "I did not! Gran!"

Aunt Bow and I tumbled inelegantly into the dining room.

Both my parents spared me a withering glare before turning their avid attention back to Ella, who was still going on about Eli.

"Did you know his band is opening at the Entertainment Centre in November?" Ella asked the table as Aunt Bow and I took our seats.

"No, dear," Gran said as she brought the ice cream in. "Do go on."

And go on she did.

Through the rest of the night, the ride home, the way to school on Monday, and any time I passed her in the corridors, she was still going on about Eli. Mum and Dad had to have tuned out because by the time I got to the committee meeting on Monday afternoon, I'd heard some of her stories eleven times. Not that I was counting.

I was sitting almost under the table, trying to get my chapter finished, when I sensed someone in front of me. I surreptitiously pulled the book down a little and instantly ruled out the legs I saw as belonging to Rica or Govi.

I'd been avoiding him all day. Any time I saw him in the corridor, I managed to find a different direction to scuttle away in. When I accidentally ran into him between classes, I was really mature and pretended my phone rang.

I wasn't really sure why I was avoiding him.

Yes, he'd basically asked me to the formal, I'd said no, and he'd asked my older sister instead. It was what everyone wanted. So I didn't know why I was feeling so weirded out about it. Sure, I liked him. But I didn't *like* like him because I didn't want to *like* like him. Ella and her rabid harpy tendencies aside, Eli and I had different hopes and dreams. Even if mine did change, I didn't want to be in the spotlight. I didn't want to be second to anyone or anything ever again.

In an effort to be consistent, I decided it was probably better if I pretended not to know he was there and I went back to reading.

"Come on, Clo," Eli said and I saw him drop to a crouch in my peripheral.

"We should get started," I said, dropping my book and getting up so hastily that I whacked my head into the table above me.

"Ouch," Eli chuckled sympathetically, his hand going to my elbow. "You okay?"

I looked at him and nodded. "Yep."

He pulled back and stood, watching carefully as I got up. "You sure?"

I nodded again as I pulled the stuff to me to mix up the papier-mâché mix. "Dandy." I grimaced, very pleased he was behind me, at such a stupid response.

"Clo, can you please–"

"Ah, shit!" Ramsey's voice cut in. "Mine's gone limp."

Even my nervousness around Eli couldn't stop me laughing at that.

"You oughtta see someone about that, mate," Eli laughed.

"Shut up, wanker. My branch. Look."

"Twig, at best," Lake said smoothly.

"Leave him be," Govi said, failing to hide a laugh.

"Yeah," Eli added. "He's a grower, not a shower."

I stifled a laugh and heard a thump behind me.

"I thought we agreed no dick jokes? Hm?" Ramsey said.

"I thought that's what we did now," Lake said lazily.

"What?" Ramsey asked.

"Break pacts," Lake answered.

"I *said* I was sorry!" Govi called.

"About what?" I heard Rica ask.

"Nothing!" Govi said very loudly and I wondered what the other boys had been about to say.

An arm went around me and I nudged her hip with mine.

"Hey," Rica said.

"Hey. What are you doing here?"

I felt her shrug. "Thought you might need some backup if you were going to be stuck with this lot again." She paused then grumbled, "Really? How old are they?"

I turned to follow her gaze and found Lake had Ramsey in a headlock while Govi was leaning over and saying something to Ramsey and Eli leant against the ladder keeping a watchful eye. When he turned that watchful eye on me, I jumped and went back to my papier-mâché mix.

"Can I speak out of turn?" Rica asked.

"You're going to anyway."

"True. Look, you managed to get over whatever brain fart you had when you first met him. You can get over this."

"I'm not into him," I hissed.

"Hey, I never said you were. But even if you don't actually want him, it's still understandable that you're a little jealous he's going to the formal with Ella. Especially the way she's been preening around all day. Ugh and the fanfare people are giving her!" Rica made a gagging noise and I had to agree with her.

I dropped my hands from the frantic busyness they were trying to keep up and sighed. "Okay. So I'm jealous. But not because I want to be with him. I just... In another life and all that."

I felt Rica nod. "I get it. Now," she said, more upbeat. "My services are at your disposal. What do you want me to do?"

"Is there any way to make our trees look half decent?" I pleaded and we both turned to look at them.

We both snorted when we saw Govi's head pop up between the branches and make a face.

"They look pretty good to me," Rica said.

I elbowed her playfully. "With a certain decoration in them, yes."

She elbowed me back slightly less playfully. "All of them."

"But they could be better."

"Maybe. Shall I start with paint?"

I nodded. "That would be brilliant. Thank you."

"You owe me," Rica said, pointing at me as she started walking away.

I bowed down teasingly. "I shall pray to my goddess at the tolling of every hour," I told her and she barked a laugh.

"Funny girl, aren't you?" She stuck her tongue out at me and I repaid her. "Every half hour, thank you!" she giggled as she started getting set up.

I was shaking my head when Ramsey sidled up to me.

"What's up?" I asked him when he didn't say anything.

"Am I allowed to papier-mâché today?" he asked coyly.

At the previous meeting on Friday, Ramsey and Govi had ended up making boogers out of the mix to flick at each other, then resorted to all-out war the rest of us had been dragged into. That was after they'd each finished a tree, so at least there had been some progress before everything devolved into messy madness. But I had also made a heat of the moment declaration that Ramsey was off papier-mâché duty.

I turned a look on him. "Are you going to waste it on Govi again?" I asked.

"I…" Ramsey started, flicking his hair out of his eyes. "I *want* to say no…"

I grinned. "At least you're honest."

"I promise I'll finish my tree before I misbehave."

I sniggered and nodded. "Okay. Here." I passed him the container and he took it away while I got started on the next one.

Another body appeared beside me. "Clo."

I took a deep breath. "Yeah?"

"Can we talk?"

I nodded. "Sure."

"In full sentences."

"Maybe."

I felt him huff a laugh. "I'll take it. Look, I just want to make sure we're…tight."

I nodded. "Of course."

"You just seem... I feel like you've been avoiding me since Friday."

I shook my head and shrugged in some sort of weird interpretive dance move. "No. Just... My job's... You and Ella... You know."

"Trees!" Govi suddenly yelled and I looked around.

"What?" I muttered as the other *Quicksilver* boys were mouthing things to themselves, Eli included.

"Five!" Govi shouted. "Four! Three! Two–"

It was Eli who answered the apparent call to arms. Or song, as it turned out. "Well, my heart knows me better than I know myself so I'm gonna let it do all the talking!"

"Woo hoo! Woo hoo!" the other boys joined in, and Eli continued on with the song.

When he was done, he pointed at Lake. "Ice cream flavours!"

Lake rolled his eyes, but I could see he was thinking.

"Five! Four! Three–"

One more roll of his eyes and Lake started a song I recognised off the 'Love, Simon' soundtrack. "Remember when we first met, you said 'light my cigarette'..."

He looked thoroughly displeased about the whole thing until he got to the bit about blue eyes and black jeans and he lay it all out there at Ramsey's feet. Ramsey silently pissed himself laughing, but nodded along with the tune.

"What can I say?" Ramsey chuckled when Lake was done. "I'm sweet and smoky, baby. What's my category?"

Lake grinned as he stood up. "Anthems, dude. And no Farnham."

I watched as Ramsey's fingers wriggled while he thought.

"Five!" The other boys started the count down. "Four–"

Ramsey frowned at them all, then shut them up as soon as he opened his mouth. "I'm bulletproof. Nothing to lose. Fire away. Fire away…"

And the whole room went silent, watching as this slouchy punk kid belted out 'Titanium' with nothing but raw emotion.

Eventually, the other kids started joining in around the room and I looked around in awe.

"Cool, huh?" Govi asked, bumping into me.

I nodded. "You guys do this a lot?"

He shrugged. "It's a good competition. Forces us to look outside the box for songs to beat each other with. Shazam, Spotify and Google are my *best* friends for this."

"How do you work out who wins?"

He shrugged again, good-humouredly. "Dunno. We just kinda all agree."

"Rica. Movie themes. Go!" Ramsey called.

I saw Rica's eyes go wide with panic. She didn't even think of it, she just started singing the song I'd guessed she would; 'Can't Stop the Feeling' from Trolls, her most recent favourite movie.

When the guys worked out what she was singing, they all threw their arms up and cheered her on. I had the feeling that Govi could tell she was a little nervous because he started singing with her and she smiled at him with the very definite beginnings of full-blown crush.

I kept ripping the paper for the papier-mâché as they sang, then the song was over and the room was eerily silent. I looked around and saw them all looking at me.

"What?" I asked.

"Chloe Cowan. Power Ballads." Rica grinned and I hung my head with a sigh.

"Really?" I asked.

Rica nodded. "Five. Four. Three. Two—"

"Okay!" I popped out of my seat and let loose the first line of the first thing that came to mind; Kelly Clarkson's 'Since U Been Gone' courtesy of the 'Pitch Perfect' marathon Rica and I had had over the weekend.

I tried not to look at any one in particular, because singing in front of people was not my thing. But if Rica had had the balls to do it then I kinda had to or I'd never hear the end of it. But as I sang, I realised I didn't hate it. The idea of singing to people was not as terrifying or stupid as I'd told myself it was. In fact, there was something freeing about belting out a song and I felt a little bit lighter for it. Lighter and heavier all at the same time.

Everyone in the room joined me on the final stretch, then I dropped back into my chair and went back to my ripping a little more vigorously than I'd left it. I was confused all over again about what I wanted out of life. Did I want to sing after all?

"That was…" Govi leant against the table next to me and made an explosion with his hands. "Amazing!" he chuckled.

I smiled. "Thanks. Not really my thing, though."

"Cool. Cool. Eli said you were devoid of…things."

I shrugged, wondering now how true that really was. "Yeah, I guess."

"Still. Amazing."

He patted me on the shoulder and left me to it while he went back to attaching branches to trees, and another round started up. This time, still on the tree theme, Govi started it with a song I'd only heard on the Mix radio station when Aunt Bow had it on, 'C'est La Vie'.

"How's it going?" Milly asked, appearing in front of me.

"Uh… Good, thanks. I can…? Do you want them to stop?" I asked awkwardly.

Milly looked over at Govi and shook her head. "No. They're fine. They're working, so it's just easier to let them be as rowdy as they want."

I nodded. "Okay."

"Listen… Can I ask you something…?"

"Chloe," I offered.

Milly's smile was warm. "I remembered."

"Oh." That was a new one. "Sorry."

"No. It's fine. I was just a little hesitant to ask, is all."

I shook my head. "No. Ask away."

"I know it's not your job at all, but I was wondering if I could lump some more stuff on you? Please? Awkwardly, you're the person I trust most to just get stuff done." She smiled at me totally awkwardly, which worked well, because I was also feel super awkward.

"Uh, whatever I can do to help…" I said, for once legitimately wanting to help her rather than just feeling obliged to deal with Ella's responsibilities.

"Great. Thanks, Chloe." She smiled again, then hurried off with an exasperated, "Brenda…"

A while later, I was sitting with Lake and Ramsey making more branches while Govi and Eli were still on papier-mâché duty and Rica was lost to her painting. Somehow talk had found its way to the formal.

"Who are you guys going with?" I asked Lake and Ramsey.

"No one," Lake answered simply.

Ramsey glared at Govi as he came over. "We were *supposed* to all be going stag. But *someone* broke the pact!"

Govi shrugged. "What?" He looked over at Rica. "Can you blame me?" He grabbed a few more branches and, as he left again, said, "I've said I'm sorry."

"Sorry doesn't have all four of us going stag to our last formal, does it?" Ramsey said pointedly.

Lake rolled his eyes. "Sure. It would have been great to just have a friends' night out, but we can do that with Rica."

"It sounds nice," I told him.

"Angling for an invitation?" Lake teased.

My cheeks went red. "I'm not, no. I really don't want to go. We had our formal earlier in the year and I'll have our last one next year."

"Well, I'm going to find someone to ask," Ramsey decided, looking around.

"Are you now?" Lake asked. "And who's going to want to go with you?"

Ramsey turned his blue eyes on me. "And you're *sure* you don't want to go?"

Lake smacked him in the chest. "Wow. Sweep a girl off her feet, why not?" He looked at me, hazel eyes shining with humour. "I apologise for the cretin."

"Watch who you're calling cretin," Ramsey snapped, but he was smiling.

"What about Eli?" I asked, as nonchalantly as possible.

"What about Eli?" Ramsey asked slowly.

"Well, does him having a date not count…? Or is that why he didn't ask Ella when he found out she was interested?"

Lake and Ramsey exchanged a look I didn't understand.

"Uh… Yeah…" Ramsey said. "*That* is definitely why he didn't ask Ella at first."

Lake nodded. "Sure. Because of our pact."

I smiled at them. "Why does that sound like total bullshit?"

Ramsey scrubbed the back of his head. "I couldn't tell you, Clo."

Lake shook his head. "No idea."

Friends without benefits

The next day, I was scurrying along the corridor as inconspicuously as possible between lessons, and I was already late.

"Clo!"

I pulled up short and turned around. "Eli, hi…" I said, then wondered why I'd turned around when I was late and avoiding him. "What's up?"

"I just wanted to finish our conversation from yesterday. Govi kinda killed it with the song competition."

I nodded absently. "Sure. What conversation?"

"If everything was okay after Friday."

I blinked. "We didn't finish that?"

He shook his head, suppressing a smile. "We didn't."

"Ah. Right. Okay. What about it?"

"Well, I think you left it at some unfinished sentences about me and Ella. It didn't really fill me with confidence…" he petered off and seemed to wait for me to pick up the thread of the sentence.

"Um… That sounds like me," I muttered, trying to remember what I'd been trying to say to him.

"I think you were trying to say something about how your job was done and after me and Ella…something…?" he pressed and I managed to remember the gist of my ramblings.

My head was filled with so many other things that day that I even managed full sentences.

"Right. Just… Yes, everything's…fine," I told him as I pulled my bag further up my shoulder. "I just figured that now Ella's got her wish, there was no need for you and me to…" I trailed off, not quite sure what I was trying to say now.

"What?" he asked. "Talk? Be friends?"

I opened my mouth, closed it, then found the courage to push on. "Were we friends though? Really?"

He looked me over like I'd betrayed him or something. "I know I'm a bit of a dick, but I didn't realise I wasn't worth your friendship."

Now I felt like the dick. "I didn't mean…" I sighed. "It was a legitimate question, Eli. In case you hadn't noticed, I haven't got a lot of friends. This is largely due to my inability to accept that people might want to be my friend

233

so I never presume to think of them as a friend until they've been around for like at least five years. It's nothing personal." I sniffed, feeling a little embarrassed I exposed so much of myself there.

"We're really not that different," he said softly. "But I thought we were friends."

I looked around the corridor nervously, feeling the hairs on the back of my neck tingle, begging me to turn around and confront the threat. But I was pretty sure there was nothing there, so I tried not to fidget the tingling away.

"I get you're not interested, Clo. I won't push it, and I'm sorry if I did."

I nodded, chewing on my lip in agitation. "I... Look, that's not the..." I sighed. "That was never the problem. Ella's the–"

"Ella can do or think whatever the hell she wants. I couldn't care less," he said and I quailed.

"No," I whispered. "No. Please care very much. For the sake of my skin and my sanity, please care very much. Much. Much more." I shook my head. "Like, right up there..."

I realised I was babbling and stopped myself. I looked up to find him looking down at me in concern, and I laughed self-consciously.

"Sorry…" I breathed, then cleared my throat and tried again. "Sorry. But I just…"

"Can't use full sentences anymore?" he teased gently.

I pressed my lips together to stop more babble and shook my head again. "My life is…" I paused to think about it. "My life is absurd. Talking about it out loud sounds ridiculous. I just… My sister can make my life hell. No, I'm exaggerating. She's just annoying and mean, and had I not been a doormat for all those years maybe they wouldn't expect me to do everything they do and then act all surprised and incensed when I don't want to. I don't know, but what I do know is that I have twelve months before I'm free and I'd like to make those the easiest twelve months I can. So can we please care very much about what Ella thinks or does?"

Eli's eyes searched my face for a moment. Still there was no sign of teasing or disbelief, no hint of 'is she for real?' or 'that's nuts'. He chewed on his bottom lip as he seemed to look for something, then finally nodded.

"Okay. Okay. For you, and you only, I will care very much what Ella thinks or does."

I sighed in relief, then tensed. "No. Not just for me. That is the worst possible reason!"

"Well it's that or nothing." He shrugged unapologetically.

I sighed then nodded. "Okay. Fine."

"Does this mean we're friends again?"

I looked around quickly. "As long as Ella doesn't feel…anything in the cold, dark cockles of her heart, then yes."

Eli sniggered. "Anything?"

"In humans and animals, it's known as emotion. Most commonly we call this feeling jealous or threatened," I told him sarcastically.

"I'll keep that in mind," Eli answered, trying not to laugh.

I rolled my eyes at myself. "No. That's not fair. I shouldn't say such shitty things."

"Why not? It sounds like she's not very nice to you."

I nodded. "This is true. But me being rude about her does nothing but drag me down to her level."

"So this is you taking the high road, is it?" he asked.

I scrunched my nose as I thought about it. "Maybe like…middle road at most."

He laughed. "Fair."

I smiled at him, then remembered I was already super late to class. "I need to go. I'm meant to be in class…" I said as I started backing away.

He nodded. "Sorry to keep you."

I shook my head. "No. I'm…glad we had this chat."

Eli bit his lip as he inclined his head. "Yeah, me too."

I hurried off to class, sliding in practically unnoticed at the back and pulling out my script. I didn't have any lines anyway – acting as, surprisingly, an understudy to one of the supporting characters.

Ever does art imitate life, I thought to myself.

****

By the meeting on Wednesday, I'd psyched myself into behaving normally around Eli again. It had taken a few awkward hellos, complete with blushing and laughing and incomplete sentences, but I'd managed it.

I was one of the first to arrive as usual and was up the ladder working on branches when hands grabbed my waist and pretended to shake me.

"Boo!" Govi laughed and I swatted him away.

"You nearly gave me a heart attack," I accused, trying my best to frown at his boyish charm.

His laughter gained a tinge of concern as he put his hands out. "Sorry. You okay?"

I shook my head. "In my own little world, and you come and scare the bajeesus out of me."

"Well, one might be inclined to ask why you had the bajeesus in you to begin with."

His eyes went wide with excitement just before he tried to fit 'bajeesus' into 'I've Got the Magic in Me'. To say it went well would be a gross exaggeration. But we were both in fits of giggles when Eli came up to us with Lake.

"Funny?" Lake asked.

Govi nodded wildly, trying to stem the laughter that was starting to make his eyes water. I took a deep breath and had a little more success explaining ourselves.

"There was a thing about bajeesus and he tried changing it to 'I've Got the Bajeesus in Me' and it went...poorly," I snorted.

Eli tried to school his smile as Lake looked us over, doing his best unimpressed expression.

"Do I want to know why Govi has the bajeesus in him?" Lake asked.

"Because I scared it out of Gin!" Govi hooted, wiping his eyes.

Lake nodded. "Okay. I'm going to see a man about some glue."

I looked up quickly. "You left Ramsey in charge of the mix?"

Eli's hand rested on my arm for a moment. "He promised he'd behave for you."

I smiled at him. "That'd be a first."

Eli snorted and took his hand off me slowly. "Yeah. I'll go check on him."

I nodded. "Wise."

He grinned before following Lake over to where Ramsey was at the table with his back to us.

"Ha!" Ramsey yelled, jumping around quickly.

Both Lake and Eli screamed and braced in surprise. But when they saw that Ramsey had nothing in his hands, they both had a moment where they pretended they hadn't freaked out and were still totally cool.

I sniggered and turned back to my work.

Govi and the boys burst out into spontaneous song now and then as we worked, they had a few more rounds of their song competition. But I bowed out, deciding that if Rica wasn't there – she rudely had other things to do of a Wednesday afternoon apparently – then I'd let it just be a band thing. After a brief grumble, they let it go.

But at least they were productive while they squabbled good-naturedly and sang among themselves. I was on my second tree for the afternoon when Eli came over to bring me some more papier-mâché mix.

"Gin, pass me that paintbrush?" Eli asked nonchalantly as he put it down.

"Which one?"

"By your elbow."

I looked at the top of the ladder. "My paintbrush?"

"The one by your elbow," he repeated with a nod.

"Don't you have your own?"

Eli leant towards me in an attempt to reach past me. "Yes, but I need *that* paintbrush."

I laughed and tried to keep his hands off my paintbrush. "You have your own paintbrush!"

"But I want that one."

"That's mine!"

"Here you can have mine."

I giggled as he brandished his in front of his face and pulled mine behind his back.

"Stop dicking around," I told him as I took the proffered paintbrush and bopped him on the nose.

He grinned back at me. "I put it to *you* to stop dicking around." He got very serious very quickly as he started wandering around. "We are doing very important busy work here, you know. No time for your shenanigans, young lady."

I pressed my lips together until I had my laugh under control. "Perhaps you shouldn't lead young ladies astray?"

Eli gasped, popping his head out from behind the tree. "I would not dare. Govi, would I dare?" he called.

"I have no idea what you're talking about, but whatever it is I'm siding with Gin!" he called back from the other side of the miniature forest that was coming along quite nicely.

"What?" Eli cried, his arms dropping to his side as he turned towards the sound of Govi's voice. "Why?"

"Because she doesn't make me drum until my fingers bleed," Govi called cheekily.

"What do we say, Govi?" Ramsey yelled from whatever tree he was up.

"I've got blisters on my fingers!" Govi cried dramatically and I snorted.

"I swear that is not my bad," Eli said, barely suppressing a smile and pointing at me like he dared me to think poorly of him.

"What? The blisters or Govi?" I sassed.

"Both," he replied, his eyes shining with humour and everything about him was gorgeous and infectious and made it impossible to not feel light and bright and bubbly.

My smile softened unbidden as we looked at each other.

"Did I tell you how good these look?" he asked me, running his hand up the dry part of the tree.

I pretended to think about it. "I'm not sure you did."

"I'm sure I did."

I shook my head. "I just can't remember it."

He looked back at me and grinned. "Should I again?"

I shrugged coyly. "Might jog my memory."

He snorted a short laugh as he bit his lip. Then he got a little serious again. But only a little. "They do look really good, Clo."

I looked around at them all. "It wasn't just me," I reminded him.

He took my hand and I looked down at it. "And yet I doubt we'd have them without you."

Never one to be good at taking a compliment, I shook my head. "No. You'd probably have something better."

Eli's smile grew wry and he shook his head. He squeezed my hand and said, "Take the damn compliment," before walking away.

I watched him go, feeling no guilt whatsoever about perving on his very fine arse as he went.

"It doesn't work!" I heard Ramsey say exasperatedly. "Stop trying to make it work!"

"I've got the bajeesus in me," Govi shouted defiantly.

"I blame you, Clo!" Ramsey yelled in my direction. "This is all your bad."

"I take no responsibility for your drummer or his blisters," I called back. "That's all on your frontman. Please direct all complaints to the appropriate lines."

"The number you have called is not available!" Eli said.

"Dishonour on both your cows!" Ramsey grumbled.

"Oh, I like *Mulan*." I jumped when Govi's voice came from right next to me. I looked at him and he smiled. "Bajeesus clearing service, reporting for duty."

I shook my head. "You're funny."

He tipped his imaginary hat. "I am the token comic relief," he told me with a wink.

"How goes your tree?"

"Good. That one's done. I'm just taking a smoko before I get onto the next one."

"You smoke?" I asked, surprised.

He looked mildly affronted. "No. But it's discriminatory to withhold breaks from those who don't smoke."

My eyebrow rose. "I was just surprised you called it a smoko."

He did that little wriggle. "It sounds more rockstar, doesn't it?"

I snorted. "Um…sure."

"So…"

I wondered where that unsubtle segue was headed as I climbed down my ladder carefully. "So?"

"You and Eli seem cosy," Govi commented as he bumped me gently.

I looked up at him in annoyance, both at his comment and the fact I nearly lost my footing again. "I don't know what you're talking about."

Govi nodded slowly. "Is that so?"

"It is."

"So it's not like you – I dunno – like him or anything and are just now realising that you made an awful mistake pushing him into the arms of your sister?"

I nudged him less gently. "No. Can a girl not be friends with a guy?"

Govi looked at me in mock-outrage. "Excuse me, but what exactly are we?"

"But two ships passing in the night?" I teased.

"Rude." He huffed. "Keep that up and I might not get you a backstage pass for November."

I hid my laugh. "Sorry. No. I'd love that. I'm sorry."

He broke out into one of his wide grins. "All good. I already put you on the list."

I hugged him with one arm, trying not to get my gluey hands on his clothes. "Thank you. That's amazing."

He wriggled another one of his cute little happy wiggles. "I kinda am, aren't I?"

I laughed. "You are."

"But as amazing as I am, you can't change the subject."

"I didn't change the subject!" I objected. "I gave you my answer."

"Uh huh…"

He looked at me, waggling his eyebrows as though that was going to get any other information out of me. As far as torture techniques went, it ranked a little below mildly annoying

"Shut up," I mumbled and Govi just nodded all too knowingly.

He's (not) all that

Annoyed with myself, I rushed back through the doors to the auditorium on Thursday and came up short when I realised the music I heard wasn't just in my head. Eli was sitting up on the stage with his acoustic guitar and a pencil behind his ear. He played a bit, grabbed the pencil, scribbled something on the floor and put it back, then played a bit more.

As I stepped forward, my shoe echoed loudly on the floor. He stopped playing and looked up. The concern and annoyance melted as a smile spread across his face when he saw it was just me.

"Hey."

I gave a pathetic little wave. "Hey. Sorry, didn't mean to interrupt. I just left the all-precious clipboard behind."

His smile widened. "You're fine."

"What are you doing?" I asked as I walked over to the stage.

"Uh, not what I want," he gave a self-deprecating laugh.

I chuckled. "You'd rather be…what? Making out in the broom closet?"

His rueful smile warmed me, but I ignored it. "While I'd never pass that up," he winked, "I'm actually trying to…" He frowned and looked down at the papers by his leg as though they'd betrayed him.

I leant my elbows on the stage and looked up at him. "Working on something new?"

He shrugged again. "Dunno, I have this…" he waved his hand next to his head, "thing going around in there, but I can't get it out."

I didn't know much about song-writing, but it made sense to me that it was hard. "Well, I like most of your other stuff. So I'm sure you'll manage."

"Was that actually a compliment?" he chuckled.

I shrugged and smiled slyly. "Maybe. Or maybe I think Govi's drum skills are amazeballs."

He broke out into a full, sincere laugh and the way it transformed him almost took my breath away. I reminded myself heavily that Eli Sweet was in no way whatever guy my head was currently trying to tell me he was. I felt goose bumps chase across my arms and I rubbed them quickly.

"Which songs don't you like? I'll bet they're all mine." Eli leant over his guitar towards me.

I grinned and looked down at my hands. "I don't know. 'One More Time' isn't my favourite, I guess."

"What?" Eli spluttered. "That's everyone's favourite?"

I shrugged. "It's just another song about another guy who wants another girl who's not good enough for him."

Eli cocked his head to the side and tried to supress a smile. "Not good enough for him?" he scoffed. "How is she not good enough for him?"

I leant my cheek on my hand. "If she didn't notice him before he was famous, then she's not worth him. He should have just let her be with the arsehole. It's 'Teenage Dirtbag' all over again."

He grinned. "Is that so?"

I nodded. "It is. I mean the track's good. But your lyrics…? I mean cliché wannabe much?"

"Well, wannabe kind of goes with the territory when you're trying to get famous, Clo," he faux-chastised.

I laughed. "I suppose so."

"But you still don't like it?"

I shrugged. "It's not my song."

He patted the floor beside him. "Come and help me write a good song then."

I snorted. "No. I play other people's music. I can't write it and I'm no good at poetry."

He scoffed. "Poetry?" He glared at me exasperatedly. "Come on. Help a friend in need?" he pleaded.

I laughed. "I'll sit with you for a bit, but I make no promises of how helpful I'll be."

He gave me one of those sincere smiles, his honey eyes warm. "Thank you."

I gave him a look that warned him no funny business and he nodded somewhat believably. I went over to the stairs and jogged up them, plopping down next to him and crossing my legs.

"Okay, show me what you have," I said.

He played me through half a minute or so of the song and I listened. As far as *Quicksilver* songs went, it was pretty par for the course. A little poppy, a little rocky, and about a guy pining over a girl based on the meagre lyrics he had down.

"Well?" he asked when I'd sat and looked at him for a few seconds.

I frowned. "Uh, it's fine?"

He laughed. "Fine? Friends are honest aren't they?"

I grimaced apologetically. "Well, the track seems a little…clunky?"

"Clunky, what would you know about clunky? You play guitar, too?" He smiled like it was impossible for a girl like me to play more than one instrument.

I decided not to bruise his fragile brink-of-stardom ego by confirming or denying anything.

I shrugged. "Can't be that hard."

He scoffed. "Come on then, I'll show you."

He lifted up the guitar and unbent his leg. I looked at it sceptically.

"And what are you expecting me to do with that?"

"I'm expecting you to park your butt. I'm going to teach you to play guitar."

I laughed. "Eli, I'll be fine."

"Come on. Can I not share something I love with a friend?"

"You're very hung up on this friend thing today."

He shrugged and I wished I didn't find it adorable. "I'm not used to having a girl as a proper friend. I'm enjoying it."

Giving him a smile, I shook my head.

"Why not?" he laughed. "Please? For me?"

I sighed, figuring a few minutes of pretending to learn to play guitar wasn't the worst thing in the world. Finally, I nodded and scooched between his legs, facing away from him. He put the guitar over my stomach, boxing me against him. He leant over my left shoulder and I was completely, totally, one hundred per cent not affected by his pleasantly warm breath tickling my ear.

"Okay. So, chords. Most important..." he said as he placed his fingers on the stings on the neck in a few different chord positions.

I totally didn't get distracted for a second by how nice his hands were, how long his fingers. The rings covering them only served as points of reference to better notice the way his hands moved flawlessly. A little bit like those white spots on those people who model for CGI characters. I was a little captivated by it until he spoke, actually.

"We start with a simple E. Your turn, put them here."

I put my fingers next to his. He slid his fingers over mine and my heart hitched before it started beating slightly more erratically.

"Good," he said softly, no hint of the sarcastic flirt I'd come to know. He reached his right arm around me and strummed. "Right, see?"

He took me through a few chords and I even got to strum it a few times. I had to say, he was a good teacher. Even if no teacher I'd ever had before had sat me between his legs as he'd taught me – which, in hindsight was probably good on a legal level. I could feel the vibration of Eli's voice through his chest and my back, feel his warmth surround me, and feel his heart beating steadily. Which only made mine pound faster as I panicked he could tell mine was running far too quickly.

His right hand rested on my waist when it wasn't strumming and his left on my leg, or they hovered, ready to help or to tutor. I told myself strictly that it didn't feel good, that it didn't feel right, that I felt nothing more about it than that I was supposed to be playing the guitar. His hands, wherever he put them, were sure and comforting and warm. They lingered on my body every time before he moved them almost lazily to the neck or strings of the guitar. He laughed congenially when I played the wrong chord and just gently helped me place my fingers for the right one.

Eli was relaxed, sincere, happy.

It was far too much contact, too close, too much of a sizzling hint of potential. But I was in no hurry to move or get the lesson over with. It was wrong and it was bad, but I liked it there between his arms, our cheeks brushing as he guided me over my shoulder. The fact that he smelled amazing – all musky and spicy with a hint of something sweet – certainly didn't hurt. The fact that his voice in my ear was low and smooth and gentle also didn't hurt. And the way his rough chuckles made a pleasant tingle shoot through me just seemed to be the last nail in the coffin.

Eli brushed my hair out of his way. "Okay, shall we put some together?" he asked finally.

I nodded, glad that his proximity was making me nervous because then I didn't have to pretend I couldn't play. I was playing poorly well enough on my own. He went through a few chords, then got me to play them after him.

"Huh…" he said and I felt his huff.

"What?" I asked.

"Play that again. A little faster."

Confused, I did.

"You know how to play, don't you?"

I felt my cheeks flush and I looked down at the guitar in my lap. "Uh… Maybe."

For a moment, I thought he was going to be pissed at me. Then, I felt him laughing. He scooted away so he could look at me, his face lit with that annoyingly endearing sincere smile, an accompanying glint in his eyes. He ran his tongue over his lip and huffed again.

"You totally can. Why didn't you just say?"

I shrugged. "I find life goes faster if I just let people do what they want to do."

"But, you just… How do you just go along with people like that?"

"Years of practise," I answered before I had a chance to think about what I was saying.

His humour dropped as he looked me over. He flicked his hair out of his eyes and the intensity with which he was looking at me gave me tingles. I wanted to look away, to break whatever it was, but I couldn't. Those pale honey eyes held me so tightly it may as well have been his arms around me.

"And, what about what you want to do?"

I shrugged again but didn't answer; it either would have been a lie or something far too real. I finally managed to look away, staring at the floor between us.

"Will you play me something, then?" he asked, his voice soft. It was a proper request, no expectation.

"Like what?" I replied, my hands moving over the strings while I thought about what I might play.

"Your favourite song?"

I looked up at him, unable to stop myself smiling. "It's not a *Quicksilver* one."

He smirked at me like we shared a secret, his eyes warm. "I'm glad." He looked at me, waiting but patient.

Finally, I nodded slowly. "All right."

I shifted so I was facing him, still between his legs. He lifted one leg to bent and rested his elbow on his knee while he looked me over as though in anticipation. I gave him a small smile, bit my lip and told myself to just go for it. I started strumming, watching to see if he'd recognise it. Slowly, a smile spread across his face. When I started singing, my eyes dropped and my cheeks heated. But, I kept going.

254

I got far too into it, as I always did when I heard that song. But, he was a semi-famous rockstar; if anyone was going to understand getting carried away by the song, it was him.

As I played the final notes of Sixpence None the Richer's 'Kiss Me', I finally had the courage to look up at him. Like the day we'd played the piano together, he looked at me with something scarily similar to respect and wonder. He leant forward slowly, closing the not very large gap between us. My heart fluttered, but I didn't pull away.

"You can tell a lot about a person by what song they choose to play," he reminded me, almost a whisper, as his eyes darted between mine, down to my lips and back again.

"Yes, like I watch too many old teen movies with Aunt Bow," I replied, willing the fluttering in my chest to stop.

The corner of his lips rose for a second. "Guilty pleasure?"

I nodded. "Little bit."

He nodded slowly and I was sure he was even closer than he'd been before. Our lips were so close I was surprised they didn't brush when he spoke. "Guilty pleasures, I get."

The distance between us was closed and I don't know who was to blame for that one.

His lips touched mine, warm and soft and far too nice. I kissed him back for a moment, forgetting who I was in the face of what he made me feel. But, finally, I pulled away slowly.

"Eli, what are you doing?"

"Kissing you," he answered simply, our noses still close enough to bump. "I might again if you don't say anything."

He waited for a heartbeat, then two. Why didn't I say anything?

When I'd remained stoically silent for long enough that we both knew it was a signal, he leant in again. This time, I'm pretty sure I met him halfway as our lips touched again.

As his hand cupped my cheek, I told myself I didn't get that warm fuzzy feeling you get in your chest when the main characters in a Kasie West novel are being sweet and adorable together and you want to just shout at them to be together already.

But, I did.

As I reached up and ran my fingers through his hair, I told myself I didn't have a split-second moment where I could imagine kissing only Eli for the rest of my life no matter how ridiculous that sounded.

But, I did.

As his lips parted mine and the kiss deepened, I told myself my stomach didn't backflip, my head didn't tell me I'd made a fantastic choice, and that my body wasn't telling me there was far too much space between us.

But, all that happened.

Eli slowly took hold of the neck of the guitar and moved it to the side, our kiss not breaking. We both moved forward and I found myself straddling his lap, both my hands in his hair and my chest hard against his like I couldn't get enough of him. And, just then, I honestly couldn't.

His scent enveloped me like I needed it to live, and he tasted like something sweet – probably all that peach coke he drank. I got this weird, light and floaty feeling in my stomach. Everything in me felt settled and at peace in a way I could never remember feeling.

One of Eli's hands was on my waist, the other ran up my leg as I pressed against him. I felt him bend his knee up behind me and we toppled over, our kiss breaking and both of us laughing. His head smacked on the stage and he winced. I bit my lip and put my hand under his head.

"You're not as innocent as you look, are you?" he asked gently, his eyes shining bright and clear and… There was something about them I'd never seen before. His voice was low and gravelly and it was only then I realised we were both breathing hard.

I smiled down at him and brushed his hair from his face. "Maybe you've just never seen the real me?"

"I might not have then, but I do now."

He looked at me then like he really saw me. His gaze was piercing and just as the vulnerability rushed through me, so did something I wasn't anywhere near brave enough to put a name to.

"Do *not* go totally cheesy on me." I smiled.

"But, that *really* isn't how nice girls kiss…"

"Maybe you've been kissing the wrong girls."

"I think I have."

Before I could overanalyse that statement or my reaction, he reached up, tucking a piece of hair behind my ear, and brought my lips back to his. He kissed me softly, confidently. I might not have kissed as many people as he had, if you believed the rumours, but I'd kissed enough to know that that was not the sort of kiss you give someone when you're just trying to get in their pants – or, if you are, you're far too good at your game and should probably be ashamed of yourself.

Just as I was shamelessly melting into him, my phone rang, jolting me out of the pleasant haze he'd created in my head. It had almost been like I'd forgotten reality; who I was, who he was, where we were. I rolled off him and wrestled my phone out of my pocket.

"Oh, shit," I muttered as I answered. "Yeah?"

"Where are you?" Ella cried shrilly.

I threw a guilty look to Eli as I clambered up from the floor and dusted the butt of my jeans off for good measure. "Uh, I'm… I just had to get something for Milly."

"For Milly?" she spat in disbelief.

I rolled my eyes. "Yes. For the Committee. She needed me to do something."

"Did you see Elijah?" she asked, her tone changing from raging monster bitch to sickeningly sweet.

I looked at him again in panic and found him watching me cautiously, a hint of a humoured smile on his face. Was it my imagination, or did he looked seriously kissed? God, did *I* look seriously kissed? A nervous bark of laughter escaped me as I turned away from Eli and smoothed my hair and my fingers trailed their way to my lips of their own accord.

"No. No, I didn't see him. He's probably gone for the day…"

She sighed like everything in the world was my fault and she should have known better than to expect better of me. "Fine. I need you to get home and drive me to this thing tonight. Elijah's going to be there and we need to be seen together if rank Milly's going to get the message she's out."

My heart thundered painfully and I had to take a deep breath. God, if Milly had been in this much shit for just looking at him, what would happen to me if Ella found out I'd kissed him? He'd kissed me…whatever.

I mean, they weren't dating – going to the formal together didn't indicate dating and *anything* with Eli Sweet didn't indicate dating – but Ella was sure he'd be hers and, like I'd said before, I was quite partial to my skin.

"Yeah, sure. Of course," I chuckled nervously. "Sure, what time do you need to be there?"

I jumped as I felt hands on my hips and lips on my neck. I froze.

There was a pause from Ella, then, "You're very agreeable today," she accused.

I laughed and hoped I was the only one who thought I sounded like a lunatic. "Nothing out of the ordinary."

"Fine. I'm leaving at five."

"Okay, I'll be there in plenty of time."

"Good."

The phone clicked as she hung up on me and I couldn't move. Eli's lips were still on my neck and it was a war between my body telling me to turn around and kiss him like my life depended on it – and my body was very inclined to think my life *did* depend on it – my brain telling me to get out of there before we lost my body its precious skin, and my heart that didn't know whose army to join for far too many reasons than there should have been.

260

I pulled away from Eli with an awkward chuckle and backed towards the stairs. "Uh, I need to go… Thanks for the guitar lesson… I will… Uh… I'll see you…" I took a deep breath as I kept backing away. With each step I took, his face got more confused. "I'll see you tomorrow."

"Chloe…" he said, moving forward.

I held up a hand, like that was going to do anything, and shook my head. "I have to go."

"Don't go," he pleaded.

I could do nothing more than shake my head again as I turned and hurried towards the doors. I heard a thump and then Eli grabbed my arm and turned me to face him; he must have jumped off the stage.

"Chloe, what's…? I–"

"I need to go, Eli," I said, looking up into his eyes and willing him to understand whatever it was I was feeling; I hoped he had more idea than me.

Concern crossed his features for a moment and his eyebrows twitched into a frown for a second. Finally, he let me go, his face looking an awful lot like he'd just worked out something he might have preferred not to, as well. I wasn't going to even begin to delve into what it might have been; I didn't think I'd like the answer. He took a step back quickly and nodded.

"See you tomorrow," he said with an awkward bluster, much more the suave flirter I hadn't seen in a while.

I gave him one more look, not sure what I was trying to apologise for, and ran out.

He might not have been kissing me the sort of way that meant he only wanted to get into my pants, but I hadn't exactly been giving him the 'not interested' vibe with the way I'd kissed him back.

As I unlocked the car and swung in, realising I'd forgotten the damned all-precious clipboard again, I realised something else.

Maybe I wasn't quite so uninterested in Eli Sweet as I was trying to convince everyone. Maybe I could actually be very interested in Eli Sweet; with his sexy smile, those twinkling eyes, that laugh that made you smile right back… Or, worse, maybe I already was.

"Because, that's just what I need," I grumbled as I turned on the car.

Brighter lights of infamy

Feeling like a right prat, I was back to avoiding Eli where possible. But I wasn't going to let my stupidity or my confused emotions get between me and Govi.

"You look like you've seen better days," I laughed sympathetically as he smiled wearily at me on Friday afternoon.

He nodded. "Yeah, Eli instigated the practically all-night practices last week and it's starting to take its toll."

I gasped sarcastically as I put Milly's clipboard down with my bag – I was in charge of it that meeting as Milly had a doctor's appointment. I'd just neglected to tell her I hadn't put hands on it until that morning.

"Maybe you're not cut out for the life of a rock god after all?"

He grinned lazily. "It would be easy if I didn't have to be at school by half eight."

"Why has Eli decided you need all-nighters?" I asked, hoping I sounded nonchalant; last thing I needed was Govi guessing what had happened the afternoon before.

Govi sighed and ran a hand through his hair. "We've got a couple new songs we're working on and he wants us to make them tight by formal. And last night was…intense. I mean, I'm all for the craft, you know. But…damn, I wish we had a bit more time."

I nodded, pretending I had any idea what he was talking about. "Are they… What kind of songs?"

Govi's smile was proud as well as tired. "Something a little different. I'm really enjoying them."

"Are you sworn to secrecy?"

He mimed zipping up his lips. "You will hear what we have at the formal."

I nodded. "Okay then."

He pointed at the trees. "Guess I'll get working," he finished with a yawn.

"You sure you don't want to pike out?"

He shook his head. "Nah."

"Does this have anything to do with Rica coming?"

Govi's eyes went shifty. "No. Why? Did she say something about me?"

I laughed. "She says a great many things about you. But I'm not allowed to repeat the majority of them."

"Oh, really?" he asked, mock-arrogantly. "Because they're too dirty?" He winked.

"No. The opposite," I said and he frowned. "They're far too cute and Rica will murder me if I let it slip she was such a softy."

Govi's smile was soft and sweet. "Aw, shucks. I'll take it to my grave."

"You do that."

Govi nodded one last time, then got to work.

My eyes kept sliding to the door and I realised what they'd been waiting for when Eli walked through them. Just the sight of him had my heart hitching and my breath catching, but I was pretty sure it was only a tiny bit of crush. Most of it was panic.

Because I was going to have to admit it now, I had the absolute last thing I ever wanted or needed. I had a crush on Elijah Sweet.

To say it was inconvenient would be an understatement.

Firstly, I was just the stand-in. I was the messenger at best. Guys on the brink of stardom deserved girls like Ella who had people fawning all over them whether they deserved it or not. Popular attracted popular. Popular wanted popular. Popular gets bored of unpopular. And popular certainly gets bored of the uninterested in being popular.

Secondly, I wanted to be rid of all that stuff, not setting myself up for more of it. I'd lived in the shadow of someone else for so long, I didn't want to be interested in – let alone with – a guy who planned to be the centre of attention. I was going to be the star of my own story, not the supporting act in someone else's.

It didn't matter that when I played music or sang now that I felt this wonderfully warm and tingly feeling, and I could pinpoint Eli as directly responsible. It didn't matter that I liked that feeling, that it felt good and right and amazing. It didn't matter that this feeling had me half-wondering if I was actually allowed to want what Ella wanted, to use what I'd be trained to do as something more than the understudy.

Not even that gorgeously confidant smile he was giving Milly as he walked in slow-motion across the room was bright enough to make me take my sights off that bright neon light that heralded my own future. Eli was nothing I wanted or needed.

Still, a girl could look even when she was decidedly not going to touch. Again.

Especially when he stopped to help Brenda with a box of material she was about to drop. He took it effortlessly out of her arms as she smiled at him shyly in thanks. He grinned that lazy half-smile as she nattered something to him, trotting after his long gait as he took the box to a table. He looked down at her warmly as she pointed in all sorts of directions, and nodded to whatever she was saying as she gazed up at him adoringly. He–

I blinked as something hit my shoulder and pulled myself up.

"Earth to Gin!" Govi called and I felt like it wasn't the first time.

I cleared my throat, sincerely hoping it wasn't true that I'd just had my elbow leaning on the top of the ladder, my chin in my hand as I mooned over Eli.

"Gin!" Govi called again.

I looked at him. "Yes?"

He was doing a very bad job of suppressing his laughter. "You – uh – all good over there?"

I nodded quickly. "Totally fine."

My gaze darted over to see Eli touching Brenda's arm briefly before he started walking over to us with a chin-kick in greeting.

"'Sup, man?" Govi said lazily.

"Same old," Eli replied, equally lazy. "You woken up yet?"

"No," Govi said sullenly.

"So blisters will be the least of your worries?" I asked him, sparing him a sympathetic smile.

267

Govi nodded. "I might die of exhaustion, but yeah, blisters are the least of my problems at the moment."

"Ninety-nine problems and blisters ain't one," Eli sung cheekily.

"How are you still functioning?" Govi grumbled.

Eli stopped beside my ladder, putting his foot on the lowest rung and holding the top as he smiled at me winningly. "Dunno. Just seem to have a pep in my step today."

"Well do us a favour, will you?" Govi yawned. "Work out what's causing said pep and avoid it. I'm really not sure how much longer I can last with you being the most energetic one."

Eli winked at me and I pulled my eyes off him hastily as my cheeks flushed.

"Seriously," Govi continued. "You're leaving me with no titles. I'm meant to be the manic one."

"I suppose titles like kindest, most adorable and sweetest don't count?" I asked him, focussing on my tree.

"Well…" Govi conceded. "They're not awful, I guess."

Eli laughed as he swung around the ladder, then wandered towards Govi. "You can be most manic again when we're finished."

"With trees, the songs or killing me?" Govi grumbled.

"All of the above?" Eli asked, then segued into song.

268

It wasn't one I knew, so I assumed it was him just making things up. The way Govi joined in, interspersed with laughter, made me think it was one of their processes. The words were mostly nonsense and involved trees, paint, papier-mâché, and a naughty little monkey I assumed was meant to be Govi.

Two other voices joined in as Ramsey and Lake arrived. I looked over and saw Rica running in behind them, holing the pocket of her overalls as though she was worried something was going to fall out. Probably her phone considering she had a habit of dropping them, sitting on them, or dropping them in paint.

"Sorry!" she called, skirting between the two singing boys, sparing them a quick, "Hey guys," before stopping in front of me and throwing her arms out. "Here I am!"

I smiled. "About time too," I muttered.

Rica looked over to Eli. "Have you…talked to him yet?"

I huffed, "If that's code for…" I wrinkled my nose at her in annoyance.

"Kissing him again?" she had no qualms clarifying. "It wasn't, but did that occur as well?"

I waved my fist at her. "No. There will be more kissing."

Rica looked me over. "There are worse guys you could be kissing."

"What?" I hissed.

Rica shrugged as she started pulling paintbrushes from random pockets. "Well I mean, he's gorgeous. Really. As far as hook-ups go, you could be doing worse."

"That's hardly fair."

"What's hardly fair?"

"I can't go…encouraging him."

Rica's look was asking me to rethink that statement. "You're worried about leading him on? Him. Elijah Sweet."

I waggled my head weirdly. "You know what I mean."

"Remind me again who kissed who."

"What?"

"Who kissed who?"

I looked over at Eli, who was mucking around with the boys. "I guess he kissed me first."

Rica gave a huge nod. "And he didn't want you to leave?"

So I might have called her on the way home and recounted the whole thing in way too much detail in the hopes she could calm the festering panic threatening to take over. Needless to say, she'd done nothing of the sort in her excitement.

"If you have a point, make it quickly," I warned her.

"Well. Way I see it, dude *likes* you. So what's the problem?"

I blinked down at her. "Are we forgetting the integral part of my continued existence my skin plays? Are we forgetting the Wicked Bitch who has her sights set firmly on a certain guy over there?"

"Since when do we care about the harpy?" Rica accused. "And it's not your fault if Eli likes you."

"Ree," I said patiently, as though I was trying to explain something to a small child for the twentieth time. "I was literally born as a backup. My parents have made no secret of this. That guy over there wants to be the next One Direction or 5 Seconds of Summer or whoever else is famous these days. Read my lips." I pointed to my lips. "I don't want to play second fiddle to anyone else's dreams for the rest of my life–"

"You're planning on marrying him now?"

I was hit with the memory of how it felt kissing him and, even though my heart rate spiked and I nearly smiled, I tried not to let it show. "You know I don't make plans that far ahead. I'm just saying that it seems stupid to set myself up for more pain than necessary."

"And if he'd give it all up for you? Put you first?"

I frowned. "To even consider letting him do that is ridiculous," I scoffed. "I want him to follow his dreams, Ree. I just don't want to be in the shadow of those dreams. Is that so difficult to understand?"

Rica's eyes slid to Eli and Govi. For a moment, I thought she was going to argue. But she nodded. "Okay. I get it. Actually," she amended, "I don't really get it. But I accept the logic."

I nodded back to her. "Thank you."

"His happiness above yours," she continued wistfully as though she wasn't being a disapprovingly judgmental bitch.

"Erica!" I snapped.

She kept on with the same tone. "Because it couldn't possibly go another way."

"I'm going to rescind your best friend status in a minute," I warned.

But Rica knew me and she only grinned cheekily at me. "I've got tenure."

I huffed. "Go and paint some trees, please," I begged.

She saluted me with her handful of miscellaneous paintbrushes. "On it."

I went back to the task at hand, wishing Rica hadn't put it in my head that there could be a different outcome. Because there wouldn't be. Either Quicksilver made it and Eli would have to put that first, or they wouldn't and I'd always worry that it was my fault.

No, it was better this way.

And I tried to remind myself of that through the rest of the meeting.

"Gin?" Ramsey called and I turned to look at him.

"Yeah?"

"We're running low on branches. Want me to make some more?"

I wiped my hands off as best I could and climbed down the ladder. "How are we doing for trunks?" I asked as I looked around.

Ramsey shrugged. "We've got about ten of the originals left. Rica's caught up on base coat and has got started on detail–"

"Leaves!" I cried as I suddenly realised we'd done nothing about leaves for our trees.

"Dead forest?" Govi offered, apparently on my wavelength.

"Not very enchanted," Lake replied.

"Zombie trees!" Govi tried.

I smiled absently as I looked around. "Lake's right. It's not going to be very magical if all we've got is a few skeletons."

"We can use some more tissue paper?" Eli suggested.

I nodded. "Yeah. That could work."

"Draped or scrunched?" Rica asked, her eyes still firmly on her detail work for the trees.

"Both?" I wondered out loud.

273

"Do you want to give one a go and we'll see how it goes?" Govi asked.

"Ramsey, do you want to make some more branches and I'll see what we can do in the way of leaves?"

Ramsey nodded. "Can do."

"Need some help?" Eli asked.

I almost said no out of principal. But if Govi, Lake and Ramsey didn't know I'd kissed him, then I wanted to keep it that way. And saying no would make me look awfully suspicious which would lead to them possibly finding out. Besides, a little crush didn't mean we couldn't still be friends.

"Yes? No?" Eli asked with a cheeky smile when I didn't answer.

I felt my cheeks warm and smiled. "Yes. Thanks."

Eli and I hunted around the table for the packets of tissue paper I knew should still be among our mess. Our hands brushed and we looked at each other. That steady heat was in his eyes again, a question as well as a statement now. I licked my lip and sidled away a little.

"Okay," I started, feeling flushed and hot and a nervous flutter in my chest. "So I'm thinking we start with some big, scrunchy balls–" I stopped as he sniggered.

He waved his hand. "Sorry. The scrunchy balls got me."

"You are so immature," I told him, trying to hold back my own smile.

He shrugged unapologetically. "I really am."

He watched me scrunch a couple of sheets of tissue paper up, then followed suit. Once we had a few of them, we went over to the closest finished tree and dropped them at the base.

"How do you want to attach them?" Eli asked.

I looked around. "I'm thinking glue or staples?"

Eli nodded, then grabbed both the glue and the staple gun from the table. "Dealers choice?"

I pointed at the staple gun. "That will be faster."

Eli grinned warmly. "Let's hope it works then."

He gave me the staple gun, dropped the glue in our pile and dragged the ladder over for me. He held it with one hand, put one foot on the bottom and pointed to it with his other hand.

"M'lady," he said, his eyes sparkling much too enticingly.

"Thanks." I ducked my head in the hopes my unbidden smile didn't encourage him and climbed the few steps.

Eli picked up a couple of balls of tissue paper and passed them to me. I arranged them on the end of a branch and looked at him.

"What do you think?" I asked.

He lifted his hands and placed them over mine to move the tissue paper a little. As he surveyed his positioning, he left his hands on mine. Every inch of my skin seemed to tingle, spreading up my arms from his touch.

My heart pounded, my stomach was full of butterflies, and my breath was threatening to get shorter. It felt like it took almost all my control to remain outwardly calm, act nonchalant as though Eli touching me had no effect on me whatsoever.

"Clo?" he asked.

"Mmm?" I turned to look at him and our noses nearly bumped. I cleared my throat and turned back to the tissue paper. "Yep. Better."

"Okay. I'll hold and you staple?" Eli's voice was soft and low.

Goose bumps chased over the tingles on my skin and I licked my lip to stop myself from blurting any misleading thoughts out loud. All I managed was a nod as I tried to extricate my very unwilling hands out from under his.

Once I'd managed it, my air felt stupidly cold against my skin where his warmth had been. I looked over to Rica, needing a little bit of… Well the most I'd get out of her was humoured teasing. But at least that would kick me out of the threatening mush.

I picked up the stapler and manoeuvred it between Eli's long fingers and fastened the tissue paper in place. We both pulled back and looked it over.

"Yes?" Eli asked, looking to me.

I nodded, trying not to look at him because then I could pretend I was unaffected. "Yes."

"Excellent. Next lot?"

I nodded again.

We got through a few more – about half the tree – when I realised that Eli was staring at me, and had been for a while.

"Eli, focus," I chastised.

"I am focussed."

"Eli…"

"Chloe…"

"On the leaves," I said quietly, trying not to feel flattered or flustered.

"I prefer this view."

"Eli, come on."

"What?"

"You know what," I hissed, not wanting the others to hear.

"I don't know what."

"You and me… Yesterday. It–"

"I'm thinking we should try that draping thing on this one," Govi said, walking up to us.

I pulled away from Eli quickly as though Govi had walked in on us in a far more compromising position than actually working on the trees. I cleared my throat and smoothed out my jumper unnecessarily as I looked around the room like I was very busy.

Stop being so weird, I told myself.

"Gin?" Govi pressed. "Want me and Rica to give it a go?"

I nodded wildly as I brought my head back to look at him. "Yes. Great idea. Thanks."

Govi looked between me and Eli, a slow smirk forming on his face. I gave him a pointed look and he shrugged subtly before moving off.

"Anyone would think we had a secret," Eli said nonchalantly as he picked up some more tissue paper.

I ignored the statement and he thankfully didn't say any more about it as we finished adding the leaves to our tree.

There were a couple of interruptions when people had questions, but most seemed happy to go on with their own things and wait for when Milly was back to check in with any problems.

Stand-in, stand down

My new plan was to keep my nose buried in a book at all times. That way I had a good excuse for being mentally absent from the world and there was less chance I'd think of Eli or how I might feel about him if things were different.

This worked well until Monday afternoon when I ran smack dab into the frame of the auditorium door instead of walking through it.

"Oh, you okay?" I heard Milly say and I looked over at her with a self-deprecating smile.

"Sure. Only thing bruised is my ego."

Milly shrugged. "It happens. How's everything going?"

I nodded as we headed in for the meeting. "It goes. Although I'm thinking we're going to need a few more hands to get these trees done in time."

Milly looked down at the clipboard I'd given back to her that morning – yes, I'd had it a whole weekend and managed not to lose it or damage it or anything. "We can do work that out. I'm sure we can. We've got a few things left to tick off, but I'm sure they won't take too long."

I looked at her in concern. "Are you okay?"

Milly nodded, but the panicked expression on her face suggested she was lying. "Sure."

"Are you?" I checked.

She waggled her head noncommittally, then shook it as we headed over to her base of operations. "Honestly, I'm freaking out. This whole thing has to be together in mere days and I'm just not convinced we're going to make it."

It was already Week Ten and only four more meetings left. We had four more meetings to finish everything and get the place cleaned and set up. The Year Twelves on the committee had time off on Friday to get things finalised, but even though I probably wouldn't be missed in class I thought it best to leave it to them. After all, I wasn't even going.

"I'm sure it will be fine," I told her.

She smiled, but it didn't reach her eyes. "I hope so. I just really want people to have a good time."

I nodded supportively. "And they will. They don't need decorations or six kinds of soft drink to have a good time. Quicksilver will make sure that, even if the DJ plays some absolutely terrible rubbish, no one will notice. You'll all be so hyped up with adrenalin and excitement that anything will be a great time."

Milly took a deep breath and I saw her visibly relaxing. "No. Of course. You're right."

"Do you want me to look over things and double check it all for you?"

She nodded vigorously. "Yes. If you don't mind, that would be great," she said as she passed me the clipboard. "And steal whoever you want for the trees."

I smiled. "Thanks."

"No. Thank you. Those trees really look amazing." She gave a small chuckle. "It's so weird that the person I can count on most isn't even really meant to be here."

I shrugged, always wonderful at taking compliments. "I committed. I wanted to see my project through to the end. Plus I didn't want to let you down."

"Unlike some people," Milly said quietly, her eyes shifting behind me.

I didn't need to wonder who she'd seen. The excited murmuring and noise that suddenly came from behind me told me exactly who it was. The added calls of her name were definitely unnecessary.

I turned to see my sister stroll in authoritatively, looking around her like she was waiting for her complimentary glass of bubbles and personal slave to appear. Only I was on the other side of the room and had no inclination to go running at her beck and call today.

"Elijah!" she cried happily and I followed her gaze to where he was by our trees.

"What is she doing here?" I muttered as Eli called, "Ella, you're here."

I'd been talking mainly to myself, but Milly answered, "I have no idea. I didn't think she'd turn up."

"Me either…"

"I was hoping she wouldn't," Milly whispered confidentially.

"Me too," I admitted.

The formal committee had been one of my only safe places, one of the only places where Ella didn't lord her superiority over me, and now she was there, crashing through the barricades and demanding worship for finally deigning to turn up. Worship that people seemed to be happy to give her. Well, most people except Brenda, Milly, Rica and Me.

"Of course I'm here," Ella said loudly as she sashayed over to Eli, followed by the simpering Lindy. "Here and ready to help."

Milly and I both huffed a sceptical laugh as people almost lined up to say hello to Ella as she walked by.

"As long as she's in no risk of breaking a nail," Milly muttered and I hid my snort behind a cough.

But Milly saw through it and grinned at me.

"I'm not sure if you want to go over there or not?" she asked.

I shook out my shoulders, passing Milly back the clipboard for now. "I suppose I'd better."

"Good luck," Milly offered, touching a hand softly to my shoulder.

I nodded to her and wondered how normal it was to feel like you were heading into a battle to the death just by walking towards your own sister. I wanted to hope it wasn't normal at all.

"What are these?" Ella scoffed, pointing up at the trees.

"Trees," Eli told her.

Ella scoffed again, as though he must be joking. "Trees? Why on earth do we want these at our formal?"

"The theme *is* Enchanted Forest..." Govi said, sliding his eyes to me as I stopped just behind Ella.

Ella's smile was more a grimace. "Of course. And this is the forest?" Even when she was trying to be sincere, she just sounded stuck up.

"This is the forest," Eli said slowly as though he wasn't quite sure what else to say.

Ella lay her hand on his arm and giggled. "You're so talented." She took a step towards him and batted her eyes. "So skilled with your…hands," she said suggestively.

My heart stuttered painfully as Eli smiled at her. "It's not my only skill."

"Right!" came Rica's jovial voice. "I am late again I know. But I bring… Ella!" she finished on a strangled note and I felt her run into the back of me.

Ella turned, finally noticing me as well. "What are you two doing here?" she asked like we hadn't been here the whole time.

I blinked, trying not to spell it out for her. "We're finishing the trees for the walkway."

Ella looked me over as though I'd turned up to the opera in my oldest tracksuit pants. "I'm sure we can manage."

"Great," I said sarcastically. "So you need about four or five extra pairs of hands to help you get these finished and in position in time. And someone who can paint them up."

I should have known better than to challenge her.

Ella looked around the room expectantly. "Listen up, people!" she called out and every one turned to look at her. "I need a bunch of people to help with…" She looked at the trees and waved her hand at them, "these or whatever."

Almost every person threw their hand in the air and I exchanged a weary look with Rica. When I looked back to Ella, she was looking at me triumphantly.

"Great," I said, putting on my best fake smile.

"So…off you go then," Ella said, dismissing me with a flourish of her hand.

"Rica's actually really good at the painting," Eli said quickly.

Ella looked at him quickly and smiled. "Of course. Rica can stay then."

"Chloe's kind of needed…" Govi started, then looked around for help.

"Every pair of hands," Ramsey offered.

Ella sighed, then looked at me like she was doing me a favour. "Sure. You can stay." He hand flourish this time was quite obviously intended to send me on my merry way.

"Uh, Clo," Eli said, clearing his throat. "Shall we keep on with–?"

"I need to help Rica," I said, cutting him off and pushing Rica to the furthest away tree.

"What was that?" Rica asked me, clearly annoyed with me.

"Just… Can we let them…do them or whatever?" I begged.

"He chose you. Again."

"I don't want to hear it."

Rica held her hands up defensively. "I just wanted it said that one time."

I frowned at her, then did everything necessary to avoid Ella and Eli as we got on with work. I frowned as I watched our extra volunteers go up to Ella and ask her what they needed to do. Ella would pause in her laughter with Eli, then shrug at them and tell them something along the lines of, 'I don't know. Make a tree?' then go back to batting her eyes at Eli.

I didn't bother telling myself I wasn't jealous at the way the two of them were or that she was the one he was laughing with. I had plenty of anger at the significant lack of work they were doing while they flirted to keep the jealousy from getting too heavy.

"Okay!" Rica cried, her hand lying gently over mine. "Can we loosen up just a little?"

I looked at my hand and saw it was white-knuckle tight around the ladder I was holding for her. I took a deep breath and relaxed my hand. It was stiff so who knew how long I'd been tensing it.

Rica batted me away. "Can you just go and take a breather, please?" she said kindly. "I think we both need it."

I nodded. "Sure."

"Go backstage. Quiet and calm."

I nodded again and tried to shake myself into some semblance of loose as I went. I finally stood in the wings and took a deep breath.

"Why are you pissed with me now?" I heard and turned to see Eli had followed me.

"I'm not…" I started, but outright lying was not a fundamental part of my character.

"Why?" he repeated.

I bit my lip to stop myself blurting it out. "I'm fine, Eli. You're just being you and I have no problem with that. You and Ella are a perfect match."

"What?" he spat. "Seriously? I thought I was supposed to be flirting with her?"

My nose wrinkled as I bit back another unwise retort. "You do what you want, Eli."

"Except I won't because what I want is the opposite of what you *claim* you want."

"Claim? I'm not *claiming* anything."

"You're claiming you're not interested in me."

"I'm not!" I got some control over myself and said more calmly, "Not like that. We're just friends."

"Really? Then why did you kiss me?"

"You kissed me," I reminded him.

"You kissed me back. Why?"

I sighed. "I don't know, Eli!"

"I do. Because you like me."

"I'm just the stand-in and the leading lady has finally deigned to take her place. So let it go."

"And you always do what you're told, don't you?"

"Yes."

"No, you don't," he fired at me.

I narrowed my eyes. "A momentary rebellion now quashed."

"Then kiss me."

I huffed in annoyance. "You are such a dick!"

"But you've just proved my point for me. You *don't* always do what you're told. Only when it comes to Ella."

"So?"

"So she doesn't get to tell you who you can and can't fall for."

"No," I told him. "She doesn't. But that doesn't mean I fell for you."

Just because outright lying wasn't a fundamental part of my character didn't mean it wasn't necessary on occasion.

I turned and walked away from him, hiding my annoyance when I got back to Rica and the boys. Rica looked up at me and I noticed she was covered in paint she was supposed to be adding to the trees. For a moment, I was sure she knew something had happened.

But she said nothing except, "Feeling better?"

"Sure."

"How is this looking?"

I took a breath in to make sure my breathing was even before replying, "Great. I doubt anyone's going to want to throw them out once you're finished with them."

My eyes scanned the room and I saw Ella glaring at me from where she was standing next to Lindy. I seriously hoped she hadn't seen Eli follow me into the wings, and I even more hoped she hadn't seen us walk out basically together. But I was pretty sure both of those were a pipedream.

Ella continued to do a spectacular lack of anything while she 'supervised' the people she'd roped into volunteering. And that was only because Eli was trying to keep busy with his own work. Not that it stopped her trying to flirt with him at every opportunity. If he needed more paper or he dropped his paintbrush, she was there quicker than the Flash. She'd bat her eyelashes and giggle and push her amble boobage at him. And he'd smile winningly at her every time.

"You did ask him to turn his attention to her," Rica reminded me again.

I frowned. "You and your logic just keep painting."

"Just say it once and I'll let it drop."

I huffed. "Fine. I'm jealous."

"And?"

"And nothing. It's just a little crush. It'll pass and we'll all be better for it."

I didn't need to be looking at her to know she was rolling her eyes at me.

"Gin?" Govi appeared beside us. "I'm just going to go grab some more paper from the art room, okay?"

"Let her go. Someone needs another timeout," Rica said.

"Everything okay?" Govi asked.

I nodded, but Rica answered, "Someone's a little testy today."

"Hush up." I nudged her ladder for good measure.

"I never noticed how lazy Ella was…" Govi marvelled.

I huffed a humourless laugh. "Yeah, you and most of the rest of the world." I pointed to the volunteers Ella had working for her. "I'll be back in a minute."

As I was walking through the corridors to the art room, I quite literally ran into Eli, who was shaking out wet hands.

"Shit!" I snapped, more at myself than him. "Sorry."

He shook his head, wearing a wry smirk. "Nah. You're good. What are you up to?"

"We're out of paper," I told him, making to move on.

He held a hesitant hand up in front of my path. "Clo…"

I sighed. "Eli?"

His eyes were soft, they were warm, they were beautiful. His half-smile was questioning, it was hopeful, it was

290

enticing. He took a step towards me and I mirrored it, feeling like I was running completely on autopilot.

His hand cupped my cheek and, even though there was plenty of time for me to pull away from him and I knew I should, I let him kiss me. My hand came up between us and clutched his shirt tightly, pulling him closer.

It was soft and gentle and full of more meaning than was wise. But I leant into him like he was water in the desert. All the while trying to convince myself I had to stop.

Finally, just as his hands were alighting on my waist, I released my grip on his shirt and gently pushed him away.

"Chloe?"

With one word, with just my name, he implored me. But I wasn't only leading him on here, I was setting myself up for a world of hurt in more ways than one.

I shook my head. "I'm sorry, Eli."

He swallowed hard, but he nodded. "No. Sure." He cleared his throat. "I'll – uh – see you in there."

"Yep."

He nodded again, then headed off. I watched him go and I could feel his reluctance like it was my own. He trailed his fingers along the wall for a moment, then laced them with his other hand on his head.

"Just a crush," I told myself. "It'll pass."

291

I collected the paper, and myself, and headed back to the auditorium.

Ella was regaling the committee with her version of 'Let You Love Me'. Most people were clapping to the rhythm and she had the bashful smile and coy eyes directed at Eli to perfection.

I slapped the paper into Govi's hands a little harder than I intended.

"Gin, you right?" he asked, his hand going to my shoulder in concern.

I took a deep breath and reminded myself everything that was happening here was either my fault or how it was supposed to be so getting angry was stupid. I looked up at Govi with a smile.

"I'm good."

He didn't look totally convinced, but he nodded. "Give Lake a hand with his tree then?" he asked.

"Please do," Lake said. "My fingers are sticking together."

His smile was a little deeper than his usual cool exterior and I felt my smile become more natural in response.

"Sure. Love to."

Lake moved over and we worked pretty well together. He was always the most aloof of the boys, but he spared me more smiles than I'd ever seen on his face, he sang to me –

usually total nonsense but it made me laugh – and generally kept me distracted enough that I barely even looked at Eli or Ella for the rest of the meeting.

I didn't know if he and Govi had set it up intentionally or not, but I appreciated it anyway.

An off-screen romance

On Tuesday, we were back in the auditorium and I was looking over the trees, pretty sure we should have made more progress the afternoon before.

I had planned to not even turn up, but Govi was adamant that they needed Rica to do the fine-detail painting and Rica was far more adamant that she needed me to maintain her sanity. So there I was, not convinced that our enchanted forest was going to be ready in time.

"How's it going?" Milly asked and I jumped, not realising she was beside me.

I didn't want to worry her any more than she already was so I nodded. "Great."

She looked around as well and she seemed to know I was stretching the truth a little.

"Do you not have enough help?" Milly tried.

We shared a look. "We have enough hands…" I said slowly.

Milly understood. "But those hands aren't really doing any work?"

"That is one way to put it."

Milly nodded. "Okay. I'll see what I can do."

More people had arrived and Milly headed for the centre of the auditorium.

"Can I have your attention please?" she called and the general rabble quietened to look at her. "We're only a couple of days out, people. Now is not the time to slack off. We need just a couple more days of hard work and I promise it will all be worth it. Those of you working on the forest, direct any questions to Chloe–"

"Who's Chloe again?" someone yelled.

Milly pointed right at me. "Chloe Cowan. She's in charge–"

"Chloe?" Ella laughed as she walked in. "Chloe couldn't be in charge of anything. I'm here for anyone who has questions about the forest."

"Like you've been here for the last five weeks?" Milly accused.

Ella's smile fell a little. "I've been *very* busy, Milly," she said forcefully.

But Milly wasn't afraid of her. "So has Chloe. While you've been 'very busy', Chloe's been the driving force behind what has become the centrepiece of our entire formal."

Eyes were darting between me and Ella and Milly now. I couldn't tell what they were thinking. But I was freaking out. People didn't stand up for me. Not as far as my sister knew. And people certainly didn't insinuate that I was a better person than Ella. But here was Milly Wallis, doing both of those things. And it looked like the rest of the committee were listening.

Ella scoffed. "She was filling in for me. But I'm here now, so everything's okay."

Milly visibly rolled her eyes. "Oh good. And here I was starting to worry."

"Well you don't have to anymore." Ella smiled around the room. "So any questions about the beautiful forest can be directed to the appropriate leader – i.e. me."

Milly glared at Ella for a moment longer, then looked around the room. "Whatever. Let's get on with it, people. Three more meetings to go!" She clapped her hands and everyone started moving onto their projects.

I turned hurriedly, keeping my head down in the hopes that Ella wasn't going to make a point of dressing me down in front of the whole committee. Sometimes she seemed to take inordinate pleasure in making me look small in front of other people, and other times she seemed to feel it reflected badly on her.

Ella appeared beside me and the overpowering floral scent of her perfume made my eyes water. But I kept on with my tissue paper scrunching while I waited to see what sort of mood my sister was in.

"Chloe…" she started, using that fake, overly sweet tone she used at her most passive-aggressive.

"Ella."

"Do you want to tell me why rank Milly Wallis has forgotten I'm in charge?"

I shook my head. "I couldn't tell you."

Ella nodded. "I see. So you wouldn't know why she thought you were of any consequence?"

I shook my head again. "Nope."

"I see," she repeated, her tone still pleasant for all intents and purposes. "Which, I suppose, means you can't tell me why *you* suddenly seem to think you're of any consequence?"

I swallowed back my biting retort and shook my head a third time. "I'm just the stand-in, Ella. Doing as I'm told."

Ella leant towards me. "Good girl. It doesn't do for the nobodies to go thinking they're popular. That will only lead to heartbreak."

There was no use in me telling Ella I didn't want to be popular. I'd tried that once, and she'd just assumed I was lying or pandering to what I thought she wanted to hear – which on that occasion was the wrong thing to do. Ella just didn't grasp the concept that I didn't need everyone to like me or feel jealous of me to be happy. The fundamental understanding that someone could hold no value in popularity was lacking, and nothing I said would make her believe I wasn't in denial.

"Of course, Ella. Stupid me. The spotlight is all yours," I said and I was glad she didn't seem to notice the slight bite in my tone.

"And you'd do well to remember…" She stood up and started primping. "Eli!" she giggled.

"Ella. Chloe."

I nodded, but didn't look up. "Hey, Eli."

"How are things?" he asked.

"Fine," Ella answered for me. "I was just telling Chloe that the trees are coming along so nicely, aren't they?"

My eyes slid up to Eli. He was watching so saw my inadvertent eye-roll and he turned his unbidden smile to my sister.

"They are," he said, laughter in his voice. "And I'm sure they'll finish perfectly now you're here."

I heard a weird noise and looked around to see Rica fake-gagging, which made me smile. Ella also turned and Rica turned the gag into a cough as she put her bag with mine and pulled out her paintbrushes.

"The paint fumes…" Rica said, putting on a weak voice as she waved her hand in front of her face and fake-coughed again. "Painters cough. Gets us all in the end."

Ella's eyes narrowed at my best friend. "Just keep your paint germs to yourself," she accused. "I can't afford to get sick."

Rica nodded quickly. "No. Of course. I wouldn't dare."

I smiled at everyone before I took my scrunched tissue paper over to the closest as-yet-dead tree.

"Oi, oi!" I heard Govi cry and looked up so see him walking over with a jovial spring in his step. "Here's trouble and a half."

"Here he is indeed," I laughed as I got to stapling.

Govi scoffed. "Fair, that."

Ramsey arrived and slung his arm around Govi's shoulders. "Right. Where do you want me?" he asked with a wry half-smile.

"If you can–"

"Ramsey!" Ella called and I kept my eyes firmly in any direction but my sister while Govi and Ramsey both turned to look at her.

"Yeah?" he called back petulantly.

"I'm in charge."

Ramsey nodded. "Okay. So where do *you* want me?"

Ella's nose wrinkle in disgust. "Just keep working."

Ramsey blinked, looking at me in confusion. I shrugged, trying my best to convey a 'don't look at me' vibe.

"On what?' Ramsey asked.

"Do you have *no* initiative?" Ella asked playfully.

Eli opened his mouth, but Govi said loudly. "Why don't we help, Gin. Yeah?"

"I'm sure *Chloe* can manage quite well on her own," Ella replied. "Why don't you sing us a song?"

Ramsey looked at me in question. I shrugged again and kicked my head towards Ella, hoping he'd just get off the radar and let us all get back to work. The day before, Ella had managed to do nothing but distract people from actually getting work done and I had a feeling that this meeting would be little different. Which meant that the people who were actually making progress – at the moment, just me and Rica – needed to keep their butts moving.

"Sure," Ramsey said uncertainly. "What do you want me–?"

"70's!" Eli called out, wearing a shit-eating grin as he looked at Ramsey.

Ramsey's face drained of colour as the countdown began.

"Five! Four! Three! Two!" There was a slight pause...

"At first I was afraid, I was petrified!" Ramsey popped out with triumphantly, giving Eli his own shit-eating grin as he continued the song.

By the time he was at "walk out the door", all the forest workers were singing with him. The Quicksilver boys were all wandering around as they sang and Ella had her eyes planted on Eli with an obsessive look in her eyes.

"Eli! 60's!" Ramsey cackled when he was done.

"Shit!" Eli laughed. "Okay. Give me a second."

"No seconds," Govi told him. "And you put that phone back in your pocket!"

"Okay! Okay!" Eli said quickly and I turned to see he was panicking.

"Five. Four. Three–"

"There she's goes, just a-walking down the street..." Eli paused and Govi, Lake and Ramsey all joined him in the, "Do wah diddy diddy dum diddy do," and left the rest to him.

As I climbed down the ladder to get more tissue paper, I bumped into Eli as he was singing and he pulled me into a dance.

"I'm hers, she's mine, wedding bells are gonna chime," he sang with a cheeky smirk and bright eyes.

I pulled out of his arms hastily, my cheeks flushing, and he winked at me before he kept going. I couldn't help my eyes sliding to Ella. She was looking at me with a calculating glare before Eli scooped her up and distracted her.

I was so flustered about the whole thing that I ran into Rica as I went back to my tree, more tissue paper safely in hand.

"You good?" she laughed.

I nodded. "Fine. Unaffected."

She smiled. "Of course you are."

Eli finished up with a, "Govi. 50's"

The countdown didn't even get to start before Govi jumped into pride of place with a, "You ain't nothing but a hound dog, cryin' all the time."

He made it the whole way through only forgetting the lyrics a couple of times, to which someone helped him out as he laughed and kept going. His Elvis impersonation was quite good, really, and I could see Rica was pretty impressed.

"Lake, my man!" Govi cried when he was done.

Lake sighed resignedly. "40's. I'm on it." He opened his mouth but Govi didn't let him go on with whatever song he'd picked.

"Ha!" Govi laughed. "Nope."

Lake looked slightly pissed off. "What then?"

"80's."

"What?" Lake whined.

"Go on," Govi encouraged none too sincerely.

I could almost see Lake's mind spinning furiously as he tried to come up with something. "I was ready for 40's, damn it!" he snapped.

"Five," Govi said, mock-apologetically. "Four. Three. Two–"

"Some boys kiss me, some boys hug me. I think they're okay," Lake started.

Govi and Ramsey let out a snort. But when Lake glared at them, they mimed zipping their mouths shut and let him continue relatively unhindered.

Meanwhile, I was still running about trying to get trees some leaves. The other committee members who'd volunteered for Ella had spent the whole competition standing around uselessly, largely getting in my way and watching the boys sing. And, to be fair to Lake, he was giving Madonna a decent run for her money.

"Right, I'm calling it," Ramsey sniggered. "Lake won. Hands down."

Govi was leaning on Ramsey, tears running down his face from his silent laughter. All he could do was nod.

"Back to work then?" Lake asked, his glare for Govi was scathing.

"Hang on," Ella said, finally sliding off the perch she'd commandeered on the table. "We haven't all had a turn yet."

Ramsey clicked his fingers at her and swivelled around on his heel. He was pointing at me, his mouth opening as Ella giggled coyly and said, "Well give me a category, then."

Ramsey snapped his fingers again, tapped his palm onto the top of his other fist as he pursed his lips and kept on swivelling back around to Ella.

"Lake?" Eli pressed.

Lake blinked, took his eyes off me, and looked at Ella. "Yes. Um... Take Pop for three Peach Cokes."

Lake pointed at Ella as Eli objected, "Dude those are my Cokes. You can't give my shit away."

Lake did some bit about flipping Eli off as Ella started her song, with Lindy on backup vocals of course. And what wonderfully poignant piece did Ella come out with? 'break up with your girlfriend, i'm bored'. To say Old Tom felt someone walk over his grave was probably an understatement.

Govi nudged me companionably as he walked by with his arms full of tissue paper balls. Ramsey gave me an encouraging wink as he followed, brandishing a staple gun suggestively. Lake looked at me apologetically as he went to check if Rica needed a hand with anything. And Eli appeared at my side, looking at my tree like he was inspecting it.

"Ella made an…interesting choice," he said quietly.

"Pop was an interesting choice," I replied, not sure what I meant by that.

"What would you have picked for Pop?"

"I'm not sure that's the point of the game."

I felt him shrug. "Humour me." He rearranged some of the tissue paper aimlessly. "Personally, I'd go with 'Don't Give Up On Me'."

My heart hitched and I took a deep breath before I answered. "Pop, yeah?"

"Yep."

"Then I'd probably pick 'Nothing Breaks Like a Heart'."

His hand trailed over mine as though it meant nothing. "Is that a message?" he asked softly.

I snatched my hand away, looking back to Ella who was thankfully busy performing to the groupies who'd gathered

305

around her. I cleared my throat and stepped well out of any limbs that might try to broach the gap between us.

"I picked a Pop song. Same as you."

Eli nodded slowly. "Sure. Just a Pop song."

I nodded as well and was saved trying to get out of any further conversation with him when Ella called for his attention. He gave me one more look, then let me get back to my work.

Ella managed to keep him distracted for the rest of the meeting but seemed suddenly very demanding about everyone else working very hard. I told myself that it didn't matter how the work got done, only that it did get done. Now and then, Eli would look at me and we'd share a smile that made me feel better about our last words. And the progress we'd made on the forest by the time Milly called the end of the meeting was significant; there was only one tree left to branch and the leaves were starting to actually look semi-decent. Of course Rica's additions were making them look all the more realistic.

"See you all tomorrow," Ella called as she swanned out, and a whole lot of people called goodbye in return.

"You coming, Gin?" Govi asked, coming over with Rica.

I shook my head. "I'm just going to finish this," I said pointing to the tree that still needed branches.

"You sure?" Rica asked.

I nodded. "Yeah. I'll be like ten minutes. Tops."

"You don't have anything to prove, you know," Govi said softly. But he just touched my arm and let Rica pull him away.

Lake and Ramsey paused, but they followed Govi and Rica.

"Want some help?" Eli asked me.

I looked over at him and shook my head. "No. I'm all good. You go."

He scrubbed his hand over his chin. "I can keep you company?"

I smiled. "I'll be okay," I promised.

"I'm sure you will. But I thought we could hang out after?"

I looked around, but we were the only two left in the room bar a couple of people still wandering out.

"She won't know," he continued and I looked back at him.

"She might."

He shrugged. "So? I'm sure I can come up with a brilliant excuse."

"If you think you'll need an excuse, then that's probably a reason not to."

"I'll tell her I wanted to ask you more about her."

I tilted my head for a moment. "Well she's so up herself that would probably fly…"

"So… Hang out with me."

"And do what?" I laughed.

Eli picked up his guitar. "Just hang. I'll sing some Quicksilver songs while you finish and you can tell me everything that's wrong with them."

I laughed. "Okay. Sounds good."

As I finished my papier-mâché, Eli played some Quicksilver songs on the guitar and I fake grumbled about each one. After he decided he'd heard enough of me bashing his precious work, he then moved onto the piano to play anything that wasn't a Quicksilver song.

My heart felt big and light and happy as we sang and laughed and mucked about, and I didn't feel any awkwardness or discomfort. Not at me singing in general or at me singing with Eli. I enjoyed it. In fact, I really enjoyed it. I was enjoying it so much that, when I was done with the tree and wiped off my hands, I went up to the stage with him and sat on the piano stool with him.

"Your turn," he insisted.

"What?" I laughed.

"Your turn. Play me something."

My hands hovered over the keys and I let them fall where they would. Where they chose to fall was 'Say Something'. As I was about to start the lyrics, Eli did instead.

I looked at him at the lyric 'I'll be the one if you want me to,' but we kept on like there suddenly wasn't about six layers of heady undercurrent in the room.

I joined in at Christina's bit and we finished the song together.

When it was done, we both sat, just breathing. My heart wasn't pounding, it was just beating at a steady, insistent rhythm.

Eli's hand came up to the keys and he started playing. He sang me a song about a girl who seemed terribly indecisive about a relationship. Apparently she was giving him mixed messages – saying she will, then she won't – and the guy was trying to work out what they were to each other.

If Eli was sticking with the tenet that you could tell a lot about someone by their song choice, his spoke volumes and I didn't know what I could say to that. It was a good song and I wanted to have an answer for him. I also wanted to know who Jenny was.

But I didn't have an answer, so I asked, "Have you written anything for piano?"

He played some random notes. "A few things."

"Why don't you ever play them?"

He shrugged as he looked up while his fingers still played over the keys. "None of it's very good."

"At the risk of complimenting you, I'm not convinced."

He huffed a laugh as he smiled. "It's all pretty rough."

"Play it anyway."

He looked at me and the tune he was playing changed. It was a little slower. It was sweet and simple and catchy, very different from most of Quicksilver's original songs.

"Has it got lyrics?" I asked as he played.

He shook his head, turning his head forward again and closing his eyes. "Not really."

"Not really?" I asked coyly.

He nodded, his eyes still closed. "Nothing set." One hand came off the keys to twist by his ear before it went back to playing. "Fragments."

"What's it about?"

A pure smile lit his lips. "Do you like it?"

I was annoyed he'd avoided the question, but I really did. "It's okay."

He laughed and the tune changed to something more upbeat. "How's this?"

I took one of his hands from the keys and he looked at me in question. I looked down at his hand in mine, running my fingers along his softly. Despite a near lifetime of learning piano and being reasonably proficient, it still

310

amazed me that people could make such beautiful sounds just by moving their fingers. And there was something about Eli that had me feeling the surreal nature of the situation even more.

"Clo?"

I looked up at him and I felt more than just surreal.

There was that warm and tingling feeling, that rightness. Him and the music and the closeness was getting to me. Looking at him then, it felt like more than just a crush that would harmlessly pass while our friendship remained intact. Looking at him then, it felt like that feeling wasn't one-sided. And in that moment that felt like the most wonderful feeling in the world.

So I leant forwards and kissed him. Soft and short, a mere press of my lips against his before I pulled away again and looked back at his hand. He said nothing for a while as I made a big show of inspecting his hand as though I'd never seen one before.

"You kissed me again," he said softly.

I kept my expression neutral. "I really shouldn't have."

He placed his fingers under my chin and tipped my face back up. "And yet you did."

I searched his eyes. "Don't read anything into it, Eli," I warned him, despite me reading a lot into it.

"Okay." He shrugged lazily. "It doesn't mean anything."

I nodded too quickly. "It doesn't mean anything," I agreed.

He wasn't the only one I was trying to convince, and I was pretty sure we both knew it.

"And if I kissed you again?" he asked softly.

My eyes flickered down, but he still had his fingers under my chin. I forced myself to look at him again before I spoke.

"It still wouldn't mean anything," I told him carefully.

"Does that mean you don't want me to?"

His eyes pinned mine and I couldn't lie to him. "That's not what I said, Eli."

A smile crinkled at the corners of his eyes. "Now who's the heartbreaker?" he teased.

I pulled away and got up. "Well I wouldn't want to risk breaking your heart."

He jumped up and caught me around the waist. I giggled as I looked up at him, my hands going to his shoulders to steady myself.

"Leave and you might…" he said softly.

And I couldn't help myself. I kissed him again. I knew I should have walked away. I shouldn't have let it go this far. I was trying to make him believe I only wanted to be friends and then I turned around and kissed him. It wasn't fair. And yet…

It was only a kiss

An arm appeared in front of me, attached on one side to a hand planted on the wall and a recognisable body on the other.

"Ella." I nodded, putting my book down.

"I don't know what you're playing at," she hissed. "But if you think Elijah Sweet is going to leave me for you then you have another thing coming."

Why could she not have done this at home? She really should have, because I was seriously over the whole thing.

"It's just Eli. Not Elijah Sweet. Just Eli. And tell me, how can he leave you when you're not even dating?"

Ella growled at me. "You think you're so clever?"

"I think I have a meeting to get to. If you don't mind."

"I mind very much. You think Elijah Sweet's going to choose you? When he can have me. You think *anyone* would choose you?"

I looked her over and wondered whether it was even worth it to tell her that he already had chosen me. That he pretty much already had her and he'd chosen me anyway. I wondered about telling her that he wasn't the only one, that I had the friendship of all the Quicksilver boys as well as more and more of the formal committee. Well Milly and Brenda. And they totally counted.

As I wondered all of this, I realised one fundamental thing about my sister; she knew all this. She knew all this no matter what she said. Behind all that conceit and bluster was nothing but a little girl frightened she wouldn't live up to our parents' expectations and that no one would like her. So she took it out on me. She kept me down so she felt better about herself.

Not that the realisation made me feel any better and it didn't excuse her behaviour, but it made it easier for me not to throw it all back in her face. It made it easier to just keep living my life until I could be my own person and it was my time to shine the way I wanted to. But biding my time didn't have to mean being walked all over anymore.

"You can have him, Ella. I don't want him," I told her as I pushed passed her and into the auditorium.

And I wasn't lying. I really liked Eli, I did. But I was finally stepping out of my sister's shadow. There was no way I was swapping hers for his. There was the small matter of the fact I kept kissing him and giving him all the wrong signals, but I was going to work on that. I was going to implement and stick to a 'just friends' policy.

Even if he was totally gorgeous and everything went in slow-motion every time I saw him give someone a sincere smile.

Which is exactly what happened as I was walking over to our forest.

Govi was waving his arms around as usual and Eli paused in taking a sip of his drink as he burst out into laughter.

The moment was ruined as Ella's shoulder crashed into mine as she hurried over to him. My book made a loud thud on the floor as I dropped it and every person in the room stopped to look at me go bright red and slowly bend down to pick it back up. Except Ella of course, who was draping herself over Eli's arm.

Even Lindy stopped, ever trailing after my sister, and looked down at me sadly. "Little Chloe Cowan. Always second."

I grinned at her falsely. "At least that puts me ahead of you, Lindy."

It took her a moment to work it out, but when she did she huffed and stamped her foot and ran off to no doubt tell Ella I'd dared to step out of line.

But I didn't care anymore.

I was a part of something. I was making more than one friend. I was letting people see the real me – who maybe wasn't the person I'd thought I was after all, but I was letting them see her anyway. I wasn't so shy anymore. I wasn't hiding in the shadows anymore. I wasn't going to let someone else dictate who I was or what I wanted.

And Ella had come in and ruined it.

She wanted me so far in her shadow that no one would ever notice me. She wanted me to feel so small it didn't matter how badly she failed, I'd always have failed harder.

Squatting there awkwardly and watching people crowd around her and her soaking it up, I realised something else. But this time it was about me.

It wasn't easier to just go along with the madness. All those years thinking I was fine just waiting for my time? That was giving up. And I might have been a pushover, but I wasn't a quitter. I saw things through to the end, and that included living life.

So I was going to live my life however I wanted and Ella be damned.

I picked my book and my ego up off the floor and headed towards the forest with a sense of renewed purpose.

As I got to the back of the crowd though, all the confidence my inner pep talk had given me ebbed away. I wasn't left with any less resolve, I just didn't quite have the wherewithal to put the theory into practice. Yet. For now I was quite happy with working on just being less of a doormat. After all, one didn't go from doormat to the queen of assertiveness just because one's decided to.

So I went about my work. I didn't pay much mind to the people who were trying to get Ella to give them some direction. On one such occasion, I felt confident enough to nod to the lost looking soul.

"The staple gun works best," I told him.

He gave me a second look, as though he hadn't actually been looking at me properly before. "Sorry?"

I went over with the staple gun and a bunch of tissue paper. I held the up against the branch and showed him. "The staple gun's faster and doesn't need time to dry," I explained with a smile.

He looked surprised for a moment, then smiled as well. "Thanks. Uh…" He looked to Ella, who was giggling over something, then back to me like he knew Ella wasn't going to be any help. "And the tissue paper's best. Yeah?"

I shrugged and looked around at our few totally completed trees. "It definitely does the most coverage. On some of them, we're mixing it with draped crepe paper." I shrugged again. "But really whatever looks good. We want a good mix of trees so they don't all look the same."

He nodded. "Okay. Sure. Uh... Thanks…?"

"Chloe," I reminded him.

He nodded again. "Chloe," he repeated. Amazingly, it sounded like he was trying to remember it.

"Here. You take this," I said, holding out the staple gun.

"You don't need it?"

I shook my head. "I'll grab another off the table."

He took it. "Thanks… Chloe."

I smiled. "No worries."

I left him to it and went back to my own stuff, trying not to let Govi or Rica distract me with their constant questions. Rica was particularly into poking me with the end of her paintbrushes. And Govi picked it up off her, when he wasn't throwing bits of rolled up rubbish at me. But at least they kept me smiling.

A little later, I heard a quiet "…Ella's sister…" and turned to see the guy I'd helped earlier pointing to me. When he saw me looking, he smiled.

"This look okay?" the girl he was with asked.

I nodded. "Yeah fine."

She smiled. "Matt said you use the staple gun?"

I nodded again. "I found it works best, yeah. But you do what–"

She shook her head. "No. We'll do it your way."

They turned back to their tree and I felt a slightly less insistent poke.

"Govi!" I snapped and turned to find Rica grinning at me. "What?"

She shrugged all fake nonchalance. "Nothing. Just enjoying people realising who the better Cowan is."

I rolled my eyes at her. "People aren't realising anything. I'm just helping."

Rica nodded, her jaw slack. "Well, duh. As opposed to her royal lowness over there who does nothing but fling body parts on Eli and tell Lindy to…" Her Ella impression wasn't really on point, but it was snooty and stuck up and made me laugh. "Like, fetch me a Fanta, Lindy."

"Yo, Gin?" came Ramsey's voice and I peered around my current tree to look for him.

"Yeah?"

"Love songs."

I rolled my eyes. "I am not falling for that."

"Switch up!" Ramsey called out and I had no idea what he was talking about.

But Govi started up a song I'd never heard before. But Rica froze beside me.

I looked between Govi and Rica, who only had eyes for each other. As he sang to her, I was transfixed. It was beautiful and I wondered if this was one of things I was supposed to remember for my Maid of Honour speech.

"You know this one?" I hissed to Rica, who waved me away.

"It's Trevor," she said quickly.

I blinked, wracking my brains for a Trevor. Finally, I gave up and just Googled it to discover it was a song by Trevor Daniels called 'Falling'.

Just as Govi seemed to be finishing, Eli decided to take over and went with Alicia Keys. He did the typical musician thing and there was a lot of pointing involved with his heartfelt performance. And I wasn't sure, but I thought there was some very pointed…pointing going on with the lyrics 'Oh, oh, I never felt this way'. Then he moved on and I was left wondering if it was a coincidental point or a meaningful point.

After the day before, I wanted to say it was a meaningful point.

But the person who knew it was sensible to just be friends wanted to convince me it was coincidental.

I wasn't going to pretend I was hesitating about Eli because of Ella anymore. I didn't care if she wanted him or not, I liked him. I was interested. He was hot and funny and charming. I liked how I felt with him. I liked the person I was with him – when I wasn't being a blushing idiot. And I really liked kissing him.

But he was also larger than life. He shone with a light so bright that it blinded you to anything else, and I wasn't sure anymore that it was even intentional half the time. He wanted a life where thousands of people screamed his name and watched his every move, and he'd have to work hard to keep it that way.

If he really did like me too and we did the whole dating thing, where would that leave me?

It would leave me in his shadow. It would leave me playing second to a life I'd wanted to run away from since I'd realised there was more than just music and dancing. And just because I was open to the idea I'd chosen Commerce as a rebellion – as the only way to separate myself from the Ella-clone I'd been moulded into – it didn't mean I didn't feel a strong knee-jerk aversion to anything related to what Ella wanted out of life.

And that aversion came with a heady sense of fear. Fear that I wouldn't be able to stop myself from becoming someone else's understudy. Fear that I'd fall into the trap of making someone else's dreams my life under the guise of a crush, or habit, or love.

"Ella?" Milly called.

"What?" Ella called back.

"Can you go and check that the tables and chairs are all ready, please? They might need to be counted."

"I really need to get these trees finished. Chloe will go."

I looked up quickly.

Milly looked over at me and I could see she was trying to decide if this was a battle that was worth fighting. Finally she nodded. "Great. Chloe, do you mind?"

I shook my head. "No. Not at all."

"I can help her?" Eli said, looking at Milly for confirmation.

Milly nodded as she looked at her clipboard. "Far be it for me to get in the way of this new *helpful* attitude of yours, Elijah," she said.

"Another pair of hands never hurt," Ella said.

Milly's eyes snapped up. "I thought you just had to get the trees finished?"

Ella gave a minute snarl, then flicked her hair back. "The trees are a very important job. I'd better stay to keep an eye on everything."

"Excellent!" Milly said loudly. "If that's all sorted. Eli and Chloe, if you can go and check the tables and chairs. Here are the numbers." She brandished a piece of paper and Eli jogged over to get it. "They should all be down in the shed."

I nodded as I started heading out. Eli caught up to me easily, falling into step with me by the time we'd reached the doors. He pushed them open for me as he looked over the paper from Milly.

"Okay. Two hundred chairs. Thirty tables. Twenty round. Ten rectangle. In the usual place." He looked at me. "Do you know where the usual place is?"

I nodded. "Storage sheds. Depending on how organised it is, there may be a bunch of sets in the way."

"How do you know all this?" he chuckled, but he sounded impressed.

"I'm ever the understudy. I spend a lot of time with the backstage stuff."

"See you say this. But these last few weeks, I've seen anything but."

As I pulled open the shed doors, I frowned at him. "I'm being literal. I'm given the understudy roles." I titled my head, amending, "I go for the understudy roles. It lets me have more time with the backstage crew, but makes it look like I just suck at acting."

"Why would you do that?"

I flipped on the lights and looked around. "Because then my mum doesn't nag me about trying harder. Ella was an understudy in Year Nine. Mum asked her why she didn't put more effort into learning her lines for auditions. It was one of the only times I'd ever heard Ella say something real."

324

"What did she say?" Eli asked as he followed me into the shed.

"She screamed at Mum about how sometimes you can give something your all and even then you're not the best. Right after that, I was an understudy. When I told Mum, she took one look at Ella, said 'We can't all be winners,' and left it at that."

"So you've been playing your mum all this time and she's said nothing because Ella yelled at her?"

I nodded. "That and the understudy is what I was born for."

Eli caught my arm and I looked back at him in question. "My parents wanted me to be a doctor–"

"It's not quite the same thing, Eli."

"I'm just trying to say that it's up to you to be the star of your own life."

I sighed. "Not every story needs a star."

"Maybe not. But every story has one.

"There is nothing…starry about me."

"Sometimes it just takes a little longer for them to shine."

"Eli–"

"You shine, Clo."

I looked up at him and wished I didn't want to kiss him so badly. Maybe if he wasn't looking down at me with a soft smile, no sign of that cocky arrogance, just a guy standing in front of a girl.

He tucked a piece of hair behind my ear as he looked into my eyes. "I don't know what it is about you, Chloe," he said slowly and I fiercely chastised the flutter my heart made. "Every time I'm with you, everything and nothing makes sense."

I shook my head. This wasn't fair on anyone. "Eli..."

"You still going with not interested?"

I looked into those pale eyes, willing him to understand something I didn't really understand myself. I knew what he meant. We both knew I was very interested. But I shouldn't be. I didn't want the life he wanted. I didn't want to swap my sister's shadow for his. That meant I had to stop this.

Eli leant in to kiss me, but for once I resisted and turned my face away.

"Clo?"

I sighed and pushed him away softly, taking a step backwards to make it more definite. If I was going to keep telling him I wasn't interested, then I had to start acting like it. For both of us.

"What changed?" he asked.

"Nothing."

"Did Ella say something to you?"

"I just… It's…" I sighed and looked at him, begging him to understand and not make this any harder than it already was.

"You're taking Ella to the formal. We… You and I… We can't…"

But he wasn't having a bar of it. "Just say it," he demanded.

I took a deep breath and said the words I could never take back. "Whatever I told myself this was, whatever it *actually* was, it's over."

"It's over?" he clarified.

I nodded. "It's over."

He didn't say anything. He just looked at me like he wasn't sure what to say or what to do. I opened my mouth, but no words wanted to come out. So I closed it again and looked down.

I felt him move and forced myself not to look at him. As he passed me, he shoved Milly's checklist into my hands. Then he was gone.

I let out a deep breath, willing the sudden prickling heat in my eyes to go away.

"Milly needs the tables checked," I reminded myself.

It wasn't quite enough to lift the heaviness in my throat, but it was enough to get the job done and get back inside with my report.

One last bow

Thursday turned into a blur of last-minute formal preparations and lessons, which made it easier to ignore the slight regret that threatened over what I'd said to Eli the day before.

It was made even easier as my day was interspersed with Milly appearing in front of me to go over, "One last detail, I swear". Every time, she apologised for relying on me again and explained that she just didn't know who else she could count on. And every time I told her it was okay and I was willing to whatever I could to help. She'd finish by checking I was sure I didn't want a ticket for the next night and I'd shake my head and say, "Thank you, but no".

"Okay. I'll see you in the meeting?" she said, again.

I nodded as she hurried off, feeling like, even though I wasn't going, it was just as much my formal now. It was something that had started as an Ella obligation but had ended with me wanting to see it through for my own sake.

Most of that was because I hated to see a project unfinished – whether it was my project or not – and I knew that was something I was going to need to work on.

As I turned to continue on to class, I ran into Lake and his hands went to my arms to keep me on my feet. He was with Ramsey, but the others weren't in sight.

"Hey!" Lake said with a warm smile. "You're in a hurry."

"Sorry, just late. But that seems to be my normal at the moment."

"You going our way?" Ramsey asked as he kept moving down the corridor.

I shook my head. "I've got Maths with–"

"Formal is almost upon us!" Govi cried dramatically as he rushed out from God knew where, jumped on Ramsey's shoulders, then took off up the corridor whooping in excitement.

Ramsey blinked in surprise as he looked between me and Lake. His arms were out by his sides as though someone had dumped a bucket of ice down his neck or something. I wasn't sure if he was bracing for another attack or was trying to work out what had just happened.

"Dude, you done got Govied," Lake laughed.

Ramsey nodded slowly. "I *think* I'm okay with that."

"You don't sound sure," Lake said, leaning down a little to peer into Ramsey's face.

Ramsey grimaced in thought, then nodded again. "Nah. I'm okay with that," he finally said with a smile. He stood up straight again. "You know I–"

"Has anyone seen a crazy dipshit come through here?" Eli asked as he came around the corner. "About yea high, green hair, fucking terrible dress sense, and higher than a–" He was grinning widely at his friends, but it dropped when he saw me. "Chloe. Hey."

It was suddenly very awkward in the middle of the corridor and I wasn't the only one to clear my throat.

I tucked my hair behind my ear and nodded at him. "Yeah. Hey."

Lake pointed the way Govi had disappeared. "Nutter and his rhythm sticks went that a-way," he said quietly.

Ramsey was looking at his shoes, but he nodded.

Eli coughed. "Right. Cool. I'll go and… Go and catch me a monkey, then…" he said stiltedly. He nodded to me once. "Chloe."

I nodded once also. "Eli."

Eli gave one last nod then walked away.

"Okay," Ramsey started, pinning me with his blue eyes. "Do you want to tell the class what that was about?"

Lake whacked him in the chest. "She's already late, arsehole," he whispered. "We'll see you at the meeting, Gin."

He grabbed Ramsey by the front of the shirt and started dragging him away.

I could hear Ramsey's, "I just wanted to know what happened."

And Lake's responded, "*I* can tell you what happened, you muppet."

I sighed, straightened the strap of my bag, and plodded to Maths to meet Rica. It was thankfully our last lesson of the day, and she could tell I needed that when I walked into the room and sidled into my chair.

"Your afternoon go swimmingly then, did it?" she asked me as we left at the end of the day.

I shrugged. "It was going fine until I literally ran into Lake and Ramsey–"

"I thought we liked them?"

"No. We do like them. If you'd let me finish…" I nudged her with my hip as we walked.

"Sorry," she chuckled. "Finish then."

"Right, so that was fine – obvs–"

"Obvs," she agreed.

"But the Eli found them."

"Ah."

"Yeah."

"How'd it go?"

I shrugged. "Weird?"

"As expected."

"Well yeah, I guess. But like, not pleasant or anything."

Rica snorted. "I was *not* suggesting that awkwardly running into the man of your dreams who you also totally rejected was going to be pleasant."

"He is not the man of my dreams."

"I see your lips moving and the words coming out, but I'm convinced it's ventriloquism."

"I thought you were supposed to be supportive? Wind in my sails and all that."

"Like Bow said, that's her job."

"Oh, so you're like the safety rudder?" I frowned. "If that's a thing."

"I don't think it is. And even if it was, no."

"What does that make you then?"

Rica puffed her chest out proudly. "I'm like that magic compass that steers you to your deepest desire, except you think your real desire is one thing so you resist my direction all the time."

"Uh huh. And where do I get my refund on that dud?" I teased.

Rica threw her arms around my shoulders as we walked into the auditorium, looking around as Milly directed the guys up on the ladders hanging the fairy lights and tulle.

"I was a gift, brought to you upon the rough seas of life, to see you through the storms that batter your poor little craft as you're forced to ride out the plunging waves with only–"

"Are you plotting a painting now. Because this is getting weirdly specific and just wee bit dark."

"I wasn't. But now that you mention it, I'll put that down on my holiday to-do list."

"I'm so pleased my great blunder has fuelled your craft," I said sarcastically.

"At least we don't have to be starving artists now," she said as she dropped her bag and started putting her hair up.

"What? What does that have to do with anything?"

"I did tell you. A lack of money or some horribly traumatising experience." She shrugged. "Trauma, it is."

I rolled my eyes at her. "Eli's not a…" I stopped.

"Ye-es?" she pressed.

"He's not a trauma. An experience, yes. A trauma, no."

"That sounds deliciously dirty. Did you withhold some details from me, Miss Cowan?"

I huffed as I took my annoyance out on the tree with the staple gun. "No."

"You tell me why that tree did to you, miss, and I'll see to it he doesn't bother anyone else."

I turned to Lake, my eyebrows raised in disbelief. "Really?"

He shrugged and suddenly looked a little self-conscious as well as defensive. "I'm not good with this stuff, Gin. Give me a break." He turned a somewhat self-deprecating half-smile on me.

"Sorry. I just—"

As I went to half-heartedly bat the tree, I missed spectacularly and my hand smacked into Govi's face.

"Oh my God, Chloe," Ella called out. "Watch what you're doing."

"At least she's working," one of 'Ella's volunteers' said as she passed with one of the finished trees, then looked up quickly as though she was surprised she'd said anything out loud.

I tried to fight a snigger but I couldn't do it with Ella's look of outrage in front of me, so I turned around and remembered Govi.

"I am so sorry," I said to him.

He stretched his jaw out as though I'd given him my best shot, then he grinned. "Nah. All good. Was barely a tickle."

"In that case, Gabriel, could you help me with this tree please?" Ella asked, sounding bored. "The forest won't finish itself and Chloe *is* so useful with a staple gun."

Govi and I exchanged a knowing look before he jogged over to help Ella.

We were getting all the trees in place when Milly clapped her hands.

"Okay, people. This is our last official meeting. If I can just have your attention while we finish working."

"We're almost all sorted and everything is looking amazing. I'd like to give a huge thank you to you all for giving up your afternoons, and to those of you who gave up their lunch times for ticket sales. I'll do all this properly tomorrow night, but…"

Milly smiled at me warmly and my stomach dropped in expectation of what she was about to say. "I would like to extend a particular thanks to Chloe Cowan for her dedication, her tireless efforts, her outstanding creativity…" Milly paused, looking around at the gathered members of the committee pointedly. "And for stepping up and helping out just because Ella couldn't be bothered to show."

I wasn't the only one who gasped. My gasp though was one of dread surprise Milly had actually had the gall to come out and say it. There were other gasps of surprise, as well as a gasp of indignation from Ella and Lindy at the very least.

"How dare you," Lindy snapped.

"How dare I?" Milly asked. "How dare I what, Lindy? How dare I speak the truth about Ella Cowan?"

"You've always just been jealous of Ella," Lindy said as Ella just sat back and waited for other people to stick up for her.

"That doesn't make her wrong," Matt said slowly and Ella whirled on him quickly. He shrugged. "What? Chloe's been here since day one, basically. She's turned up, she's done the hard work–"

"She's kept these arseholes in line," Ramsey added as though he wasn't one of those arseholes, lovable or not.

"She's actually helped us when we needed it," the girl who'd been working with Matt the other day said.

"She's nice," Brenda said with a nod.

Ella looked around and laughed. "Seriously?"

There were a few hesitant faces, and mine was bright red out of nerves and embarrassment and just feeling totally weirded out about the turn of events.

"Elijah…" Ella tried. "Tell them."

Eli shrugged. "Tell them what, Ella?"

"Tell them Chloe's nobody."

Eli grimaced. "I… I can't do that. Chloe's not nobody."

"What?" Ella asked. "She's just Chloe."

Eli nodded. "Yeah. She is."

Ella's laugh was completely covering for a lack of confidence. "Are you saying you prefer my sister?"

"I'm saying that Chloe put in a lot of effort to make *your* formal happen. That's all."

My stomach flipped, but I told myself it was for the best.

Ella straightened herself up and flicked her hair back. "Well, of course. And thank you, Chloe."

A few people fell for the routine, presumably finding it easier to ignore the behaviour that went against their view of Ella. But there were those who had obviously seen Ella for the person she was and weren't going to forgive her quite so easily.

"Yes. Thank you, Chloe," Milly said.

I nodded. "Uh, it's…fine. I'm glad I could help." I nodded again, willing myself to stop being awkward but failing spectacularly.

"And let's keep on, people!" Milly cried, with another hand clap.

I spent the rest of the meeting avoiding the apologetic looks from Eli and the harsh glares from Ella and Lindy, but at least he Wicked Bitch and her minion were pulling their weight for once. Which not only served to keep them busy from being able to talk to me, but also seemed to serve to help a few more people forget the dressing down Ella had received.

But I wouldn't forget.

****

Norbert's head nuzzled against my leg as he rearranged in his sleep and I patted him absently.

After school, I'd gone by the auditorium and had one final look over the formal preparations. The tables were in, the fairy lights were in place, the forest looked enchanted, and the dance floor looked ready to see some action. It was bittersweet, but gave me some ideas for the next year if I felt courageous enough to put myself forward for head of the 2020 Formal Committee as Milly suggested.

I'd then come home and done what I did most Friday nights; lock (not literally) myself in my room with a book while my sister and parents ignored me (and each other if I'm honest) and Norbert kept me company. Although that night, Ella was at another popular girl's house to get ready before the Before Party.

Govi and Rica had promised to send me all the pictures during the night because they were convinced that I secretly wanted to go. Rica should have known I'd be perfectly happy with my book, but Govi wasn't having a bar of it. And I thought it was absolutely adorable that Rica was siding with Govi in that fight. For the record, she did not like this and I got a whack for my giggles.

Norbert whined and I couldn't tell if he was complaining I'd stopped patting him, was having a dream, or if he was wondering if there was a noise outside that required his attention.

I ruffled his ears one more time, then hopped up for a toilet break.

I paused as I walked back to my room.

"…goodness sake, Arlo!" That was Super-G.

I vaguely wondered why she was over, but it was normal that when she and my father were in a room that she was exasperated with him.

"Don't tut at me, Mum," Dad replied.

"You've got two incredible daughters! Two of them! And you choose to foster the ego of one to the detriment of the real talent."

"Ella needs the encouragement, Mum," Dad huffed and I paused to listen to the conversation.

"She needs encouragement like I need a shot to the head," came Aunt Bow's voice. "Gin, on the other–"

"Gin doesn't need encouragement, Rainbow," Dad said testily.

"My foot she doesn't," came Aunt Bow's voice. "She tiptoes around–"

"What Gin does as naturally as breathing, Ella has had to work hard for."

"So she deserves all the praise? Because, what? Gin's a natural?" Aunt Bow scoffed.

"I wouldn't expect you to understand–"

"With all due respect, Mr Cowan…" That was Lake's voice, cutting in clear and calm through the emotions of the adults.

Super-G and Aunt Bow made sense, b why was Lake at my house?

I padded over to the bannister and looked into the void. It wasn't just Lake at my house. It was Lake and Govi and Rica and Ramsey. The boys were all in suits – Ramsey in full black of course with Docs and a stud belt, Lake in a far more traditional black and white tuxedo, and Govi in white suit pants with a green velvet jacket, and black shirt with, naturally, green Converse and a top hat. And Erica Gorman! She was in a floaty tulle skirt and cropped singlet ensemble in a dark, dusky pink. She completed the look with soft wisps of hair escaping the paintbrush she was using as a hair clip.

"Remind me who you are?" Dad said.

"Lake Walton–"

"The bass player for Quicksilver," Rica added and I fought a very loud snort.

"For what?" Dad asked.

"That band from Winters, Arlo!" Aunt Bow sighed.

"The band?" Dad asked, then blinked. "The famous ones?"

"Semi-famous, at best," Govi said.

"And you are?"

"Gabriel Costa, drummer extraordinaire."

"I see." Dad looked him over, then turned to Ramsey. "And you?"

"Ramsey Power, guitar and–"

"Your last name's Power?" I couldn't stop myself shouting as I leant over the rail.

Everyone looked up at me in various states of pleasure. Or lack thereof.

"What?" Ramsey said, shuffling his feet self-consciously. "It's my name."

"Your friends are here, Chloe," my dad said. "And others." He looked at his mother and sister.

"What are you guys doing here?" I asked.

"I was just trying to ascertain that myself."

"We're here to take you to the formal," Lake said.

I shook my head as I started backing away from the rail. "I said I wasn't going."

"Gin!" Aunt Bow called, then she appeared up the stairs, followed by the slightly less elegant Rica. "Baby, if this is about that boy–"

"It's about that boy," Rica interrupted.

I rolled my eyes. "It's not about a boy. It's about me not wanting to go."

"Bullshit," Rica said.

"You put in so much work, Gingernut."

I shrugged. "So? I'll get to go next year."

"Or you could go this year," Rica said, pulling a garment bag from behind her skirts.

I frowned at her. "If that's for me…"

Rica shrugged unapologetically. "Then you'd have to go or look like a totally ungrateful bitch."

I sighed and stormed into my room. Norbert looked up from his place on my bed.

"Some guard dog, you are," I grumbled.

"Hiya, Norb," Aunt Bow cooed at him as Rica hung the bag up and unzipped it.

"Everyone wants you there–"

"Except me and like all but about four people," I said.

"Come on. Whip those clothes off. On with the dress."

Rica pulled it out of the bag and it came in two pieces. As in, intended to come in two pieces.

"Is this the year of the bare midriffs?" I asked Rica sceptically.

She grinned and patted hers. "I can't be all exposed on my own."

"I guess I'm meant to consider myself lucky mine doesn't have the plunging neckline?"

Rica nodded. "Yes. At least you can wear a bra with yours." She winked and I doubted she much cared if she was wearing a bra or not. Not that she needed it with her stupid naturally perky boobs.

"A strapless. The most uncomfortable of all bras."

Rica's finger went to her chin. "Oh yeah. The worst of the worst…"

"Thank you. I guess." It was all sarcasm and she knew it.

Rica shrugged, swishing her skirt around her legs. "In an effort to make sure you looked smokin' hot, I may not have considered lingerie. I'm sorry."

"Underwear, at best," I said, trying to stifle my smirk.

"Just get dressed," Aunt Bow said. "The boys are on at eight."

"What do you know about it?" I asked.

"Oh, baby. I know *everything*," she said.

"*Everything*," Rica agreed with a wink.

I sighed. "I'm not getting out of this, am I?"

344

"Terribly inconvenient time for her to go and get some lady balls and stop doing what she's told," Rica muttered in what was definitely supposed to be overheard.

Aunt Bow snorted. "Terribly inconvenient. Go and find her nice shoes and I'll fix her hair."

"My hair is fine, thank you," I told her.

Aunt Bow shook her head and pointed to my desk chair. "Sit."

I rolled my eyes as I dropped into it. "Fine. But no makeup." I saw her look before she spun me around and amended, "Minimal makeup."

"No promises."

Aunt Bow had never been gentle with a brush and that night was no exception. But I just winced and grimaced through it while Rica found some music to put on and danced around the room.

I went from hair to makeup to putting on my dress in twenty minutes, which goes to show how simple Aunt Bow thankfully kept the whole thing. Rica finally flourished my 'nice' shoes – being one of my only pairs of heels – and then they both pulled me in front of the mirror.

"Well?" Rica asked, bouncing on her toes.

I nodded. "It could be worse."

And it could. It was a dark blue, off the shoulder cropped top made of glittery material and the skirt was multilayered

345

tulle that nowhere near as wild as Rica's skirt. It went well with my silver heels and didn't clash horribly with my strawberry hair. It even made my blue eyes pop. Or that could have been the eyeliner Aunt Bow had slathered on.

"You look…" Aunt Bow kissed her fingers. "Gorgeous."

I fluffed the skirt and nodded. "Okay. Fine. I feel it."

Aunt Bow and Rica squealed as they hugged me. Then I was dragged downstairs again where the boys were standing around awkwardly as Super-G, Mum and Dad sat awkwardly in the front room.

"Ta-da!" Aunt Bow said and everyone looked at me.

I looked at them hesitantly. "This really wasn't necessary."

"Pfft!" Govi waved away my words. "After all the work you did? It's the least we could do."

"No," Lake said. "The least we could have done was leave her home alone with her book while all her friends were out having fun."

"Books are fun!" I objected. "And it's not too late."

My eyes caught Mum and Dad and I looked down as I cleared my throat.

"Shall we go, then?" I asked, and started ushering everyone out who wasn't related to me.

The filed out with a smile and a wink.

I looked at Super-G, who was giving me a warm smile, then to my parents who were…looking at me in a way they never had before. I coughed and pointed to the door.

"I should… I'll see you tomorrow." I nodded and headed out as well.

"Uh, Chloe…" my dad said and I turned to see he, Mum, Aunt Bow and Super-G had followed us to the front door.

"I know. I'll be home by one."

Dad looked taken aback for a moment. "Actually, I was just going to say you look beautiful."

Mum nodded, hanging onto Dad's arm like it was the only thing keeping her up. "You do, Chloe. Amazing."

I felt Rica pause beside me and I had no idea what to say. I couldn't remember the last time either of my parents had given me a compliment. Looking back on it, I wasn't confident enough to say it had never happened. I just couldn't have said when it had.

"Have a good night."

Just as I closed the door, I heard Super-G's chastising, "You say that like it's never happened before."

I'm ~~not~~ gonna write you a love song

I stumbled to a stop at the curb and laughed. "Of course you got a limo."

Lake smiled as he put his arm around me and bundled me forwards. "Of course we got a limo."

"Gotta begin as we intend to go on, Gin!" Govi said.

"Is Eli meeting you there?" I asked as we all slid into our seats and the others froze. I huffed in annoyance. "What? I don't even get to mention him now? You all expect me to be friends with you and think he's not going to come up?"

The boys all looked at each other and nodded.

"Fair," Ramsey admitted.

"Yes. He's meeting us there," Lake answered.

"He…uh…was going to back out… With Ella," Govi said.

"Doesn't like going back on his word," Lake finished.

"He's a good dude when it comes down to it," Ramsey said, clearing his throat.

I looked at them. "Is this some misguided attempt to get the two of us together?"

"No."

"Definitely not."

"Why would you think that?"

"Really not."

"We know better than that."

"Out of curiosity, would it have worked?"

I smiled. "I appreciate the loyalty. But Eli didn't say the wrong thing, I didn't mistake him hooking up with someone else, he didn't break my heart or anything…" I shrugged.

"So what's the problem?" Govi asked.

Not wanting to go into all the details, I remembered something Eli had said to me. "Maybe I'm just not the right girl for the right guy?"

"And do we have an ETA on when you will be the right girl, or…?" Govi petered off and Lake patted his knee.

"Leave her be, mate," he said softly, giving me a sad smile.

"Yeah," Ramsey added. "It's not like we have to choose between them."

"If we ever do, can I get Gin in the divorce?" Lake asked.

Ramsey nodded. "Yes."

But Govi looked less sure. "If you get her, do we all get her?"

"Then who gets Eli?" Rica asked.

"You?" Govi offered.

They squabbled about who they'd get in the divorce if any number of people broke up – some they knew, most of them they didn't and that was because apparently Ramsey's life partner had yet to be built – the rest of the way to school.

Govi helped Rica out of the limo like a true gentleman, then Lake and Ramsey fake fought over who was going to help me out. While they were busy, I helped myself.

"This damsel doesn't need rescuing," I told them and they both whistled in appreciation.

"I can get behind that," Lake said.

"Little class, please mate," Ramsey chastised with a chuckle as we followed Govi and Rica inside.

"After you," I told them, taking a little bow and pointing inside.

"Why thank you." Lake curtseyed and Ramsey nodded.

I let them lead, giving myself a moment to just enjoy the whole thing in its proper glory, and it was just as I'd pictured it.

The trees lining the walkway were shrouded in partial shadows and dappled light, making Rica's knots look like little faces peering out at you. The glitter sparkled as though the whole forest was full of magic. The fairy lights and tulle above our heads spread that magic out further.

Once we got through the forest – pausing for our entrance photo, of course – the room opened up with the rectangle tables down each side, full of drinks and snacks that were presided over by the teachers. The round tables were set up towards the back with the chairs around them for if people wanted to sit and chat. The stage was set up with instruments for the band and a DJ booth was sitting in front of it. And of course there was a big space under the disco ball for the dance floor where people were already dancing.

"Oh my God," I laughed as I looked around.

"It looks pretty freaking awesome, huh?" Ramsey said.

"It wouldn't look half as good without you," Lake said.

"Hey, I did a lot of helping with that forest," Govi said, appearing beside us.

Lake swatted Govi's top hat off, but he caught it and glared at Lake.

"I was trying to give her a compliment," Lake said by way of explanation.

"I don't think she's interested in you…" Govi hissed in a terribly unsubtle stage-whisper as he walked by.

And he wasn't wrong.

Because I'd just spotted Eli and he looked amazing.

He didn't cut nearly as suave a figure as Lake did. He wasn't ahead of his time like Govi. And he wasn't half-heartedly sticking it to the man like Ramsey. He wore a simple black suit, a white shirt, black dress shoes, and one of those really thin ties that never seemed to be able to be tied properly.

But it didn't matter what clothes he was wearing. All that mattered was that smile he was wearing as Govi strutted over to him. Eli stole Govi's hat out of his arms and tried it on, and I saw he was still wearing his silver rings though.

"Boys, you about ready to go on?" Paul, one of the music teachers, asked as he appeared next to us.

Lake nodded as Ramsey started stretching his neck and bouncing on his toes.

"You want us up there now?" Lake asked.

Paul nodded towards Eli and Govi. "Get those two and make your way over."

Lake nodded again. Ramsey was quite clearly in some sort of zone.

"We'll see you lovely ladies later," Lake said.

Rica punched him on the arm enthusiastically. "Break a leg!"

"Any limb will do." Lake grinned, then smacked Ramsey on the chest. "Come on, Lord of the Dance. Let's nab us a monkey and a wanker."

"Show time," Ramsey grunted and I wasn't going to judge whatever pre-show rituals the dude had.

As they left, Rica and I sidled closer to one of the snack tables so we could pick at the offerings while Rica watched Govi do his thing.

We lost sight of the four of them as they made their way to the stage, then they were there in the spotlights, instruments in hand, and personas in place.

Govi was much the same as he always was; exuberant, warm, in his favourite place on earth. Ramsey was cocky and brooding, with a determined glint in his eyes that was only offset by the half-smirk. Lake was cool, calm, collected, the picture of emotionless sophistication. And Eli. Their frontman was all sexy charm, with a smile made for trouble and the easy body language of someone who belonged up there.

"Good evening, Winters Class of 2019!" Eli cried and there was whooping and cheering and screaming. "We've got some of your favourites for you tonight, as well as something just a little bit different. So hold on to your corsages, button those lapels, and find yourself someone to share it with. We're Quicksilver and we're going to–"

"Rock your world!" chorused through the auditorium just before the boys started their first song.

It was a good set. As promised, there were covers and there were the band's original songs that almost everyone in the crowd knew word for word. Rica and I swapped between eating and dancing, but we had to just watch and laugh as Ramsey and Lake had a battle of the Aussie pub songs, complete with crowd voting. In the end, it was very difficult to work out who had won and no one seemed to mind.

"It's time for a new one now, guys," Ramsey announced, and it looked like he was having trouble keeping the smile off his face. "If it sounds like we only learnt it in the last few days, that's because we did." He grinned and there was a smattering of laughter through the auditorium as they started playing. "This one's for all you lovebirds out there. We don't want to see any room for the Holy Ghost!"

It sounded similar to the one Eli had played me the day we first kissed. Similar if it had had four brains pouring over it to polish it. It was like any other Quicksilver song, but also not quite. I had to admit I tuned out a little, even if I was subconsciously bopping along with it.

"Yeah, I'm not sure that worked," Govi said into his microphone as the boys repeated the last few bars of the previous song.

Lake shrugged as he looked at Eli and moved closer to his mic. "We might have to get super corny, dude."

Eli shrugged dramatically. "Aw, shucks. And I left my piano at home."

Ramsey disappeared off stage as they kept repeating those last few bars and I wondered what in the hell they were doing. It had to be said, those boys had brilliant stage presence, even if they were being a little weird.

"That's okay," Govi said. "Here's one we prepared earlier." He played a 'ba dum tush' on his drums in the middle of the repeating bars and there was some laughter here and there.

Ramsey came back on stage, 'helping' a few guys push a piano onto the stage.

"What are they doing?" I asked Rica.

She shrugged and made a very noncommittal, "I dunno," sort of noise.

"I dunno, guys," Eli said. "Do they even want a slow song?"

The gathered students cheered in answer to his question.

"Yeah, but – like – *we* wrote this one," Eli said, acting surprised.

There was another cheer and a few people yelled unintelligible things.

"I think they want it, dude," Ramsey said.

"Make a choice either way," Lake added. "This base line is getting mighty tedious, man."

More scattered laughter from the students.

Eli shrugged again. "All right. All right. I'll do it."

Govi drummed out a flourish as Lake used his smooth, deep voice to announce, "All right, everyone. Grab that special someone and hold them tight. We're about to get a little mushy on you."

They moved almost seamlessly into position – Eli at the piano and the others disappearing off stage – as though they'd practised it a tonne of times.

"Be gentle with me, we're trying something new," Eli laughed into the microphone, then started playing.

I recognised it instantly as the piece he'd played me the other day, but a little different. Like the other piece, it was more polished. As far as melodies went, it was similar to 'Piano Man' or Stephen Speaks' 'Out of My League'. It was a sweet piano piece with a tune you wanted to remember and whose chorus you could sing along to by the end of it. And the way the couples in the room swayed to it, smiling wistfully at their partner, it looked like it was going to be a hit when *Quicksilver* finally landed that record deal.

But it wasn't until the second verse that I started to sense there was something else going on with the lyrics. Super-G was the one to blame for any connections I came up with, but the mention of 'Alabama' so close to 'Four Pillars' had my mind whirring.

"What was that?" I asked, grabbing hold of Rica's arm.

"What was what?" she replied unhelpfully.

"Slam…Alabama…" I muttered. "Four pillars…" My eyes went wide and shot to Eli, heading into the third verse. "Alabama slammer?"

"I need you more than Danny needs Sandy…" Eli sang.

"A pink lady?" I wondered, then looked at Rica. "It can't be…"

"Can't be what?" she asked coyly, but the smile she was trying and failing to suppress told me I wasn't wrong.

I listened to the rest of the song and even if I was making it up, it made sense. Especially when the last lines were, "Just let me see those sapphire eyes. Don't let the last word be 'it's over…'"

Damn Super-G and her obsession with all things gin.

"Sapphire… Bombay…" I breathed. "Oh my God."

"We have a winner, ladies and gentleman," Rica whispered.

As the last chords of the piano faded out, Ramsey and Lake started up with their guitars.

"That was Eli and our entry into the illustrious halls of corny with 'Gin Fizz'," Ramsey announced with a wink and my breathing went from heavy to hyperventilating.

I didn't even have a chance to be excited, I was too busy looking for Ella and hoping I could escape without her making a scene. I spared one last look up at Eli, whose eyes had just found me, then I hiked up my skirts and did my best

357

attempt at a runner, Victorian novel heroine style. All I needed were some shrouded moors and I was set.

"Gin!" Rica called after me, but I ignored her.

Thanks to her, the people around us started muttering. It didn't take an inordinate amount of brains to work out that a song called 'Gin Fizz' plus a swiftly vacating person labelled 'Gin' was probably connected.

If only Ramsey hadn't told them the title of the song...

"Chloe!" I heard behind me, but it couldn't have been him because the band were still playing.

But the hand that caught my arm and turned me around was definitely attached to Eli Sweet.

I looked around. "What are you doing?" I hissed, ripping my arm out of his grasp.

"I'm not caring anymore. I'm taking a leap. Take your pick."

"Oh God," I muttered. Because of course people were watching us. Eli freaking Sweet just sang a song presumably written for me and had then run after me.

"You're not some stand-in, Clo," he said adamantly. "You're Chloe Cowan. You sing and you dance, you're terrible with a texta but amazing at papier-mâché. You play piano and guitar, and you're *good*. But you're not just good, you enjoy playing. At least you would if you let yourself. You're kind and funny and wicked smart and constantly

358

putting other people's needs before your own." He looked at me, beseeching me. "You don't have to do the opposite of what people want you to do to be free. Being free is being the person you are in your heart, however that person was made."

"Eli…" I begged, really not wanting to do this here.

"Chloe!" I could hear Ella calling as she pushed her way through the crowd of people. "Chloe!" she cried again as she practically fell out of the last row of people before us looking like a pale blue marshmallow with a tiara that was threatening to fall off. "What is going on here?"

"I'm trying to convince your sister to give me a proper shot," Eli told her and I think that was the first time both Ella and I were I sync.

Both our mouths dropped open as we stared at him. But he was completely unabashed, unapologetic, and unfazed.

"Eli!" I hissed angrily. Standing up for me generally in a room full of people was one thing. This… This was another.

"You what?" Ella spat.

Eli shrugged. "Sorry, Ella. But I think I'm a little bit in love with Chloe."

My hand flew to my mouth and I wasn't sure if it was pure shock or I was trying to hold in some kind of retort.

"You what?" Ella spat again. "Her?"

359

Eli just nodded. "Yeah, her."

"Why would you be interested in her?"

Eli shrugged again and looked around. "I don't know, Ella. Maybe because she's not a pretentious drama queen who sends other people to woo a guy."

Ella only spluttered in response.

Eli nodded. "What did you think was going to happen?" he asked. "Did you really not foresee that I'd fall for the girl who was actually there, right in front of me and real?"

"But… But… It's Chloe!" Ella whined.

Eli nodded again and turned a leg-melting smile on me. "Yes, it is."

"Ugh!" Ella humphed, stamped her foot, then stormed away.

Eli was still looking at me – me! – like all his dreams had come true. Once again in slow motion, he reached one hand towards me.

"May I have this dance?" he asked.

I looked around and saw everyone was still watching us.

On one hand, I wanted to dance with him. But, on the other…

"Can we…?" I paused and cleared my throat. "Can we not do this entirely in front of your whole year?" I asked him.

360

He finally looked around. "Ah…" He nodded once. "Yep. Sure." He grinned and waved at everyone then took my hand and pulled me out to the corridor.

We almost got out without too much fanfare but, just as the door was closing behind us, I heard Govi yell, "Give her a kiss, Eli!" and my cheeks flamed super-hot.

"Clo, I–"

"Eli, you can't just write me a song–"

"Two songs, actually. Not counting the one Gove has in the works."

I sighed. "Regardless. You can't get up on a stage and sing me some song full of cringe-worthy gin references and think it changes things?"

"Did you not hear everything else I said?" he asked.

I nodded. "Yes. But this isn't some fairy-tale romance where I'm just yet to believe I'm worthy of your love or whatever."

"Then what is it? Because either I've completely lost my mind or there's the potential for something real here. And I'm not talking about the kind of real where we do the happily for now ending and then fade into obscurity. I mean *real*, Chloe."

I sighed in frustration. "There's more to life than that."

"Than what? Something real? What else is there? Because if you've found some higher power, then I think you could probably market that quite nicely."

"Just!" I grunted. "There's more to life than defining who you are by who you're with. I'm more than Ella's sister, than your girlfriend, that Rica's friend. I'm Chloe Cowan and I'm my own damn person."

"You think I don't know that?" he asked. "I don't just want you to be Eli's girlfriend. I want to be Chloe's boyfriend. I want to be two separate and amazing people, coming together and creating something epic–"

"I don't want to play second anymore, Eli!" I interrupted. "I just crawled out of one shadow, I don't want to fall under yours."

"Clo…" he said softly, taking a step towards me. "I would never–"

The door opened and Old Tom the English teacher walked out. "Let's break it… Oh…" He looked between us. "This is not what I expected to find…"

"Were you expecting something a little more explicitly rated?" Eli asked him calmly.

Old Tom nodded. "Yes. But…" He pointed between us. "Attempted negotiation?"

Eli and I both nodded and said, "Yes," in unison.

"Right. So sorry to interrupt. Just…if this ends favourably… Can we celebrate back inside with a dance rather than a heavy petting session?"

"No long-winded metaphor?" Eli asked.

Old Tom shook his head. "No. I suspect you two will exchange plenty of words to make up for it." He nodded once more, then slipped back into the auditorium.

Eli looked back at me. "What was I saying?"

"I don't remember, but it doesn't matter. You don't get what you want just because you want it."

Eli huffed. "No. I don't. If I did, you'd have fallen for me too and you'd be here with me instead of Lake."

"I'm not here with Lake."

"You know what I mean. Shadows!" he said triumphantly. "I was talking about shadows. Right. Look, I get I wasn't in your grand plan. I'm looking for a life like Ella is and you want anything but that. And I wouldn't dare to suggest I'd ever put you above my dreams because I know how you'd feel about that. But why can't we have both? You wouldn't be in my shadow, you'd be beside me. Every step of the way." He tilted his head and amended, "As far as you want to go."

"And if this is as far as I want to go?"

He swallowed. "If this is really it, then okay. Tell me this is the end of the line and I'll go back onstage and let you go back to your life."

I opened my mouth to tell him that was it, the end of the line. But I couldn't. And he seemed to know it.

"I'm not going to say I'm never going to be a dick. I'm not going to say you won't have to put me in my place a million times. Probably in the next week alone. And I'm not going to say that I'll be easy to live with. But I will say that I really like you, Chloe. Like a crazy amount. And I would really like to give us a proper shot. No mean older sisters with crazy-arsed agendas getting in the way."

Everything in me was pulled in two different directions. I wanted so badly to be as far away as possible from anything resembling a shadow again. But I also couldn't bring myself to tell him that. I opened my mouth, hoping the words would just come. But they didn't.

"I… Can I have some time to think about it?" I asked him slowly.

His smile was hesitant, but he nodded. "Take all the time you need."

I nodded. "Thanks."

"If you're thinking, does that mean I can't dance with you?"

I looked up at him quickly.

"Just as friends. With our other friends. No pressure for anything else." He leant towards me conspiratorially. "It's just… I think my date might have left me."

I bit my life against a smile and gave him a nod. "As friends. With friends."

"Exactly," he said.

We shared one more unnecessary and awkward nod, then moved back inside.

The rest of Quicksilver were off the stage and the DJ was back in the saddle. I wasn't sure if the band had some sort of code, but no one said anything about anything I didn't want to talk about. The rest of the year were a little less inquisitive. Not that anyone said anything to my face.

Most of the Year Twelves hadn't been on the formal committee so most of them didn't know who Rica and I were. They were probably all wondering who this girl was who'd somehow not only stolen the spotlight from Ella Cowan, but also the attentions of Elijah Sweet.

But we didn't let that get in the way of a good night out with good friends.

Will the real leading lady, please stand up

Norbert breathed out heavily and I nodded. "I agree."

I heard his tail thump on the bed and flung an arm out to scratch him. But Norbert couldn't help me work out what I was going to do. Only I could do that. And I could only do that by looking long and hard at myself. Which, let's face it, no one likes to do.

But despite all my reservations, I hadn't been able to tell Eli that was the end of the line for me. All the noise clamouring in my head said it was, and yet I couldn't do it. I couldn't completely sever that thread.

So I had to look at why.

"It's time to get real, Norb," I told him. "Okay? We need a step forward or an ending. No more pussyfooting about."

Norbert whined what I chose to think was encouragement and I took one more breath in an attempt to find the courage I needed to be totally honest with myself.

Thankfully, Norbert had always been a good sounding board.

"All the nonsense about playing second to Eli's life is ridiculous," I told him. "There, I've said it. If I'm going to let myself be open to going into the Arts after all, I can't be all precious about him already knowing that's what he wants to do."

Norbert whined again.

"I know. I know. Commerce or Arts. That's a whole different problem. But one at a time." I paused and tried to remember what I'd been saying. "I just need to give myself permission to want to do music, if that's what I want to do. I mean, I'll know it's because I've chosen to rather than because I've been told to. So no more running away from the things Ella wants. And If I do that, why couldn't it work out with Eli?"

Norbert's whine was more unsure this time and I turned my head to look at him.

"No. Ella's not a problem." I huffed and looked back at the ceiling as I amended, "No more than usual. I don't care what she'll say or whatever crazy bullshit thing she might do if I openly like Eli. I have zero reasons to be loyal to her, even when it comes to boys."

Another whine, a little more optimistic this time.

"Right. So putting aside that and the fact I can't use my personal distaste for Eli's dreams as an excuse anymore…" I took another deep breath. "And that I need to learn not to be afraid to go after what I want…"

The whine this time sounded like a question.

"What's stopping me from being with Eli?"

I looked at Norbert and I felt very judged.

"Me," I admitted and Norbert's tail thump made me feel a little bit better about that. "I'm stopping me from being with Eli."

And for no good reason.

I was still scared of what the future might bring, of what or who I'd turn into, of looking back and realising I'd made mistakes I may not be able to fix.

But even fear wasn't a good reason not to live.

All my fears could happen whether I was with Eli or not. They could happen because of another guy, because of a friend, because of a child. They could even happen because of me trying so hard to not become what I thought other people expected that I'd do anything else.

So why not be with Eli? Why not be happy now? Why not make music now? Why not…

My phone vibrated, distracting me out of the circle of questioning that would quite possibly have never ended otherwise. I picked it up and saw a message from Govi. It was an audio clip after the words, 'Snagged this in rehearsals.'

Curious, I clicked on it.

Nothing happened.

I hit pause, rewound it and started it again.

Still nothing.

I went out of the clip and back in.

Still nothing.

I hit the volume button completely by accident and went bright red as I realised I'd muted media on my phone.

I looked at Norbert in warning. "Take that to your grave."

I took his answered tail thump as an agreement and turned my attention back to the audio clip. I opened Govi's chat and hit play again.

There was a bunch of laughter and chatter I recognised as Eli, Lake, Ramsey and Govi.

"Yeah, but are you going to tell her?" Ramsey asked.

There was the twang of a guitar, then Eli's voice. "What exactly am I supposed to tell her to make her change her mind?"

"How about that you're hopelessly in love with her and she's changed you," Lake offered.

"Yeah. I don't think that one's gonna work, fellas," Eli huffed.

369

"Did you try that already?"

"No, I didn't…" There was a pause. "Me telling her how I feel isn't going to change anything."

"How else is she supposed to know?" Govi asked.

There was another pause and some background noise I couldn't place. "Same way I know how she feels. She knows, man. But if that's not enough, then there's nothing I can do but hope I haven't lost her friendship, too."

"Okay, but are you sure you shouldn't tell her? Because in all the movies, he tells her, man," Ramsey said and I huffed a laugh at how earnest he sounded.

"Can we just get back to practising?" Eli asked.

"Just tell her once," Lake pressed.

"Dude! I *think* that counts as harassment."

"Okay," Govi said brightly. "Then do 'Gin Fizz' tomorrow at the formal."

"She's not going."

"Do it anyway."

"If you wankers are up to something…"

"Just promise you'll do 'Gin Fizz'," Ramsey said.

Eli groaned. "Fine! I'll do the bloody song. Can we get on, please? For a song you say you're so excited about, we are far from getting it down."

"It's catchy," Lake said as though that justified it.

"Gove, you recording?" Eli asked.

"You know it."

"Count us in."

"One, two, three, four."

I was about to close it down when I heard a song they'd played at the formal. The new one they'd apparently only learnt the week before. I liked it as much as I'd liked it that night, but this time the lyrics jumped out at me. Lyrics like 'rose-gold hair', and 'playboy rock god wannabe', and 'say something' and 'if it was only a kiss'.

"Only a kiss," I breathed, sitting up violently and freaking both me and Norbert out in the process. "Only a kiss. Two songs." I looked at Norbert. "This was the other song."

Norbert looked thoroughly unimpressed, although that could have been me projecting my self-consciousness onto him.

"It wasn't that," I told him just in case. "I'd already decided. Remember? I'm not just going to go ridiculous because a cute boy wrote me a song."

Norbert huffed.

"Two songs," I agreed.

"Chloe, are you ready?" I heard Mum call through my door.

"Yeah. Just a second," I replied, swinging myself off my bed, grabbing my bag and heading down to the car.

I'd spent the last two weeks of the holidays arguing with myself and Rica about Eli. Round and round the argument had gone until it had felt like one of those arguments even the best of friends couldn't come back from. But at that point, Rica had handed 'the problem' – being me, mainly – over to Aunt Bow and avoided any mention of it since.

We'd spent the time the way we usually did, watching movies and TV together but in our own bedrooms while we Skyped or messaged. When we saw each other, it was shopping or games or me trying to decide what my future held – with no mention of romantic entanglements.

A couple of times we hung out with the Quicksilver boys and Rica and Govi were adorably cute together in that awkward phase of not quite knowing how to act around each other. Neither Eli, I or anyone else mentioned the elephant in the room on these occasions but I still felt awkward about keeping Eli waiting.

Ella had only spoken to me when absolutely necessary in the last two weeks and it had been with as much disdain as ever. She wasn't going to forget that Eli hadn't actually wanted her, she wasn't going to forget she was basically a pity date, even if she pretended not to remember why. She'd busied herself with her fans– Sorry, friends and told anyone who'd listen that Eli was a shallow little boy she'd quickly outgrown.

Now that school was back, I wasn't looking forward to seeing how she dealt with everything.

It started well enough.

Ella pretended I didn't exist as she bound out of the house to Lindy's waiting car and I went to the car we in theory shared, but she never drove due to her belief that Somebodies didn't drive. Which suited me fine.

Ella pretended I didn't exist as we practically walked into the school building together. This also suited me fine.

Ella pretended I didn't exist while members of the formal committee whose names I'd forgotten came up to me and asked me how my holidays were, and again complimented the forest. I enjoyed watching her prove just how much I didn't exist to her.

Ella pretended I didn't exist when Lindy ran into me between classes and knocked all my books out of my hands. I let it go, knowing any scene I made, Ella would try to make it into how unfortunate I was. I wasn't going to be a doormat anymore, but I didn't have almost eighteen years' practise at stripping away every ounce of someone's self-worth with a single sentence.

Ella found it a little difficult to pretend I didn't exist when Eli and I ran into each other after their music lesson.

After spending the whole morning psyching myself up to give him an answer, I was ready for this. I was full of hope and optimism and courage.

I wasn't going to look to those bright neon lights in my future anymore. If I kept focussing on them then I'd miss out on life. I was going to live in the lights I created now. I was still terrified of what the future might hold, but denying what I felt for Eli only dimmed them, casting a different kind of shadow all of my own making.

I gave him a small, hesitant and terrified-in-the-face-of-actually-doing-it smile. "It was 'Only a Kiss'," popped out and he looked at me in despondent shock.

"What?" he breathed.

I shook my head. "The other song."

He blinked. "The other song?"

"That you wrote for me."

His confusion lifted and he nodded, a hesitantly hopeful smile spreading. "Yeah. It was."

I nodded. "I liked it."

He bit his lip like he wasn't sure what was happening but he liked it. "I'm glad."

A thought occurred to me. "Meet me in the auditorium after school?"

He looked me over, a slight tinge of confusion returning, but also curiosity. "Okay. I'll see you there."

I grinned and nodded before hurrying away.

It was difficult enough getting through a Monday afternoon, especially when it came after two weeks of lazy days. It was even more difficult when I was going to try to do some wooing of my own with two lessons still to go.

"What are you planning?" Rica asked.

I breathed out heavily. "A song?"

Rica nodded. "Yep. That makes sense."

"Piano."

"Anything else? Do you need a map?"

"To what?"

"Where the fingers go?"

I nudged her. "I don't know. What's good on piano?"

"Let's Google it."

It was amazing the number of things that popped up with a quick Google search.

'Good piano songs'.

Not very specific. But it did the job.

"Ha!" Rica said. "'Someone like you'! Adele's perfect."

"Is that not about the complete opposite of what we want to achieve?"

"Okay. How about… 'Love Me Like You Do'?"

"I don't know that one."

"Can you learn it?"

I looked up at the clock on the classroom wall. "In just over an hour… In a Maths lesson?" I asked her.

Rica nodded. "Yep. Nope. Gotcha."

We kept scrolling.

Suddenly, Rica's finger hit my phone screen and she looked utterly triumphant. "This one. You loved this one. I know you know it."

I looked at it and sighed. "It could work…"

"It's perfect!"

"It's a little…" I stopped to think of the right words. "It won't give the wrong impression?"

"He's a musician, he knows about metaphors."

"It's not really a metaphor, though. Is it?"

Rica waved away my trivial concerns. "Exaggeration, then. He gets exaggeration."

I sighed. "I do know it…"

"You do. And you love–"

"Girls, are we working?" the teacher asked.

"Yes," Rica replied, putting her arm over my phone.

The teacher stopped to look at us. "Really?"

Rica nodded. "Yep. Very focussed…on the…Maths."

The teacher looked unconvinced but didn't seem inclined to argue. I suspected after years of teaching Maths at a specialist Arts school, she'd given up the fight. Finally she moved away.

"So, it's agreed?" Rica hissed.

I breathed out heavily. "Sure. It's agreed."

"This is going to be awesome."

I was glad Rica was so convinced about it, because I wasn't. But I was going to go through with it. Even if I failed. Even it if backfired. Because I wasn't going to live in fear. And also because Rica would never let me forget it. We could be ninety and sitting in the nursing home, forgotten our own names, and she'd remind me of that time I couldn't manage to sing one little song.

I got through Maths, promised to tell Rica how it all went, then hurried to the auditorium.

A part of my brain was trying to convince me he wasn't going to come. But I pushed it away as I walked up onto the stage and sat down at the piano. I looked at the keys and took deep, steadying breaths.

Finally Eli walked in and I started playing, so nervous that it was nowhere near perfect.

I was never going to be the kind of girl who wrote someone a love song. I'd leave that up to him and Govi and Lake and Ramsey. But I could pick a song that meant something and I could play that for him now. And the song I'd chosen was little hyperbolic, but the general gist of it was right.

I was going to be brave.

He walked towards me slowly as I started singing. My smile lifted, my heart soared. I sang for me as much for him. Because I hadn't just been afraid of loving him, but of loving myself as well.

When I spared a moment to look at him, he was smiling. Warm. Open. Hopeful. Happy. Proud.

"And all along I believed I would find you. Time has brought your heart to me."

Eli joined me for the last lines. "I have loved you for a thousand years. I'll love you for a thousand more…"

I looked down at the piano and I played the last few notes, the smile on my face impossible to deny.

He waited until my hands slid into my lap to say, "A person's song choice says a lot about them."

I laughed. "Is that so?"

He jogged up the stairs but paused halfway across the stage to me. "It is."

"And what does that particular song choice say about me?"

He opened his mouth, closed it, and tried again. "That there's something you want to tell me. I hope…" he added.

I swung to face him and stood up. Taking a deep breath, I stepped towards him. "It wasn't *just* a kiss, Eli."

His smile grew a little, but I could see his optimism was cautious. "It wasn't?"

I shook my head. "No."

"Are you trying to say something, Clo?"

I smiled widely and took another step towards him, stopping when my skirt brushed his legs. "I'm saying I'll be yours."

"Yeah?" he asked, his whole body relaxing.

I nodded. "Yeah."

He wrapped me up in his arms and spun me around. I couldn't help but laugh with him. Finally he put me down and looked at me.

"Thank you."

"For what?"

"For letting *me* see the real you."

He leant down to kiss me and my heart felt like it ballooned inside my chest.

"Don't you dare!" came a shriek just before our lips touched.

Eli and I stopped and looked towards the door.

Ella a whole bunch of people were standing in the auditorium.

"Don't you dare kiss him, Chloe!" Ella shrieked and the people behind her were looking at her in confusion.

"I thought that's why we were here," someone towards the back of the crowd called.

"Kiss him and I'll–"

"You'll what, Ella?" I asked.

She huffed and stamped her foot. "You'll regret it."

I looked at Eli and smiled. "No. I won't."

And I didn't care that there were people watching. I kissed him. I heard Ella yell in anger, but it was soon drowned out by whooping and cheering. And I heard the distinct voices of Rica, Govi, Lake and Ramsey. I laughed, took Eli's hand, and pulled him backstage for something a little more private.

So in the end, Ella got her comeuppance (well, enough…for now) and I got the guy. I still had to work out what I really wanted to do with my life, but I was halfway there.

I wasn't just the stand-in anymore.

I was the star.

Quicksilver

songbook

Gin Fizz

I take my Gibson down to Arnaud's Bar.
Old Tom greets me with a smile.
The whole school said they'd be there,
But, you're the one I wanna see.

I know we've had our ups and downs.
I know you hated me before.
I might have tried to win you over,
But, darling, you won me.
You leave me with that fizzing feeling,
Don't let the last word be 'it's over'.

You see straight through the rogue I am,
I find paradise when I'm with you,
You slam me harder than Alabama
Four Pillars couldn't hold me up without you.

I know we've had our ups and downs.
I know you hated me before.
I might have tried to win you over,
But, darling, you won me.
You leave me with that fizzing feeling,
Don't let the last word be 'it's over'.

I need you more than Danny needs Sandy,
You're my tonic, make me fly,
You shake me up, don't stir me.
I'm a broken spectre in your wake.

I know we've had our ups and downs.
I know you hated me before.
I might have tried to win you over,
But, darling, you won me.
You leave me with that fizzing feeling,
Don't let the last word be 'it's over'.

Life's darker than a London fog without you.
Won't you settle down with me?
Just let me see those sapphire eyes,
Don't let the last word be 'it's over'.

Only a Kiss

There's this girl that I know,
She drives me wild,
But she don't see what she does to me.

Her rose-gold hair, I stop and stare.
That girl's so fine, I gotta make her mine.

But all she sees, when she looks at me,
Is the playboy, rock god wannabe.

Don't tell me you don't care.
Don't walk away girl, don't you dare.
What we have's damn hard to find.
Say something, say that you'll be mine.

If it was only a kiss,
Why does it feel like this?

She makes me laugh.
She makes me smile.
When I'm with her, I can run 10 miles.

She'll tear me down when I deserve it,

She's not afraid to give me sass.

Sometimes I wanna tell her that I love her,
But I know just how she will react.

Don't tell me you don't care.
Don't walk away girl, don't you dare.
What we have's damn hard to find.
Say something, say that you'll be mine.

If it was only a kiss,
Why does it feel like this?

Girl, you've gotta know,
I'm not the same anymore.
Those baby blues make me weak around you.

If you're so uninterested,
If you didn't want me too,
I wonder, why do you kiss me back?

If it was only a kiss,
Why does it feel like this?

She doesn't care if I'm famous.
(She doesn't care if no one knows my name.)

How do I show her that she's changed me?
(She's caught my heart, my mind, my soul.)

How do I tell her that I need her?
(That together we can make it through.)

Tell me, girl, why do you hide it?
Tell me, why do you deny it?

Don't tell me you don't care.
Don't walk away girl, don't you dare.
What we have's damn hard to find.
Say something, say that you'll be mine.

If it was only a kiss,
It wouldn't feel like this.
If it was only a kiss,
Darling girl, it wouldn't feel like this.

The Stand-In

You can check out the playlist for this book on Spotify. Just click or scan the QR code.

Thank you so much for reading this story! Word of mouth is super valuable to authors. So, if you have a few moments to rate/review Chloe and Eli's story – or, even just pass it on to a friend – I would be really appreciative.

Have you looked for my books in store, or at your local or school library and can't find them? Just let your friendly staff member or librarian know that they can order copies directly from LightningSource/Ingram.

If you want to keep up to date with my new releases, rambles and writing progress, sign up to my newsletter at https://landing.mailerlite.com/webforms/landing/y1n6q2.

Follow me:

Thanks

First things first, thank you to my arm tendons for hanging on for that last push. I swear you will get at least a week's rest now. Okay, maybe a few days. Let's not go wild.

Secondly, I'd like to thank Spotify and Google for their tremendous efforts in helping me find songs to use in this story. People wanted a playlist that was actually used in the story? Hopefully this didn't go too far in the other direction.

As usual, thanks go out to the beta team - particularly Charny and Anna, without whom Govi would be dressed in a plaid suit and Ella would have ended up with half the dressing downs she gets. We'll have to see how many of those ideas for the sequels make their way out of my head and onto screen.

Thanks always to my husband who still keeps the house running, who lets me bitch and moan about my writer's arm without reminding me (much) that I shouldn't have left it until the last minute. Again.

My Books

You can find where to buy all my books in print and ebook at my website;
www.elizabethstevens.com.au/YoungAdultBooks.

About the Author

Writer. Reader. Perpetual student. Nerd.

Born in New Zealand to a Brit and an Australian, I am a writer with a passion for all things storytelling. I love reading, writing, TV and movies, gaming, and spending time with family and friends. I am an avid fan of British comedy, superheroes, and SuperWhoLock. I have too many favourite books, but I fell in love with reading after Isobelle Carmody's *Obernewtyn*. I am obsessed with all things mythological – my current focus being old-style Irish faeries. I live in Adelaide (South Australia) with my long-suffering husband, delirious dog, mad cat, two chickens, and a lazy turtle.

Contact me:
Email: contact@elizabethstevens.com.au
Website: www.elizabethstevens.com.au
Twitter: www.twitter.com/writer_iz
Instagram: www.instagram.com/writeriz
Facebook: https://www.facebook.com/elizabethstevens88/

Made in the USA
Monee, IL
22 December 2019

19457078R00233